The Yonder Side of Sass and Texas

a novel

Joanna Beth Tweedy

Melissa,
It is a joy to
share these pages
with you!
Joanna Beth Tweedy

The Yonder Side of Sass and Texas

a novel

Joanna Beth Tweedy

Southeast Missouri State University Press • 2009

The Yonder Side of Sass and Texas: a Novel
by Joanna Beth Tweedy

Paperback: $19
ISBN: 978-09798714-67

First published in 2009 by
Southeast Missouri State University Press
MS 2650, One University Plaza
Cape Girardeau, MO 63701
http://www6.semo.edu/universitypress

Copyright: 2009, Joanna Beth Tweedy

Cover art: Scott McCullar
Cover design: Liz Lester

For Christopher Heath,
Jennifer Kathleen,
Clayton Lee,
Jill Elizabeth,
and my red-haired brother

Acknowledgements

Ultimately, the blessing of love is responsible for these pages: whether a devotion to language, family, knowledge, others, life, or the all-and-mighty of this world, those who have taught me about such love by their own are responsible for this book; and although its imperfections are not theirs, everything in these pages is owed to them.

Specifically, to the following literary entities who distinguished excerpts from the novel by publication and/or award acknowledgement: *Glimmer Train*, the Southern Women Writers Conference, the *Alsop Review*, the Canadian Federation of Poets, *New Millennium Writings*, the Ray Bradbury Creative Writing Contest, *Long Story Short*, and the Illinois Humanities Council. Your recognition provided splendid encouragement along the way. Thank you for the work you do on behalf of writers.

To my mama and dad, Judith Ann and John M. Tweedy, who taught me at an age earlier than understanding how to grow my heart out into the rest of life; because of this blessing, I fall in love at least ninety-three times a day: with a word-weave, a belly-laugh, a thought that will live its whole life in the quiet of a glance, a turn of measure, someone's story in the rough on their hands, not knowing, wishing I did, unassuming words steeped in unconscious wisdom, coyote harmony on the breath of night, the color of meridian sunshine, semicolons, the tiny brown spider who took up residence underneath the space bar of my keyboard. . . . Thank you for giving me a crush on life.

To my sisters and brothers, to whom this book is dedicated: from nemesis to champion, we have been rooted in each other's childhood understanding of this world deep and through, and I am powerful grateful for the almighty grace of your presence in the curious and wonderful love story of our lives.

To my grandmother, Hazel Teresa White, whose faith taught me that truth encourages inquiry, and whose example taught me that inherent in Catholicity is letting loose your heart deep and wide to everything and everyone you encounter, experience, are, aren't—no matter what, come what may; and when what-may comes: offer it, examine it, and go on loving, utterly and flat-out. That anything less is downright selfish.

To my grandma and grandpa, Helen Elizabeth and Cecil Tweedy, who gifted my family with a clear understanding of bounty and the unending love of kinship, who shaped our hearts with theirs and showed us how each fits into the space of the other, striking the peculiar and perfect imbalance that equates all we ever need to know about the exquisitely impossible ties that bind.

To my aunt, Teresa A. White, who gave me a crush on books, a gift that gave me a keener awareness of a wider world and left me with marvel, in constant wonder of the way words can connect, across time and culture, writer and reader in an embrace howbeit fugitive—one that eclipses division and solidifies understanding.

To my family, boundless in number and affection: while some live life out loud, stirring up love in spicy gumbos of emotion; others are of a mind to live life in the shadowed warmth of that cauldron, conjuring love in the underneath parts of word and action. Yet all of them love mighty and without measure, and because of that—whether clamorous or calm, eloquent or exigent, in communion or in confusion—I have tasted and felt love in every blessed interaction with my family.

To my hilly home-soil in Southernmost Illinois and its sundry wonders both merciless and steeped in grace, for the reminder that there is always a place along life's hardroad that is buffered without end by winding byways swampful of devotion, support, and cicada-song.

To Tom Annis, who ate a pie a day, spent half his life inside the earth to keep hearths on top of it fired, and typed vigorous letters to me throughout my undergraduate years—missives full of take-thats, ha!s, and recipes for pickling: we steadfastly disagreed in all things save pickling, but our tussle proved that even in utter contrariness there is love.

To the English Departments at my almae matres, the Universities of Illinois in Urbana–Champaign (UIUC) and in Springfield (UIS), for caring deeply about writing.

To Sara Cordell, Lucia Cordell Getsi, Marcellus Leonard, Ethan Lewis, Jim Ottery, and Nancy Genevieve Perkins, for your manuduction, preceptorship, and friendship: thank you for your devotion to the cultivation of art and of others.

To the writings of John Paul II, for setting me square in my understanding of a triune God, and to Sr. Ann Mathieu, who deepened exponentially my abiding appreciation of Mystery.

To colleagues at Springfield College–Benedictine University (SC-BU) and UIS, who love what they do and inspire by their doing. Your passion is contagious, and your support is tremendous.

To the students at SC–BU and UIS, who I have had the joy of teaching and with whom I've had the pleasure of working on everything from creative craft to animal rescue: you are the delight of my daily work in higher education, and there is a punch-proud part of me that belongs flat-out to you.

To Gina Cagle, Dakin Dalpoas, Josh Doetsch, Scott McCullar, Betty Parquette, and Amy Sayre-Roberts: thank you for the gifts of your friendship and your artistry: treasures of heart, mind, and spirit. And to Chad Baldwin—missed, loved, and celebrated—to whom this book is also dedicated; you are all over its pages and my heart.

To David L. Logan, for reading umpteen drafts of the manuscript and offering meaningful feedback on each occasion; for unqualified support; and for your capacity to love, a wellspring. You are an extraordinary man, and from your cogent appreciation of the comma to your acute understanding of the human spirit, you have my admiration and my affection.

To Susan Swartwout, an outright demiurgic literary champion: your passion effuses wisdom, energy, wit, and vibrancy. In researching the Press and its mission before submitting a manuscript, I recall thinking how wholly fortunate were the students of its editor-in-chief; and now, I beg mercy from gratitude that I will never be able to say *thank you* enough for having the privilege of being counted among them. I will always and gratefully be indebted to you and to Mandy Henley for the precision and care that went into bringing *The Yonder Side of Sass and Texas* to life.

To writers: the quantity of quality work in this world is downright inspiring. How fortunate to be immersed in such abundance. Thank you.

To readers, with whom I feel honored to share this work. At any given time, I'm in the middle of a mess of books, swapping finished favorites with others, and I long ago stopped keeping track of what I'd passed along to another. When I cannot locate a book I have relished, it thrills me to think that another is sharing in it, and I am happily reminded of the number of books that have been passed along to me—and also the number I have yet to read. Should it please you to pass this one along, unending thanks for the fugitive embrace.

Table of Contents

State of Affairs

Arkansas MacTerptin

Time came on fast heels toward dawn, and I busted blue through the surface of the sky, falling fast toward a pillow of pines afire on the horizon where the eyeline of daybreak winked a promise of return across earth's curve to the fading moon.

That was all I remembered when I woke, but pieces of that dream tumbled through my thoughts for the rest of sunsquint that April afternoon as I tied pie pans in peach trees, becoming a loose tangle of plaited impressions that finally started making some clear sense a few weeks and one duplicate dream later, just as day set down to keep its covenant with a full milk moon. Baxter Octan Brodie suppered with us on that bright night, the capital-b brother of the Baptist fanatic that had been my daddy's mama, but enemy to the catechism of Mama's mama.

While I remember vividly the explosive evening that followed the second dream—the night Granny knocked the pulp from the pulpit—I can't recall the exact date when the dream first visited me. But I do remember that the barn was getting a fresh coat of paint, the first it had received since the day after my younger sister was born, when my dad and Dog Dentleman got the notion to paint *It's A(nother) Girl* in proud simple letters on the side facing the road.

The day of the first dream, with evening oncoming and the barn's outer side being gussied to a new shine—letters disappearing, each in turn under the fresh coat—my older sister and I leaned against the barn's inner side in secret, perched on dried stacks of last year's final alfalfa harvest, peering through splintered slits and listening to the paint go on. "She'll end up like Bonnie Grace, goddammit." Grandpa Jelly tossed a single work glove toward a makeshift bench and passed a jar to Dog. The drink inside was tea-colored, but now that I had a closer-up view, I was sure it was one of Grandpa Jelly's special jars, not Mama's tea jars. I knew because the men only ever passed tea jars across their brows, never to each other like with Grandpa's. I heard Slug's swishy swallow, which came just after Dog's.

"Do you think they mean Ms. God Bless Bonnie Grace?" I'd scratched on the pad of paper between my sister and me, then scratched at the bale where it dimpled my bare legs before shifting to a squat.

A hush-it glare came first in return. Next came words on the pad, "They're talking about me," with *me* underlined twice by my sister.

Each man in turn passed the jar. "Say the word, Tim. I'll run him out," Slug begged permission. "Hell, I'd be happy to scat the lot of that migrant breed."

"That's not the answer, Slug. Henry's family's worked my trees every summer since the flood. They're good people. Solid family. I just wish his boy had stayed a boy."

"Yeah, and not turned into the goddam Michelangelo," Slug said the last part into the jar, before swallowing hard again.

"You mean the *David*, Son," Grandpa Jelly offered.

"Naw, Jelly, I'm not talking about the boy, see, I'm talking about a work of art here, like the Don Juan or something." Shine spilled from the jar as Slug gestured.

"Don't tell me," Grandpa Jelly would have underlined *me* twice had his words been put to the pad, but instead he stopped short to sigh to three like Granny never did before an upsurge. Then, collected, he took the jar from Slug, raised it, "You mean," swallowed hard, "*the David*."

"Never mind, Jelly." Slug figure-eighted his head from side to side, rolling his eyes. "All of that must have been taught after your time. But it don't matter. It's all chicken in the skillet, right? Anyway, I think the kid's name is Darin, not David."

"Easy, Jelly," Dog recognized the ruffle in Grandpa's breathing, now heavy, no counting. "Raise the drink, now, let's all just have us a rinse."

Grandpa raised and swallowed a second time, "The kid's name is Joseph, and you mean *the David*, by-god. Here, Tim. Finish this. I've had just about a goddam 'nough. Now by-god, what are we going to do about Texas?"

I looked over and saw my sister's tears, scooted closer, forgot all about the itch around my ankles. I remember wishing I could turnturtle whatever had capsized her heart. "What are they going to do to you, Sis?" I filled the line all the way to the margin with question marks, satisfied with how dire that made things look on the page, precisely as they felt, which was anything but satisfying there next to her on the bales.

Staring at my marks, I waited for a spoken or written answer to either question, but all I saw and heard were sweeps—the first from my older sister's hand, swiping tear-tracks from her cheeks before she climbed down and walked away from me without looking back, without making sure I could get down without a tumble. Then from the brushes in the men's hands, erasing my younger sisters' welcome into the world.

That birth announcement, once the chuckle of the county, is now covered by several layers of paint. But the dream I had the day my sisters disappeared from the barn is still alive and acute, and I smile wide at its familiar might while an Atlantic neap tide laps softly against my sun-drenched rock, seeping into sleep.

Eyes closed and memory released, I strip the barn to my favorite of its layers and allow the delicate wash of water against rock to rinse my mind inland, deep into the hills of my past. It carries me to a place where so-called ridge roads don't cut through them, but rather wind over them to paint sunset stretches of dirt-ribbon strokes at dusk. I breathe deep and smell the loamy earth in a sunken part of a foothilled fraction of the world, where seasons are still sacred as a river, and roads with crooks and creeks in their names are the chosen routes.

Beaucoup Bend boasts the longest curve in the state. A sign had sworn to it once but was long-past destroyed by someone used to straighter parts of the world. Grandpa Jelly says the road is older than time's uncle and that folks can't help swerving toward the place it steers; and in my mind I'm swerving toward that place—where rednecks roost and rut, professors retire, and Cajun hippies recover, all sharing piles of pancakes downtown at Dorothy's over patterned patches of newspaper coffee-talk. Aside from Tump's and Bottom's Up, Dorothy's of a Saturday morning is high-near the only place Dad and Grandpa Jelly can go to escape what they call the *female fluster* of our house.

Girls run in our family. Like the goddam pestilence, Grandpa Jelly says. He doesn't fix fault on Granny for it, even though it's her side of the family—two greats back and a whole country ago—that started the epidemic; he just likes to collywobble. We don't aim to buck the laws of heredity; it just works out that way. Facts as they are, the only time a boy makes it onto the tree is when he's a twin, and that usually occurs just once a cousin-cluster. The single fluke in the entire mystery is Mama's brother, who turned up all by himself and all boy—an event so significant he got named for it, as happenstance goes.

Uncle Hap aside—like hairy toes, knob knees, and bad singers—we girls just run in the family. Folks bluster on unending about how it's not possible and doesn't make a cat's bark of sense, blast-all boy-howdy and what-have-you. Some suppose it's because Granny and Mama salt their watermelon or burn too many candles to the blessed martyr Agnes. A few allege it's some kind of Creole voodoo hex, but Granny pishposhes that. According to her account of occurrences before her own, it was the footprints of blown-in-the-bottle Burgundians that pressed permanently into this Mississippi shore, not Biscayan mutts.

Grandpa Jelly prefers the voodoo version, though, and so that's the one that gets ballyhooed. But even though he likes to jaw all about his personal scourge, he never runs short in reminding us that plagues are—after-all, howbeit, and nonetheless by-god—commissioned by God for a special purpose.

Whenever I ask him what he thinks that might be, I get a clean-sprung answer. My favorite one so far this week is that we were custom-made to stir up smiles and force folks into fits of happy. I should write that down before I forget it. I fresh forget most answers to the questions I ask, and I ask all the time. Especially about my family. We seem to warrant it.

I catechize so long and loud that Mama, who says I'm more distracting than a tornado over a tin toolshed, signed us up for a set of *Funk and Wagnalls* so she could scat me off to the bookshelf when I start up inquiries. It's a heap better than having to wait for a town trip where the two-feet-thick Britannica book of answers lies open on a pedestal at the library, guarded expertly by Frieda Harbar, who Grandpa Jelly calls a cricket-like woman. She calls us *tatterdemalions* and makes us wash our hands before we climb the stepper to touch and turn the see-through pages.

Frieda hardly has the bitterweed look about her, so I wonder why she always treats us so low-down. Granny says it's because back in his sour-mash thug years, Grandpa Jelly jaw-splitted and whelped an eye-tooth from her husband, Old Doc Harbar, who at the time was a crack Pitch-player and typically Grandpa's partner when they weren't dealing a hog game. But Grandpa Jelly, who played for lark, got fed up one night too many with his partner's spar mouth and decided he needed it hush-upped for a while. "To get himself thought out," Grandpa Jelly'd explained.

The book of answers can never, ever be checked out. This is Frieda's rule. Even cardholders can't move it from its elevated shrine. And con-sidering we live too many hills from town to have check-out cards, we're lucky even to touch our fingers to its oven-paper answers.

Once, when I was looking up Holy Ghost with fingers still damp from Frieda's imposed suds-up, my pinky stuck on a page mid-turn, and when the paper gave way, there on my flesh-tip was a spot of ink: an *i* next to an inverted *h*. Falling backwards off the stepper, I keeled into my sisters and upheavaled an echo of havoc through Frieda's quiet, a sonic boom of bedlam through her blessed order. She reached our sides from across the room in three soaring strides, verifying Grandpa Jelly's cricket theory. We'd barely had a chance to right ourselves by the time she landed upon us, her face a terrifyingly serene, silent demand for answers.

A fearsome quiet sat among us for a longsome heartrattle, with my bruised sisters having no idea why I'd smashed through them and not about to stab blind at what they should say. A soundless Frieda would typically terrify me, but I had just received a *hi* from the Holy Spirit, and so I didn't start like my sisters when of a sudden the silent air whip-cracked a book smacking flat against marble, which may well have been a bullet in Frieda's backside the way she big-eyed and stiffened at once before bounding into a forest of shelves to miss catching our red-haired brother as he squirreled down from one of them just in time to sprint silently and sockfooted back to where he'd abandoned his shoes, not far from us, before ditching them to sneak off and suss how he would save his sisters and thereby extract promises and chore-doings from them afterward, a task he forgot to execute once I showed him and my sisters the letters pressed against my skin, a divine answer right at my fingertip.

"The Holy Spirit put it there," I low-voiced.

"Stigmata," my red-haired brother awed in a whisper.

At this, my oldest sister crossed both her eyes and self in a single God-forgive-them-for-they-know-not-that-they're-knotheads gesture. Then she took my brother by his hand and led him atop the stepper where she tongue-swiped her finger and planted it hard to the page before peeling it up to reveal the imprint left behind.

He spent the remainder of his time there that day pressing letter by letter to his skin as many four-alarm words as he knew. I spent it pressing book-ink to skin too, trying and failing over and again to then move the words from my skin to a white page—finally realizing it wouldn't be pos-sible to transport the book of answers from page to skin and then back to page, by-and-by creating a complete copy of it.

My red-haired brother sussed out that if we were to visit the library every day, removing a single page from the book each time, Frieda wouldn't notice, and we could have the job done in seven-and-a-half years. But it's not answers he cares about; he just likes a stir-up.

The *Funk and Wagnalls* Mama signed us up for has been sliced into volumes with sturdy pages polished slick as egg-white pie-tops. We get one a month. Next month is *Q*.

I get some of my most important answers from my oldest and quietest sister. She's a questioner too, but hers fall silently—in the form of silky-speared lashes flickering scrutiny, or single-dimpled smirks imparting a wrinkle of doubt across the otherwise smooth sunshine of her cheek. To me, my sister's questions are as public and plainsung as the probing litany of thundercracks I rain down upon the house incessantly, but no one else seems awake to them. She somehow gets answers, though.

And her answers, always remembered, come clear to me in silvery whispers through the moon's shadow across the quilt we share. Except when she gets mad. Then her silhouette secrets stay that way and my tears start, because by that time the reason we fought seems beeheaded, and the regretful side of me that mourns and haunts is sorry that a single one of our nighttides has been wasted to stubborn squabble.

On the good nights, her argentine answers make me feel beatific and safe, like I could wrap myself in the protection of her moonlight curls and know the wide world inside out. She assures me it's not that I forget things; the way Texas puts it, I'm just too young to suss facts and so they simply don't stick. She says it happened to her way back when she was my age, two years ago, and that as my brain gets bigger like hers, I'll be able to fit more things into its growing gaps and spaces—as long as I keep them tidy and spruced. But I doubt it. I don't fold or tuck anything like she does; I wad and stuff.

Grandpa Jelly says looking things up will help me remember them. He makes me special bookmarks out of sack and twine and adds labels to them when I tag pages for later. He also helps me find the volumes when my red-haired brother hides them. My red-haired brother is a twin. Mine. That's how he got in. Because I let him.

Turns out the encyclopedias have backfired on Mama and me, as by-and-large they provoke a heap more questions than they answer, which over the course of a day conjures us both into a swivet. If there's a quiz at the end of life, I'm guaranteed doomed.

All I know for sure is we defy mathematics and genetics. And according to my quest through *Funk and Wagnalls* all the way up to "Pisa, Leaning Tower of"—we've disobeyed the laws of identification as well. Folks are supposed to have people-names, not place-names. But tell that to my family. The state of names around here is all about location.

Mama and her sisters have Irish names, but not the bona fide person-kind. Instead, they're named for the home-soil sites of Grandpa Jelly's parents, my mama's grandparents. Aunt Ailee is a river, my aunt Fanore's a fishing village, Mama is a county called Clare, and Aunt Quinn is a pub. The first three are in my *Funk and Wagnalls*, and I'm about to go buggy wondering if Aunt Quinn is there too.

I've been scouting and fine-toothing, looking for folks named after states, but the only ones I've found have normal-sounding ones, like Georgia and Caroline—not Montana and Alabama.

Why my parents did this to us I can't figure. They plain went cold-duck cockamamie after the first child, and things have gotten out of hand. But then again, you can't just name a daughter Texas and stop there. So that's how I came to be Arkansas and my little sister, Montana. The baby is Abalama, but only because she can't say *Alabama* yet. Michigan is on the way.

Sometime around the beginning of peach harvest last year—before anybody knew anything about the newest state we'd be gaining, and just after letter *H* arrived—my red-haired brother started troubling up a bother about his name, which has since spilled over into out-and-out vexation. In January he downright outlawed its use. I have to comply on penalty of Mama learning about the fruit bat I've been feeding, watering, and letting roost in our closet all winter.

I look up the state of Alabama's nickname, hoping I can give my baby sister one that will work in her tongue, but *Yellowhammer* isn't much better and now I want to know what that is. My nickname is boring: I'm the Natural State. Granny says I should have been Utah, because it's the Beehive State. Or so she tells me; I can't confirm this yet. Grandpa Jelly undertook to fix up a nickname for me by overhauling the pronunciation of my state and whacking a chunk of it off. Still and all, I fancy Florida, because it's all about sunshine.

I ask Mama when she thinks *Y* will get here.

"Hush-it, Sass." That's me for short, Granny talking. "Now run out and ask Dog if he wants rub on his chop." I scrunch my brows and glower through the tattered porch-door, abusing it on the way out, but not enough to incite a wallop.

The hills inch by bit into silhouette as late afternoon's suntide washes from my mind its sunrise recollection of dawn's ember flush across their slopes. Like the dream that woke up full and wide in my head this morning, beclouding all my by-and-by thoughts with layers of Mystery, day is beginning to molt; and with the help of a swelling sun, it sloughs in stretched-out shreds of shadow, trying to eclipse midday memories of its squint-eyed, due-south warmth on my shoulders—warmth that I will recall later, when twilight misplaces time and moments do become shades, the same warmth permanently imprinted in the freckles across my sister's moonlit skin. Two weeks ago, when day equaled night and night equaled day, under the jillion eyes of the stars and by the shine of a paschal moon, we counted every single freckle we had. She beat me three to one.

A wisp of chilled wind, like a leftover wraith of winter, traces hints of petal-blossom from the orchard where row after rolling row of long skeleton shadows reaches over the hills and toward the house, the elongated profiles of cropped trees studded with buds that every other equinox show up just in time to gussy-up pruned limbs and summon the midsummer bounty that will hang heavy and rich as the bursting sunsets of lingering Julys.

July's horizon afire in my mind conjures back a layer of my dream, where the junction of dirt and sky blazed like a swath of sunbreak spilling over hills to grow a glow across earth's curve and surge upwards toward an onionskin moon, dissolving it into answers and light. As notions of my dream continue to drift back to me, I breathe openmouthed and can taste the sun on the breeze, despite oncoming April dusk.

Beyond our bluff sinks an oakwood valley, drooped on three sides by cemeteries. There's Our Lady of Divine Mercy Cemetery, where Catholics go to be resurrected, and Pleasant Hill Cemetery, where all folks were buried before the living who got born twice decided to separate their departed from those who were only born once. The third is the Baptist Cemetery, so named to make certain there will be no confusion, I reckon. That's where they put Ms. God Bless Bonnie Grace.

Beyond the segregated dead land, and all the way up to the box canyons that cause the Mississippi's bend-arounds to double back on themselves, stretches the kudzued tupelo bottomlands, where the migrant cabins sit on stilts, and the trucks that haul Henry and his family up to our hills have silt-packed tires that periodically drop squared chunks of dried river mud in our yard. My red-haired brother and I collect these, intending to build our own river one day when we have enough good sludge to line it.

The two of us are going to run the orchard someday, just like Granny's family before Mama and Dad. We've agreed to add banana and pineapple trees—ever since discovering in *Funk and Wagnalls* how tall these could get—to the squat peach and apple ones that drape our hills. Mama knows, but we haven't told Dad about this idea yet, planning to surprise him one morning with fresh bananas and pineapples in his oat mash. We just haven't figured out how to hide the orchard from him while the trees grow in the meantime. My brother suggested sending him off for a season to be a gandy dancer like Grandpa Jelly was, but Mama says she'll take him to Hawaii instead, which my brother agreed was fine so long as they don't come back with another sister for him by that name or any other of the forty-five they haven't tried out yet.

Sundip continues its gradual swell toward evening, trying to rinse recollection and bathe my bareness in cool caresses of distraction; and my feet press cold across hard ground. But I can feel in my bones the dream-heat of my tender fancy. And I can hear Dad, Dog, Grandpa Jelly, and Slug before I see them, their tone telling me they're leaning against the toolshed, laughing and likely wiping Mama's tea jars across their fore-heads—not because they're hot, but because that's what everyone always seems to do with their tea jars around here. I recognize it as the type of talk that will stop when I appear, so I walk soft and slow, pretending to admire the paint on one side of the barn so Granny won't holler at me to haul it.

The barn got a fresh coat this afternoon, the first it's had since Dad and Dog last tackled it, the day after Montana came, topping its layers with her birth announcement—in tall, straight letters: *It's A(nother) Girl.* An exclamation point was added when Abalama came, Dad lifting us each in turn atop his shoulders to help fill in the big blue dot.

A new and necessary layer has begun turning to shade that very point and the proud declaration it amended into a jubilant holler. Not yet swallowed by a second coat—that comes tomorrow after buttermilk eggs, Dog's favorite—the message still shows slightly through like the faded recollection of a smile that will grow farther and fainter, along with the eyes that once encountered it.

When I had gotten low about it earlier, Granny told me to shuck the mope, that there was cake to make. That helped, but Granny could still read the hangdog across my brow when she'd handed me my spoonshare of the batter—which my red-haired brother on every occasion carped was bigger than his, and for this once I couldn't dispute it. She looked me square, handed me the leavings in the bowl, and told it plain, "Sass, things aren't what they used to be and they never were. Now go share that with your brother." I didn't know if she meant the batter or the words she'd just spoken.

Not in the mood for either, I sulked to the sideporch and let him have both in one big huff. He wanted to know what in the hell was the matter with me, and just as I was about to announce I was off to tell on his "hell"—first covering my ears with my hands—he put aside the bowl, stuck the handle of his spoon crossways through his front teeth, took me by the shoulders, and instead of pulling my ears, sat me down. Handing me back my spoon and the bowl, he crossed his heart and hoped to die that it was safe for me to let go of my ears and take the bowl and spoon.

I let go of my ears but shook my head at his bribe. "That's okay. I won't tattle."

"Take it, Sass."

"Fine." Texas had Montana in her lap on the swing, and I heard my older sister fib to the younger one that Granny had given us the bowl because we didn't get as much as everybody else the first time around.

"Don't worry," my brother assured, "I won't tell on you, either."

"You know about the crawdads? How?"

"I was talking about the bat."

"Oh."

"What's with the crawdads?"

"I'll tell you later."

"No you won't."

We finished our share in silence, and when Texas came round to collect and tote them back to Granny, my brother made it known that he was going crawdad hunting and did I want to go. Even though I'd been practicing my drop-off-the-edge-of-yonder look for just such a moment, I didn't even bother. Texas must have noticed where my gaze was focused, because before she left she leaned over and reminded me I could always close my eyes and strip the barn to my favorite of its layers.

Thinking back on this latest answer from my sister summons a whole-teeth grin and a happy-dance, and I'm suddenly sorry I terrorized the screen door. The men have set down their jars and gone back to painting, and I step back toward the trees to see the message dimming with the afternoon. Through shadows, it smiles back from beneath the first of several coats to come, and I forget all about my errand as I hightail it back toward the house to haul out Texas for a barn-spy and ask her if she's sure it always will.

Hellfire

Arkansas MacTerptin

Grandpa Jelly is at Dorothy's, punctuating the morning summit with by-gods and goddams, when thrushes carrying the day's melody wrest me from a dream about John Denver living inside his guitar case with my cat. Gathering up the stolen parts of the sheets from my sister's side of the bed, I roll right up in them, not because I'm cold—June is approaching heavy and thick like August, threatening peanut blossoms before their time—but just because this is what I do in the morning. This places me nose-up to the patches of screen barb where last night I'd spent the awake hours of lights-out tickling gallinipper toes through the shreds they probed.

Spider Cecil's web still clings from the window latch, paint-bonded in the unlock position since long before lead-free, to where the top of the lower window stops—a line halfway down from the bottom of the upper. Cecil is the reason we haven't budged the wood scrap propping up our window since the May-first morning my older sister and I woke up and found his insect afghan spread between us and the sun like a happy welcome to the itchy part of the year.

That weeks-ago morning had been a good one even before I'd opened my eyes to its shiny web of wonder. I'd had the dream again, the second time, only this time I floated toward the horizon, held aloft by a parachute of cicada skins. I described it to my sister during the periodic lulls in our sleepy semi-squabble over the spider's eventual name. I won because she drifted back to sleep just long enough to forget that Cecil was my first choice and not hers.

The sound and smell of the skillet had eventually lured us down toward the kitchen and away from the softness of hushed and brand-new mornings. I'd known Brother Brodie was sure to show when our bare feet met the bottom step and I pirooted Granny using the phrase *Protty rot.* That—along with creamed peas, lemon pie, and tamale cakes with extra drippings—always seemed to summon the by-and-by arrival of Brother Baxter Octan Brodie. Most folks liked Brother a heap better than Granny did. A few even claimed he might well could be a prophet. Granny agreed that that word was certainly suited to his version of the Bible, but she chose to spell it with an "f-i-t" in place of the "p-h-e-t."

Granny had better things to say about his sister, the one I would have called Granny too, if I'd known her better. But as it was, all I really knew her by—other than the worry her memory stirred up in Grandpa Jelly over Texas—was her grave marker, which said *God Bless Bonnie Grace Brodie MacTerptin*, so that's what I called her. I called her husband Grandpa Hopper, but he wasn't with us tonight because he lived two whole states over, and he didn't much care for his capital Brother-in-law anyhow. Neither did my red-haired brother. Earlier he'd told Mama the only good thing about Brother Brodie's visits was the lemon pie she always made for them, but she hush-upped him fast and firm, saying he needed to learn a thing or three about family. I liked Brother's visits though, because he said *if you will* seventy-three times in one conversation, and that just slayed me.

Brother turned up that night several-ago just after sundown and told us over peas and cakes that God should be praised through these storms of spring, which made me wonder if he'd been in the haybarn with Grandpa Jelly having some corn mash before the blessing, because there had been sun for eight straight days. Just then, Granny glowered and growled something I was sorry I'd missed, being across the table and all, but Brother Brodie just kept on *if-you-will*ing us at such a rate it caused Mama to shoot me a look that got my insides to giggling, though it was supposed to have the opposite effect. I tried my best to distract myself by pushing a pea through the gap where I'd just lost a tooth, and my red-haired brother's glance was triple-dog daring me to fake a sneeze and try and splat it against the opposite wall when Brother *will*ed again and I did cough, bona fide and choke-like, never knowing where the pea ended up.

I excused myself for some buttermilk, knowing full well Mama'd fall face-first into her sweet peas before she'd let me dunk my cakes in front of company, but she could tell that one more *will* would split my spleen, so she let me go, telling me it was only polite to bring back some for the whole table. Granny knew what I was after, so she poured for me when I got back, spilling some onto my plate and blaming her arthritis, which she no more had than I did, smiling and winking as she saw the cornmeal crumbs on my plate sopping up all they could. Mama set her lip and flared her nose at Granny, and I wondered when I'd be old enough to do that to my mama, in full view of her at least.

The mention of bone aches launched Brother into a sermon on pests and plagues and how the Lord's love would see us through. Granny was glaring the whole time like she was about to crack him on the head with the jar of molasses between them, but he didn't see her. He was on about afflictions and scourges, blights that in God's holy name made His people stronger, if we will, that pestilence was our test and scripture our saving answer. Brother obviously didn't realize that locust larvae could be easily controlled by leaf-litter burning at the end of each season. Myself, I'd always thought locusts—and all bugs for that matter—were a splendid invention by a God who appreciated whimsy, but I knew enough to keep closed.

Not my red-haired brother. He piped up and told Brother about the mosquito spray Granny made from cedar sap and corn shine, and how it worked just fine without any Bible words mixed into it. I saw sparks surge from Mama's eyes and sting static upon the skin of lowercase brother while the uppercase one explained how insects and alcohol were our burdens to bear, the curse of a sinning world. Grandpa Jelly was looking just like he needed to excuse his own self for some buttermilk, but instead he stayed to grab Granny's wood-chucking hand in case it went for the molasses.

In the end, she opted to wallop with words instead, interrupting Brother's speech with an all-out bless-out, heralding that the only vermin on this earth in violation of divine law were those pests who gazed on a field of fireflies or a Saturdee soiree and saw nothing but the blazes of hell and sin, and that it was these reprobates, *God* willing, who needed exterminating. It was then that my dream-web snapped into clear sense, and I knew Spider Cecil was an eight-legged gift from a wiser God whose cicada cadence was a celebration, not a scourge.

That night is now more than three weeks old, and even though I haven't had the dream again, I wake up happy because our spider has been there to greet us every single sunup. Perfectly protected between two panes, Cecil can come and go as he pleases through the small gap where aluminum and wood won't agree to meet. He makes short work of anything else that discovers this gap, and sometimes when we think he's bored, we blow paint chips up into his web, so he can keep busy wrapping these up too.

Cecil is probably a girl, but we gave him a boy-spider's name because they've been underrepresented since Charlotte. Granny even pressed him a goodnight kiss once, and her lip print is still against the glass. We don't disturb it either.

Nose up to wire mesh below Cecil's silky one, I know it's going to be my day all day long as soon as the split willow outside my screen screams a song that spring has long turned to summer, no matter what the calendar says, and higher digits are just around the corner. Three more days and I'll be a whole decade. We'd been counting it down in the dirt circle around the burn barrel for a whole two weeks when an afternoon full of mean clouds came in to erase morningshine and sent us scrambling for the cellar as soon as we saw how the horses were acting.

But I'd already known it was going to be a gollywhomping day the dusk before when I'd seen Mama at the sink tying up apple-stuffed hocks in salt rags. Granny's bread bowl was brimming with cowpeas and water, and next to it was Mama's dented-up tin measure cup, the one she used for cutting powdered biscuits. As soon as I'd seen it, I'd known she'd saved back some beans from soaking just for me. Mama never asked what I did with those beans, just put them aside for me ever since the first time I'd asked for a handful and gotten so thrilled when she piled them into my palm.

The lemon pie that had been put to cool in the open sill made me think Brother Brodie might be showing up about the time it set up for slicing, but then I remembered the night of Armageddon and realized we wouldn't be *if-you-willed* for quite a spell. His sinfire and brimstone blazed across the peas and buttermilk that night, but it was no match for the radiant glare of Granny, whose communion with the Almighty had neither patience nor truck with those who insisted that the wide world's sacred scriptures could be confined to the pages of a single book.

She had smiled and muttered something in the spitfire gumbo of her French mama when Brother said he'd pray for her, but only after he'd moved through the screen door, out of range of the molasses jar and into moon-washed twilight. His early retreat from the battle between the forces of good and evil incited Mama to send the entire house straight to bed as contrition and Brother home with the entire pie as consolation. He took it, too.

I'd gone to bed low about this but had forgotten it upon awakening the following morning with my younger sister's long and springy little-girl curls mixed with mine across the pillow she'd all but taken over. A downright-dedicated sleepwalker, she rarely got up in the same place she went down, and my older sister and I had gotten used to her frequent travels to the sheets we shared.

She is curled into the curve of our bodies on this morning too, squirreling the sheets and stirring little when I tug them toward my side and roll right up. But I'm too atwitter to stay put for long, and just as soon as my bare toes hit the slatted floor, they start smacking cool wood to the rhythm in my head from the words Mama'd whispered into my pillow last night right before the full-and-sweet dreams part. She said a few banjos from the box-canyons had heard about my birthday and decided it was worth some picking—more than that even. She said they'd rounded up a few other finger-strings too. Not just Uncle Hap and Squint DeWitt, but real strings from west of the rivers' mixing point: tubbers from Turkey Run, fiddlers from Rattlesnake Ferry—spoons and wind harps too, she'd reported with far-away in her voice, which made me think for a moment she'd gone a bit noodle-noggined about the whole thing. There were always spoons and harps, after all.

As my toes slap across the floor, I close my eyes and concentrate hard on the hop-step Grandpa Jelly had been teaching us ever since April's end had freed up afternoons from sweet-smelling orchard chores, and how during our lessons he whirled my world into a feverdance and fired my feet into frenzy to match the fiddle. Thinking about it makes me go so giddy-goosed I tap smack into my red-haired brother who hates mornings and everyone associated with them. My punishment is light, and I'm in such high spirits I might not even tattle on him.

Usually when he pulls my ears, I run and squash them back to my head with my older sister's pillow because it smells like the petalwater she has lately started using to rinse her hair. She is much more careful with her curls, and for that reason they spring up better than my tangles, which are always having to be lopped off for some knotted infraction or another. I think about this almost every time I have to press my ears back to the sides of my head in case my brother's stretched them, because the last thing I need is balded ears as big as Tuffer Danner's to make life even more difficult.

I hate doing this, though, because it makes me hear the footsteps. Granny says it's really just my body's own blood pulsing through my head, but a part of me still trusts my red-haired curse and what he'd told about the footsteps that started out each time a person was born, setting off for marching around the whole world; and then once they got back to where they'd started from, that's when the person died. I believed him because of the way he looked without blinking when he told me how I could hear them inside my head but had no way of knowing how far along they were in their journey because only the footsteppers themselves knew how wide their strides were. I pray a lot that my footsteppers aren't related to Frieda.

Mulling this is about all it takes to change my mind about telling on him, and before I can stop frittering and unwrap the salt pork like she's told me twice, Mama's furrowed face is marching up the stairs past Granny's cold-cream quizzical one, and I'm a little sad that I've said anything to make the day's beginning any less than perfect.

I almost take to tears myself when I glimpse my brother's puffy eyes underneath copper-colored brows stomping toward the pocket room— the only room in the house off-limits to what Mama calls *clatterracket*.

The only exception is Christmas Day. Every other day of the year, the ultimate punishment is that room, shades pulled—for cooling off, Mama says. Its namesake doors won't slide closed in muggy months because the floors warp all up from one side of the house to the others, spreading up toward the sultry solstice in delicate, humid-laden arcs.

Granny raises her brow at me when she smuggles past Mama and into my hand a bacon-shingled biscuit to deliver to the prisoner, so I do her silent bidding and ask him if we can get along for the rest of the day. He says that depends on me, but only after I've handed him his breakfast intact. Hunger makes peace in the end, because as soon as he sees the tackle-and-destroy in my eyes, he mutters that if I'll leave him alone to eat, we can maybe be friends today.

I tell him it's all dandy with me either way, but secretly I miss the days we used to spend side-by-side beneath the softwood swamp trees, splashing in Sugarmouth Creek and swinging through sunshine slits of cypress like the superheroes on our Underoos until berry cheeks and barking bellies sent us home to steal dollops of sweet cream from the top shelf of the icebox where Mama thinks we can't reach it. This makes me wonder when we'd stopped spending the sunset parts of Pitch Sundays sneaking Grandpa Jelly's harp from the top drawer of his dresser, having to climb each other's shoulders to get there, then pouring down the back stairs and across the ribs of a hollow porch and into the yard where the dogs lay in a shadowed dirt-heap near the seedshed until the hum of harp hit them and sent them howling like the shades of shenanchies toward the house and the Mama-holler that would make it all stop, sending us in the opposite direction to wait until wrath turned to worry and made for a safe return.

As I turn from the pocket room, I think about maybe later asking my brother if he ever misses these things too, until I hear muffled through a biscuit bite something about the size of my ears. He ducks and the seed-stuffed cushion misses him, smacking the wall behind him and tumping crosswise the Virgin on the side table before crashing into Dad's carved duck decoys on its way down. We big-eye each other as Mama from the kitchen wants to know what's going on in there, so I run to tell her nothing while he rights things, relieved to encounter the apron full of apple peels that will keep her from investigating.

We end up getting along for most of the hours before noon, and when Grandpa Jelly comes home smelling like pipe and pancakes and orders us both out into the vines to pick toe babies for the picnic, we go side-by-side and willingly. Our usual contest to see who can cram the most berries in their mouth is unusually won by me. But it doesn't start

the racket those types of moments typically promise because we both
know a whole day of possibilities is still in front of us at the lake, so we
save our strength.

Curving toward the Kinkaid Bluffs surrounding the lake, the sign
announcing Sharp Rock Falls has been recently crushed, not by tumbling
blades of boulder bits but by Slug Milby when he tried to launch his
blazer over it at the urging of Cockeye Murk. They said the hobo pillow
Slug kept duct-taped to his steering column for unknown reasons was
the only thing that saved the few ribs he didn't fracture. The one thing
he does remember about the occasion is how the air-intake pipe met
him halfway through the windshield and gave him the notion to move it
to the other side of the hood for future mud outings. But it didn't look
like those would be coming soon for Slug, whose dance with death had
slowed him up and eased him down. The nurses even said he'd been
polite to them. The doctors declared Slug's head was still unsettled,
though they admitted its inner blaze had been a speck soothed, owing to
the accident.

When Dad heard word of the mishap, he and Dog went straight
to Tump's Talkeasy to toast Cockeye because a busted-up Slug made
Tump's a safer place to be, and they were getting tired of the long drive
to Bottom's Up—where bar fights were scarce because slugs of all kinds
had been banned ever since the night Scrapper Duroche accidentally shot
himself in the foot and made everybody jumpy. Mama didn't receive the
news of a laid-up Slug quite so well. Not that she was reeling off Rosaries
on his recovery, but she had liked the way distance from drink had kept
Dad off the snags, so before he left the house that day to celebrate, Mama
told him in a voice that made it clear how she felt about frequent trips
there, that the last thing this world needed was for the ruffian regulars at
Tump's to live without the promise of eventual annihilation.

But after Dad left with Grandpa Jelly close behind, Granny reminded
Mama that so far it had been a Communion-wine-only week, which gave
Mama a catechistic hernia right there on the spot and launched her into
a transubstantiationalist tirade that ended only when Granny—for the
twenty-first time that year—swore off sacrilege and promised penance.
The truce sent the two women to the slatted shade of the sideporch with
glass in hand, Mama's a dark bottle from the icebox and Granny's a jar
from the haybarn. They toasted to Slug and a God that maimed malice
but kept crazy intact. I watched my two mamas set the sun that evening,
silhouetted voices of laughter and love.

Though Sharp Rock's sign is gone, the spiky stones that gave it
its name aren't, and Dad makes us wear shoes on the flinty beach even

though my feet are tougher than Slug ever was. Most of the meringue has sweat off the pie by the time permission is given to eat it, right from the pan—the best way. Forkfulling it into our mouths, my red-haired brother and I are finished with our portions long before our soft-curled sisters are. My brother has claimed the remaining bites that our younger sister leaves behind, but I have wisely chosen the older's leavings as my entitlement, because we share secrets as well as a room, and I know how she feels about the way her hips are starting to balance out the long-and-tall of her. Our baby sister is too young to take on proper her share of pie, but Mama says no when we ask can we split it.

My cheeks are on fire and my nose is already starting to shed layers before the sun is finished for the day. We start to pack up and head for the events on top of the hill while Mama instructs us to cover up and spray down. But I beg her to let me stay in my towel-skirt and swim top, even though they have rub on them from when I'd overloaded my mouth at the exact moment my sleepwalking sister bellowed her cows-at-the-mooovies joke, which slays me every time. Mama agrees to the towel ensemble that makes me feel like a hula-girl on account of I've stuck cattail reeds from all parts of it, but only after she's added a load of deet to my lake-water and grill-smoke smell.

At the top of the hill, water-born breezes greet us like deep breaths of contentment. They hang generously in the treetops and swing the yellow bulbs strung from branch to branch. Mama puts our blanket too far from where the band will be, I think, but I hardly have say in these matters. A sliver of strawberry moon gets smaller as it heads heavenward, and I am so beside myself waiting for the fiddles to fire up that I nearly forget to take it all in, since usually our sunburned bodies are tucked into cool sheets by the time there are this many stars showing.

Most Saturday nights about this time, Granny sets up her rocker in the doorway joining the two rooms that five of us share and tells Big Foot stories while Dad has Mama all to himself and swings her around the concrete slab that is definitely too far in front of us right now. But Mama is a friend to fiddle-worship, and birthdays have a way of bending rules, so tonight the Saturday festivities will be crawling with kids from the Kinkaid Cliff clan.

Soon all our cousins have shown up, the girls smelling like the day's sunshine and the boys like boys, all mixing with the shampooed-aunt-and-whiskeyed-uncle smell of my family. By the time the band is boozed enough to start playing well and long, my whole heart opens up to swallow their first bona fide harmony in a great big happy hug. I look around for Texas, who is supposed to keep an eye on me and my red-haired brother, but I've lost track of her. So I look for Joseph, who has grown long muscles in his legs and was walking with Texas when last I saw her. By now they must be deep into one of their walk-and-talks, so I decide to wait them out near the dance floor.

I'm thinking what a slap-up idea it would be to start a wiggle-train when I spot my cousin Sally Rose, who looks like Audrey Hepburn and Natalie Wood mixed together, sitting on a log rack along the dance floor, tossing drop-n-pops at random into the two-stepping crowd with her boyfriend from town next to her looking all darty and hamster-like. He's puffy and has been a hero at the high school since the day his freshman cleatfoot hit the football mud, but he's not a meatball like most of the other testosteronic everyball players she's dated. He likes to tell stories with stars and moons in them, eats mashed crackers in milk, and his piggybacks are about eight times better than Grandpa Jelly's, though I'd never let my grandpa know it.

I hear him ask Sally Rose why doesn't she just get it over with and throw the whole box at the wapiti rubes who are probably waiting for the first opportunity to crush him. She turns toward him with that same squinted look that Mama had when I'd explained why she couldn't displace Cecil, and delivers along with it words telling him to relax, that the hog spit isn't long enough to share with any more corpses and townfolk aren't that tender anyway.

Things like this are what make me want to be Sally Rose someday, but my sympathies lie with her boyfriend, who should probably have worn an untucked shirt. In one divine flash, a mighty whim leaps to me that he could clearly use a cup of apple mash, so I light out for where my red-haired brother and like-minded cousin-cronies packed off with an entire jug of it while Mama wasn't looking. Except their disappearance on top of Texas's has turned Granny into an eagle-cat, and I can't even get two towel-skirt shimmies from the dance floor when she's pouncing on the sly look my eyes have betrayed. But I can tell Granny things, so I spill what I'm after.

She says Sweet Jesus won't my brother ever learn and who put me up to a whompasaddled notion like that. So I tell her about the agitation on the logs next to Sally Rose and my strategy for keeping his nerves from erupting into his head. She declares it a noble plan but assures me that not even a garden hose of Grandpa's strongest shine would get that boy to relax right now, and if he so much as goes home smelling like a rabbit-pop of it, he'll never be able to see Sally Rose again, which makes her think she'll just go and round up some for him. I don't understand whatever she's muttering in French when she walks off, but I know it means I won't be seeing him around anymore.

I feel sorehearted for him. I think he was pretty smitten. But Granny is the county seat of our Kinkaid hills and Keep Her on Your Side is a rule my cousin's boyfriends always learn too late. A twist of fate spares him for the moment and embarrasses Sally Rose for the rest of the song when a zydeco tune inspires Grandpa Jelly to whirl Granny from her aim and into a polka. I take the opportunity to spring off just like the gazelles I read about in *Funk and Wagnalls*, wondering how much of our picnic will resurface after my brother reaches the bottom end of the jug and how much time he'll be spending in the pocket room after Mama smells the ferment on his breath, despite all the burnt-marshmallow sucking he will undergo to remove it. He never learns.

I stride fast and quiet toward where I hear stupored voices laughing behind the trees, and I scare the tar out them when a dog-sized dirt hole wrecks my momentum and tumbles me howling into it, crunching cattail reeds and revealing an empty jug and spilled marshmallow sack just in front of my crash site. He's in for it. Just as soon as Mama catches it on the breeze, this grand night will be over and we'll be driving the lightning-bugged backroads home in silence. This makes me want to scuttle back to the fiddles, yet the somersaulted collapse hasn't knocked my brains so much as my bones, and I extract at least a week's worth of kindnesses from the deluded pleader who actually thinks he will get away with his actions undiscovered.

When I reach the slit-eyed gaze of Granny once again, I notice that the breeze has out-and-out stopped. The hill is a-swirl with hop-stepping, hip-swinging, and bottle-swilling, and the wind has ceded its stir to the eddy of bodies. Music topples over the shifting swarm, notes upended, harmony tripping over itself. With nowhere to go, the end of one tune slams into the start of another, as though this is exactly where the night's notes belong, not carried off to other places. The moon has shifted in the sky, but the night air refuses to move on.

Granny is marching toward me with the look that always triggers my bladder, and I am mystified that she can mind-read the extortion I have exacted from my red-haired brother while she was bouncing and bobbing across chalk-smooth concrete. She reaches me at the same time as, astonishingly, Mama, whose out-of-nowhere appearance so confounds me, I am too awed to answer when they ask where in the hell is my brother. Hasty hands pull leaves from my hair and broken reeds from my towel as I try to determine how much they know about what has transpired back in the trees, gauging whether I should confess whole-hog or just bits. It's the first time I've heard my mama say *hell*. She wet-thumbs my cheeks just as the band stops and calls my name.

Calls my name!

If the whole hill had swallowed me right up in it outright, I would have been less bumfuzzled. It's when *Happy Birthday* is struck across the strings that I realize I'm not on trial—that this whole moment is a celebration of song dedicated right to my heart where it will stay and come back to me when I need it most.

Everybody whoops at the finish, and the sum total of my reckoning cartwheels as the band boy-howdies about what marvels a ten-year-old has in front of them these days. I feel dreams on my shoulders, and with all the surefire expectation that piggybacks hope going on ten, I look up, a decade new, knowing before I see it the meteor hellblazing across the heavens.

Threshing

Texas MacJerplin

Sass is steepled atop my shoulders, concentrating on the words just over the alfalfa stacks, listening hard for the name *Joseph*. My hands grasp the balls of her feet, their arches pressing hard into my shoulders. We are wobbly, a trembling tower of anxious curiosity. Sass signals down toward me, aiming and nodding her head in the direction she needs me to take her. I am the feet; she the ears, and together we are discovering my fate. Henry, Joseph's papa, saw me with Joseph in the pond, laughing and splashing. Now Henry and Dad are deciding what to do next.

The season's second haul of windrowed alfalfa, now baled and stacked for packing off to Stretch Waters's mule-farm, stabs at my nostrils without touching them. Clear liquids seep from my sister's eyes and nose but she dares not wipe or sniff, keeping us balanced and concealed. She is a champ, and I love her more in this moment than ever I have. I hold tight to her feet, grateful to them for risking their summer freedom for this venture. I want to tell Sass my heart; she would keep it close: when it comes to hush-ups, Sass is the grave. But I don't tell her because she's already taken account of the growing distance between me and my siblings, and if she knew it was because of Joseph, she could never love him too. She thinks this is a routine spy mission; she has no idea that if Joseph must leave, then I will too.

There are other orchards in this world, and I can work alongside him. I know everything he does about peaches and apples. I even know some of his language. He taught me in secret to drive his motorcycle, despite neither of us being old enough to take to the hard road—he doesn't think he is, anyway; no one but his passed-on mama could swear to his years without a bona fide birth certificate. Joseph told me she was born of Peruvian basalt, warm and soft in youth, hard and cold by the time she fell sick and died of bad blood. Even though his papa can't remember Joseph's true age, he lets him run his motorcycle everywhere anyway, and I know it will carry us to a place that doesn't give a fiddle that I live bluffside and he in the bottoms.

Sass big-eyes me, every bit of her face radiating fret, so I know something terrible's been decided. There's no reason for any of it. Each year, bluffside folk make a show of bringing bottomside their used furniture, books, clothes, and toys to fill the migrant families' cabins before the occupants arrive to fill them with cook-smoke as evanescent as their stay and song as rich as the applewood aroma cured permanently into their temporary walls.

I remember finding Sass one Christmas afternoon, hurling a play-sized model McCormick thresher against the cellar walls. It was part of a kit our brother had just opened that morning. Assuming the twins had had another come-apart go-round, I hollered at Sass to give it back to our brother. My sister rolled her eyes and explained yet another of their twinship pacts, "It's part of our plan, see. We're giving half our presents to the migrants, but we have to disguise them as un-brand-new so Mama won't realize Santa just got them for us and make us keep them."

"Mama will know, Sass. She got that for him." My sister's eyes split wide at this disclosure a hair-trigger moment before I realized what I'd done. The revelation sent her wiggledancing the dirt floor into a dust storm, and I realized it was the biggest of her mind's constant mysteries solved to date. She had always squared off with the idea of Mama not only allowing a soot-covered man into her best room, the pocket room, but permitting him to eat in there to boot.

Even though I knew Mama would know, I knew also that she would approve, so I added my new lace socks to the donation pile after wearing them very carefully and only once.

I remember them lying folded and borax white atop the box of clothes we took to the cabins that year. The back of Dad's truck was piled high with the dried branches the families liked to cook with, the damaged or used-up parts of our trees that had been pruned.

It makes me wish I were used so it would be alright for Joseph and me to occupy each other's space.

The Rambler

Arkansas MacTerptin

I am ginned up about the drive, with the moon reckoned to rise early
and fat and just in time so it looks like it's pulled skyward by the setting
sun's red-ray ribbons—the horizon-stretched ones that make shadows
their longest and shoot straight across just above the highway to light
afire corn tassel-tops and tint crimson and magic the whole world at
five feet the ground up. I can tell that it will happen soon, that the sun
is about to spring its glow across midair in a final stretch before bedding
the day, and I aim to catch its blaze in my palm, hoping to catch Mystery
and gift it to my sister in order to cure her sulk. My ready hand is on the
window roller and my head is counting down seconds that have turned to
mississippis like they always do when waiting happens.

My sister is hangdog about it all, the packing up the car, the slam-
ming shut the screen door, and the hard-door latch-click—the sound
that never you hear unless no one is on the other side of it waiting to let
you in and dance up the dust that won't stay outside no matter what gets
planted in the yard. She is inside of another shut-up place, dancing barefoot and silly and then slow in shallow waters to the songvoice music of
the one she is lowdown to leave behind. Next to me and the eight o'clock
moon is where she wishes she weren't sitting now, wishing it was next to
him instead, ankle-washed and heart-thick on a bottomland riverbend,
thinking burn-up-the-sun thoughts of each other.

My granny up front—talking thunder and raining down a litany of
convection, about the Holy Communion of Saints and the heavens split-
open to bucket-down intercession upon us—is not tipped in the mind
like a person who is not in this car yet still can see the sky may think
because of her tempest-talk. She's on about the one we left behind. The
only truck clouds have with this sky is their fire-finger reach across the
sun, drawing on the moon. I feel brand-new to the day even on account
of it being mostly over, but my sister looks tired when Granny moves
from the rain to my sister's notebook, eyeing it cattywhompas and noting
that my sister is powerful busy this evening.

My sister hikes the pages more closely to her and more aslant to our
granny but keeps on penciling, words tumbling mighty to the page, leapfrogging from heart to thought so alive and gussied they fall spot-into-fit
on the page's white and become the whole world, summoning up secret

smiles and the kinds of notions that make hearts beat crazy-like. I know because these thoughts are at her side, and that's where I sleep at nights, which she has come-lately acted unhappy about, saying she is too old to have to share sheets anymore, setting Granny to wonder who should be turned out so the queen might enjoy her own chambers.

My granny adds as how my sister and I are on our way to learn about Ms. Bonnie Grace, God bless her soul, and what happened when she took up keeping with a rambler, which square from utterance I want to know what's that. Granny is all the time using words I think I know already until I hear them shaped in her mouth. It's an icy eye-roll scold I receive from my sister, looking like she wants to take my bones apart and put them back together wrong on purpose. But Granny is happy to set out her definition for me, which I would be happy about likewise except that it requires further inquiry I don't dare undertake on account of staying off the snags in Her Majesty's crown. Calling her that in my head causes a smile she catches and returns but only half-like and without thinking, like a reflex gone feeble, and she is tearing out the page she finished, tucking it behind the others when she asks what I'm staring at.

I look away for the moon's cool white swell at the end of the blood-veined cloud-wisps and listen for my sister's wild heartbeat, the one she told me about last night while she wrote in her notebook about loving him all the way to yonder and so far beyond that distance hollers mercy just thinking about it, which reminded me of the day in science we visited the zoo and I heard a camel gut-noise a holler out into the world like he'd swallowed all its air and didn't like the taste so he caused it to backwards right out his mouth. I'd shucked tears laughing over it, but my sister just wrinkled her face and wanted to know could I sleep with the light on because she was going to need it for a while, so then I told her my new scratch-and-sniff opera joke, but she wasn't listening a snip and kept on writing with me there next to her, getting puffy in the eyes on account of the changes between us.

The last of the sun breaks free and blazes color mad across an earth-curve just above us, and my arm is pumping at the handle with a fever inside to match the blaze I am reaching toward when the pages of my sister's notebook start to riffle and then take to the air before either of us can react to stop what happens next when her burn-up-the-sun words flutter hard out the window to ride the flame fast away from us. I big-eye my sister who is looking toward Granny who is satisfied with what she sees in the rearview, and we both know the likelihood of her stopping the car is the same as rain. My mouth is open a little, with my throat not knowing what sound to make and my heart wanting to fold in on itself when my sister's gaze turns toward mine struggling to hold back every bit of what's inside her, and I would be afraid that this very moment has ruptured every after between us, except for in it I see that we are sun and moon red-ribbon tied, that whatever we may be in this moment and every after, we are for keeps.

The Problem

Toddy Milby

My little brother is on the kitchen floor cramming stars and moons into all the holes in his head while my mom glues sugar to the wall. *Makes no sense*, I stand in the hall and think as my grandma and her yowling arms squeeze past, taking some cats out to dry.

"It just doesn't make any sense," I announce as I place my books and paper on the counter and slide into the red stool before remembering that it's gone all wobbly. Been that way for two weeks. Ever since Dad's accident made him soft and he and my mom seemed to stop knowing each other. Dad, who everybody (except me and Lucas) calls *Slug*. Even his own mom, my sane grandma.

Once, when I was little like my brother, I'd asked Dad what his real name was and he'd told me. I was expecting it to be an awful name, like one you'd never forget. But it wasn't and I'd forgotten it almost right after he'd said it. I felt weird about that. It's one thing not to know your own Dad's first name, but a whole nother to forget it entirely.

I can't stand sitting on the red stool. Makes me crazy. So I scoot over to the yellow one, sliding my homework down with me.

The problem Deacon Peanut had assigned us on Friday kept me vexed all day yesterday and now today too. His name is actually Deacon Neaput, and he's standing in for Sister Aquiline, who had something unfortunate happen, but no one will tell us what, so we make it up at recess. Her predicament gets worse every day.

But secretly, I'm praying for Sister's miraculous return because I'm having a hard time with probability, and I don't ever raise my hand in class to address Deacon with my questions because I'm afraid I'm going to slip up and say *Peanut* to his face. *Aquila the Hun* is easier to keep straight from *Aquiline*, so I understood a lot more when she was there.

This was my first year for math with the Hun, and when Sister had called Mom for a conference after only the second week of school, I just knew it was going to be a terrible one. Except it turned out Sister wanted to put me in with the ninth-graders on account of I'd tested three years ahead of myself, or something like that.

And even though the switch in my schedule meant I'd have to take art with the third-graders, I was over the moon about it—until Tuffer Danner told me being "gifted" meant you were soft. But then he assured me that as long as I learned to cuss and hit somebody every now and then, I'd be alright, especially since my dad was crazy. Tuffer found out right then and there I already knew how to hit.

"Are you still working on that problem?" My mom is almost finished brushing granular crystals onto the blue wall, *to give it a nice sparkle*, she'd said. "The dice one?"

"Yeah. I just don't get it. It makes no sense."

"Read it to me again."

I open to the page I have marked, the one that has taken away my whole weekend. Two fugitive cats, Rumpus and Fluffalo, wet fur all matted up, dash into the room, scanning for cover. My brother takes a Lucky Charm from his ear and one from his nose, eats them, then reaches over to pet first the beefy grey cat and then the smaller black one on her only white spot, the one she was named for.

"Players take turns rolling two die at once. To score, a person must roll doubles. In a game with two players, what's the probability that doubles will be rolled by each player twice in a row?"

"My goodness," my mom says to the brush as she sugarcoats it. She kneels on the green stool to reach the part up by the ceiling on the fourth and last wall. Behind her, the dog has finished licking off most of the sugar up to about knee-high on the wall she'd started with. Then he starts licking Rumpus.

"What's *probility*?" The word wrestles with my brother's tongue. He is standing next to me now, his head just below the lip of the counter.

"It's *chances*. The chance that something might happen."

"Oh. I know all about that," he assures me.

"Do you now? Then you don't need for me to tell you."

The cat scrunches up but doesn't run away while the dog licks the top of her head. She is the only cat who hasn't tried to blind our dog and he likes her for it. I turn back to the book.

"Okay. Tell me."

I ignore him.

"Tell me!" Rumpus starts and bolts from the room.

"Lucas, you're bothering your brother. Let him do his homework."

"It's okay, Mom. Tell you what?" I turn to my brother. Below me, his eyes are wide and the dog starts eating the cereal-spill Rumpus caused on her way out.

"Tell what is it," he says, then remembers to add, "please."

"What's what?" I smile.

He huffs. Then tries hard, "Probility," barely getting that much out. Polishing off the last compressed marshmallow, the dog starts in on the second wall.

"Prob-i-bility."

"Yeah, that!" My brother stomps his footed pajama feet and swings his arms, hitting his wrist on a drawer knob.

He looks up at me to see if he's okay, so I start explaining before he has a chance to cry. "Okay, Lucas, listen. I have a penny, and I throw it up into the air. What are the chances that it's going to land tail-side up?"

He's still holding his wrist, but tears have been forgotten. "It might."

"Exactly. But what are the chances that it might?"

"If it does, then it will."

I look up and see my mom smiling. Just like always, she feels me looking and turns toward me. Then she sees the dog. "Oh word! Put Lucas outside, will you?"

"Why, Mommy? I'll be quiet."

"No, not you, honey. The dog." It had been my brother's idea to name the dog after himself when he was too young for my mom to tell him what a stupid idea it was. So it happened.

"I can't, Mom," I tell her. "Grandma's out there baptizing the cats."

"Oh, my lands. Has she dunked them again?"

My brother is now trying to climb the red stool so I pull him onto it before answering her, "Yeah. And the orange one is starting to lose some hair too."

"Pumpkin's going bald!" My little brother giggles and throws his feet out in front of him, which is just enough for the stool to throw him off backwards and into the aluminum pan of modge-podge and sugar.

The word *hell* slips out of my mom's mouth as she and the dog scramble toward my wailing brother. The dog wins. Dad used to always cuss around us, but Mom hardly ever did. It seems like at the same time they stopped knowing each other, I stopped knowing each of them too. I turn to my mom, and hell is all over her face as it finds mine. "Go fill up the tub, will you? Hurry."

I trip in the folds of the old shower-curtain tarp on the way out of the kitchen, my toe all twisted up in it. When I come back, my mom has stopped my brother's crying by telling him he is a paintbrush with an important job. He is flat against the wall, dripping, smearing himself over the bald spots caused by the dog who is busy lapping at his pajamas.

My mom is on the yellow stool with the thumb and index finger of her left hand pressed to the corner of her eyes. It makes me not want to tell her what I have to. "Mom? The tub's all backed up. Cat hair and other stuff. I guess Grandma baptized the fern too."

She is quiet, her hand still pressed to her eyes.

"Should I get Dad?"

"No. I'll call Stretch. Your dad doesn't . . . won't . . . I'll just call Stretch." She wipes her fingers on her jeans and sniffs slightly, raising her eyebrows and blinking hard and quickly a few times. She looks at my brother, now sucking on the bristles of the real brush. The dog at his side. Then me. Smiles a little, shrugs, "Well, at least it's non-toxic."

I don't look right at her, but I smile back as I take the green stool next to her. She pushes my books over to me, and I think about the problem.

The Hoover and the Homework Ghost

Sister Aquiline

Responsible for the fourth- through eighth-grade instruction of math and religion at St. Brendan's for more years than not, I'm known around here as Aquila the Hun, and I'd swear on my gradebook a gigantic Hoover lurks outside my classroom door, charging up all day, awaiting the final bell's cue, at which time twenty-odd preteen bodies are instantly ingested. Afterward, at my desk, sagging behind the perpetual piles of paper I wish the Hoover would swallow, I breathe the unnatural air of stillness that hovers in the wake of each mass exodus, a peculiar current of quiet that will remain until the next flood upon the room.

I stare at the tidal debris left behind: broken pencils, a calculator battery cover, shreds of spiral-bound perforation, and an abandoned note, its message already forgotten. Turning to my paperwork, the outside edge of my vision barely discerns the fleck of white as it washes in silently on an invisible wave. It drifts on the edge of perception until curiosity stirs my focus from the task at hand, shifting my attention from the stack on the desk to the sheet on the floor. Numbers stare up at me from a page of loose notebook paper soiled countless times over with the dusty silhouettes of the very latest trends in shoeprints. A homework ghost.

Like this one, they are usually unsigned, and I typically place them where they might be recognized and claimed at a later date. Sometimes, an identifying characteristic will catch my attention and I'll return the ghost to the locker where it belongs, leaving its owner to wonder how it was there the whole time. Once, I kept a copy of one. A name written on it had caught my attention, but it wasn't the name of the assignment's owner, though this one had been signed proudly. An expressive essay assignment for Sister Celeste's English class, its author, Sass the Indomitable—the granddaughter of Mother Cosma's friend and nemesis, Hazel Genevieve Lefebryon McGann—had chosen to write about her First Communion.

The narrative had already been graded, an A, and an assessment that should have merited a stern word with Sister Celeste. The essay warranted more than Sister Celeste's grammatical mark-ups. It warranted Reconciliation and a study of no fewer than three treatises on each the Blessed Sacrament, transubstantiation, and idolatry vs. iconography. But instead of pursuing admonishment, for reasons I hold close and still can't exactify, I'd only attached a brief note to the end of the essay after copying and then returning it, anonymously, slipped through the grill of a locker.

Mother Cosma would have reprimanded me for my neglect, as the narrative was filled with notions embraced by a young mind heavily influenced by what Mother referred to as *free-wheeling*, lowercased-catholic beliefs; and Mother Cosma was constantly looking for inroads to allow more capitalized, *free-will*ing catechistic beliefs to take hold in the young MacTerptins. The struggle between the tenacious German Mother and the fiery French grandmother was constant but rooted in love. Mother Cosma felt catechism was best understood and most firmly gleaned through structured teaching, but Hazel Genevieve Lefebryon McGann felt Catholicity was best gleaned implicitly through its roots: Grace and Mystery.

In the essay, it appeared Sass's grandmother was winning, but it was the name of Sass's *other* grandmother that caught my attention.

> *This morning for breakfast I had myself some peaches and cream divine, which called to mind the bless-out I received in second grade for broadcasting to First Communion class a couple of clean-sprung sacramental food notions that piggybacked right out my mouth before I noticed the look from Father Manzelough telling me I was in big trouble with Jesus. Still, I reckoned my notion was a heap better than the grape-juice one Baptists like my grandmother Ms. God Bless Bonnie Grace Brodie MacTerptin had come up with.*
>
> *I remember pressing the issue, using all the big and sacred words I knew, thinking I could make Father understand how sophisticated and informed my idea was, but my efforts were in vain. I might as well have aimed my sentences backwards for all he understood. He assigned me away with an entire Rosary to recite even though I'd confessed nothing, and with each Hail Mary, I knew the Holy Mother of God agreed with me that Jesus might at least enjoy hearing about my idea even if it didn't end up panning out after all with what He and His Dad and Their best friend the Holy Spirit had in mind.*
>
> *Shortly after this, Father Manzelough taught us about St. Francis and how in his time, the Church wasn't ready for his ideas. I don't suppose I knew what irony was at the*

*time (but now I do thanks to your class). Still, I reckon its
impression lighted itself square upon me then, and ever
after Mr. Frank Assisi has been my favorite saint. When
I told Granny, she gave me a book with his ideas in it (I
don't know if you've ever read any of his poetry or mystical
ramblings—probably so, because Granny said you have
sense—which means you know how the man can make a body
itch what doesn't scratch. His words move inward toward
you and land heavy upon your reckoning like late-July heat
so thick instead of pushing through a screen it pulls right
open the summer door and walks on in. I think if more people
read Mr. Frank's words this world wouldn't recognize itself
amen.)*

    *But anyway, the day of my very First of all times
Communion, I was watching Father hold high the fancy
silver cup and saucer and undertaking hard to fix my mind
on all the hallowed notions it was supposed to be having, but
I still couldn't shake wondering if the body and blood of the
Holiest Man Ever might could taste the same as when I bit
my sister or fell off the minibike and sunk teeth to tongue,
and that if I were the kin of God, I would think about maybe
suggesting pralines and peachmilk instead.*

    *Then I saw Father hold up the mega-oversized host—
the one the priest gets to eat special—and then he said some
things to the saints on the ceiling—asking for extra blessings,
I reckoned—before breaking it in half, which when I first
ever saw I thought surefire was an accident. How much
trouble are you in with Jesus when you break him in half?
But that time when I saw it, all I could think was I wanted
the other half.*

    *I could think of no reason why I wanted it other than
selfishness and excitement and the fact that I understood it to
be a miracle in the making. The Answer to end all questions.
Lost in this state, there are few things can snap me out of it.
One of them is the furious-eyed, angle-browed glare of Sister
Aquiline, and it addleclutched me fierce as I stood up from
my kneeler, remembering there was a hymn I was supposed to
be joined in singing with the rest of the class. This made me
recollect the prayers I was supposed to have been thinking the
whole time I'd been fixated on getting a hold of the wonder
wafer. I just knew I was going to the Down Place.*

> *As I approached the altar, I thought sure the Devil's fires*
> *were licking my ankles and was on the drop edge of breaking*
> *left and hotfooting it for the door when Father Manzelough*
> *caught my eye and smiled. I know it sounds hard to believe,*
> *but he did. I pulled back my veil and checked. It was touch-*
> *and-go there for a while inside my seven-year-old soul, but*
> *I decided to stick it out in that alphabetical line and keep*
> *shuffling priestward, because I felt sure the Virgin was going*
> *to send me a sign about how right I was.*
>
> *The Blessed Lady did not disappoint, and I nearly*
> *fainted forward onto Father when he handed me the host and*
> *I saw the broken piece of Jesus lying in my hand. It wasn't*
> *the Other Half; it was more like half of a half of that Half.*
> *Still, it wasn't the perfect little round flat stamped disc that*
> *glued itself to my tongue, but a jagged shard of a jumbo God*
> *that melted there. It didn't taste like pralines (which was*
> *what I had predicted the Blessed Lady's miracle sign would*
> *be), but it felt extra blessed surefire.*

The note I'd added read simply, "I like peachmilk and pralines too, but nothing compares to the Precious Blood and Body of Christ: 'Above all gifts from God is the grace of overcoming self'—St. Francis of Assisi."

It is perhaps this about the ghost that haunts me most—not because of what the names on the page mean to me, not because I'd missed an opportunity to catechize, and not because of what I'd written, but because the person to whom it was written believed the note had been penned by the saint himself.

I move to pick up the ghost before me now and place it in one of the many metal basket-trays on my desk where I will recall and retrieve it at collection time when its frenetic owner sifts through folders and back-pack, swearing on younger siblings' lives that the assignment was completed. But I stop sharply as the severe little figures on the page confront me, each digit lined up in column according to place value—not simply in every individual problem but throughout the entire page's assignment. It is then I realize whose paper I hold in hand. Staring at myriad zeroes added to occupy spaces that would otherwise be blank, I wonder how it can possibly be, but it is.

Toddy. *Order is the rule and chaos the fool* Toddy. Gifted, troubled, heartsore. I look again. Tomorrow's homework. Imagining the panic that will ensue, I brush off what loose dirt I can from the paper while I walk to the doorway, smiling as I imagine being brought face-to-face with the awesome power of the giant Hoover.

Shuffling down the hall in a gait that accommodates my too-big shoes, I stop in front of Toddy's locker, folding the paper and then sliding it between the crack where metal meets metal and each school day begins. Halfway through, it gets stuck. I wiggle it. Ripping it.

Rupturing zeroes, cleaving columns. Realizing the confusion I have triggered among the numbers and their place value, a part of me feels ridiculously delighted at having thwarted the system. But then I cringe, recalling Toddy and the numbers that rule his world, that help it make sense, that keep it from collapsing inward on him.

I gently coax the paper from its jam when Squint DeWitt passes by with a listless mop. Squint has quietly roamed these halls—talking little but smiling lots—for more years than not, taking his custodial job the summer after his high-school graduation longsome years ago.

His father and mine worked Number Seven. His father and mine. If Squint ever knew they were the same man, he never let on. I had a good twenty years on Squint, but his first ten were so full of fustle he looked like the twenty years were his on me. At ten, Squint's trouble died along with his father and that's when mine began.

I'd grown up in St. John's Glen Addie Orphanage several towns north of here. At twenty, I came to St. Brendan's to teach math, not to discover I was the illegitimate child of two parents who were still alive, one barely—yet that's what ended up happening despite.

At sixteen, my mother had accepted far too many offers of an escort home from one Mr. Harlan DeWitt, far too many years older than she. He last delivered her to her doorstep pregnant. Then he married Elsie Tatum—also sixteen, and also pregnant.

Seven babies later, most of them Elsie's, Squint was born. Squint nods a polite acknowledgement toward me now, and I watch as the folds in his face curve and tighten into his well-worn smile as he sees me at the locker and interprets my task.

Shortly before our father's death, Mother Cosma told me of my past, only after a visit from Bonnie Grace Brodie MacTerptin had made her aware of it—and of the harm that might come from me hearing about it elsewhere. Bonnie Grace, who had known a daughter immediately upon seeing her, knew it was best to offer up such ecstatic pain, and for ten years she kept her own heart silent to keep her daughter's from disruption. But when a visit to Harlan DeWitt's deathside made Bonnie Grace realize he had not only confessed to Elsie the existence of another daughter, but also his suspicions that her name was now Aquiline, Bonnie Grace requested permission for her daughter to know the truth if she hadn't been told already.

Bonnie Grace feared that once Harlan DeWitt died, the contempt Elsie held for him in her heart, the same contempt his now-dead fists had kept her from acting on, would beat freely into the lives of others, with the potential for devastating them, a devastation Elsie was all-too-familiar with. Before Bonnie Grace visited the news upon Mother Cosma, she'd paid a visit to Elsie DeWitt's side. But the widow was unmoved by Bonnie Grace's plea that the town's biggest secret remain that way.

"They've talked about you and him all my days, Bonnie Brodie." Elsie spoke the name like a curse. "Do you know how many times I've had to hear that brother of yours preaching hell in my ear about my own kin? And to think, his own mutt kin is a Roman Catholic bride. Rich, ain't it? No. I ain't holding my tongue on account of you keeping your secret sacrosanct for no Christian cause. Why don't you ask your Jesus if he knows my cause? I can't walk this town twice at midnight for folks seeping pity on me in the dreams they're having behind doors. They think I don't know about you and Harlan and all the others. You all been right in front of me my whole life and I had to just take it. Well, I ain't going to sit there and just take your presence anymore. I'm going to stand right up in it and call y'all out."

"Elsie, please. This town has talked unending about me too. You and I were just girls when it happened. I had no idea Harlan was your beau. Please, Elsie. This has naught to do with us any longer, anyway. You can stand up and call me whatever names you like until the end of time. Just don't bring my baby girl into it. Please, *please*. It's her and Tim I want to protect from harm. I only got to have one more after my baby girl. And it's these two babies I have to protect above all else in life. You're a mother five times over, Elsie DeWitt. Your heart knows that charge. And that's what I'm speaking to right now. Please, listen to your heart as a mother and you'll know why I have to ask this of you. I have to protect my family."

Elsie sat quietly and still, her heart racing. "Then leave."

"What?"

"Leave I said. I've had to take their talk of you all my life, and I've wanted to hurt you for it all my life. And now that I know how to, I'm afraid I will unless you just get the hell out of my life. I have nowhere to go, Bonnie Brodie, or I would have got out long ago. Listen to your heart as a woman and you'll know why I ask this of you."

Bonnie Grace did not hesitate. "If I leave your sight forever, Elsie Tatum DeWitt, do I have it on your word as a mother that you will not harm my babies?"

"You have my word, Bonnie Brodie." And this time, Elsie did not use my mother's name like a curse.

It wasn't the first time my mother made a sacrifice on my behalf.

It seems that upon discovering her pregnancy, Bonnie Grace's parents had sent her to live at an establishment for young mothers in Chicago where I would be given away at birth. But on the way to Chicago, when the train stopped in the town of Belleville, Hazel Genevieve Lefebryon, my mother's best friend who had accompanied her on the ride north and had heard enough about the orphan trains to know the State was no fit ward for a baby, spotted a hand-lettered sign she understood as a much larger, God-written one. The paper sign had been tacked over a wooden one that read *Glen Addie State Orphanage*. Rippling in the wind were the words posted over it: *Now St. John's Home for Orphaned Children, Operated by the Order of Poor Clares*.

"You can't go wrong with the Franciscans," Hazel Genevieve had assured my mother before riding the train the rest of the way to Chicago by herself to pretend to the agency that she was Bonnie Grace and had lost the baby some days before. For months until Bonnie Grace's return, Hazel Genevieve visited the Brodies daily, bringing them their mail. As she'd hoped, they mistook her visits for a kind and Godly interest in their daughter who had strayed, and they never noticed Hazel Genevieve remove from the letterbox any inquiries from the agency in Chicago, mainly because none ever came. When Baxter Octan started mistaking her visits for much more than a kind and Godly interest in him, Hazel Genevieve waited patiently until Bonnie Grace returned—whisper-thin the town thought—before setting him straight with a blow that bent him at the middle.

I am glad to know all of this, but often I wonder about God's reason for landing me back here for this knowledge when there seems naught to do with it. Mother Cosma and I are the only ones still alive with any knowledge left to act upon. Elsie apparently never told a soul as Bonnie Grace had feared she would. Instead of an explosive secret, it has become a large and private void, a black hole in my existence.

When Mother Cosma gave me permission to transfer to another school elsewhere, I had refused, asking only for permission to attend the funeral and sit in the balcony above the long wall where I could hear the voices of the wakers as they approached the casket. So I could hear about my father, their recollections, their stories, to know what they knew. *If they knew.*

And perhaps that's why I'd simply written a note on Sass's essay instead of calling her out. *Because I knew.* Knew that she who called me *Sister* could call me *Aunt.*

I watched my brother that day as I watch him now, patient and quiet. With long and hairy fingers, he works the combination lock, and I notice for the first time that his right index finger is crooked, inciting me to share with him the many miseries of my own pinky toe and the reason for my too-big shoes. Surprising me with uncharacteristic talkativeness, he in turn shares each painful detail in the decades-long life of a long-suffering finger, and we both dutifully perform the concerned-look headshakes that accompany the shared understanding of such marathon tales of tragedy.

For a moment we forget the locker dangling open between us, its pristine organization revealing books and possessions at precise right angles to one another, awaiting their own tragedy. I deposit the paper carefully on top, and in silence we three mangled bodies part ways. Somewhere in the muffled distance, a vacuum drones.

The Longwall

Stretch Waters and Dog Dentleman

"Always thought it'd be the goddam black lung. Never reckoned on this."

"Doc Harbar said the sonofabitch died hard."

"Died hard, my ass. Only thing hard about it was the one who done the dying. Callous bastard."

"I think that's what Doc meant, Stretch. Harlan DeWitt died a long-some time ago. He just refused to lie down until now."

"Damn right. Died hard, then. Died hard."

"You know I thought I'd seen tough until I worked that longwall excavation with Cockeye out near Seven. I've never known a man DeWitt's age so strong."

"Strong and stubborn. I wish you could've seen him the day of the collapse. Hell, we was buried right up to our goddam eyeballs when that rib broke loose, and DeWitt hollering the whole time that we was all no-account, couldn't haul ass with a wheelbarrow and all that. No-account, my ass. It was on his goddam account we got into that length of soft-top. Sonofabitch wasn't no sharper than a sack a' wet mice and him trying to tell me about my affairs."

"DeWitt was no fool. Foolhardy, perhaps."

"Well, the only thing sharp about the damnfool was the dadburned flint where his brain oughten to have been. Tough nut to crack, by-god. Quicker than shit through a runt hound, though. I'll owe him that 'til the day these bones quit their jig. Hadn't been for him, we wouldn't of got out of that fall."

"I'll never tell a soul I heard you say that, Stretch."

"Well, we wouldn't of got into it, neither. Goddam soft-top. I'm getting out of that hole. Going into plumbing. Working the shit of the earth's better than the pit of the earth all day long."

"I thought you hated town. Isn't that where most shitpipes are found these days?"

"Naw, just the fancy ones. Maybe I'll just get some mules bred instead. That's what Mama wants anyway."

"Well, it doesn't appear that this world is going to run out of asses any time soon, so it looks like you're solid no matter which work you choose."

"What about you, Dog? Think you'll take charge of Cockeye's survey outfit someday? Be a nice cushy gig. You just might could have to settle down."

"I told you, Stretch, just like I told Milby, you'll find me naked and singing church hymns on top of that coal hopper before you'll see me at the altar."

"Well, little Miss Marjorie J. is damnsure going to be disappointed to hear that."

"Lord save us all from Miss Marjorie J."

"Oh shitfire, speaking of hoppers, how about Tim's parents packing across the Cumberland? What's that about?"

"I reckon that's their concern."

"Well, I never thought I'd see the day Bonnie Grace and Hopper MacTerptin hauled out of here. Tim ain't going, is he?"

"Lord, no. The only thing that could separate him from Clare McGann is a draft notice."

"I sure wish one of Jelly's girls would get all tore up over me. Finer than fiddle strings, that crop."

"Amen."

"Mama said she saw Ms. Bonnie Grace at the Motherhouse a few days back. Said she and Mother Cosma walked the grounds for near the whole morning with Ms. Bonnie Grace in tears more than a few times."

"Beautiful place."

"Now, you know as well as I do Ms. Bonnie Grace is as far from Catholic as a Baptist like her is from gin and dice, the poor sorts. I can't figure why she'd of been there."

"Now, Stretch, don't go judging folks by your own half-bushel. You know nuns can talk to Prots without hell having a hailstorm."

"I know that. I just wonder if it was about this business here with DeWitt. You know the talk well as I do."

"Listen. When we get up there, don't you so much as breathe anything foolheaded on Elsie DeWitt, you hear? She's like to know most of what other folks only think they do, and the last thing she needs right now is a reminder."

"Jesus, Dog. I wasn't going to say nothing to her. You're the one's about as subtle as horse shit in a milk bucket. You suppose Elsie's taking it alright?"

"I think Elsie's been taking it all her life."

"True. I reckon she's a mite potholed, but she'll fix."

"She's got fortitude."

"I just hope the woman's still got a few miles of easy left. She'd of walked through hell in kerosene britches for that sonofabitch. Takes a right-fine woman to stand by a man like that, don't you think?"

"I have no idea what it takes, Stretch."

"Damn right, by-god. Right fine. Best of her litter. Too bad he had so many without her."

"When did you turn into such a tabby, Stretch? I've never seen you on about other folks' business so much."

"Well, this whole uprooting to the Bootheel business is just leaving a stink in my mouth like the lick side of an envelope, that's all."

"And that's not our seal to break."

"But what of it, Dog? If Ms. Bonnie Grace was needing some God on the issue, why wouldn't she just of consulted with that pansyass sermon-monger brother of hers?"

"Perhaps because he's a 'pansyass sermon-monger'?"

"Well, Jesus Christ, ain't he? I mean, just who in the everwho does he think he is, preaching like that? Goddam fool talks in cursive, by-god."

"You're right, Stretch. I can't imagine why Ms. Bonnie Grace wouldn't want to have a change of spiritual venue from time to time."

"Have you seen him at work down in the bottoms with those orchard migrants? Stays busier than a one-legged cat hiding his scat on a marble floor, trying to pry them statues and rosaries loose of their hands. Yammering, stomping, praying. Earning every bit of what folks pay him to fight voodoo."

"Voodoo? I thought you were Catholic."

"I am. I don't pay that preacher nothing and I ain't the one saying that stuff's voodoo. I'm just saying the man's hard a-work as he sees it."

"Guess he's just doing his job, then."

"Doing his job, my ass. Unless doing your job is living off the backs of folks."

"Best money's in God and garbage."

"Don't you know it. And war. Slug Milby's called up, you know."

"We're next."

"Don't you know it. Shitfire, it's hot. You ready to go pound some corn after this?"

"Does a frog bump his ass when he jumps?"

"Don't you know it."

"Stop saying that."

"Goddam, Dog. I think I'm gonna miss the sonofabitch."

"Milby or DeWitt?"

"Both, but I ain't in no hurry to join either."
"I do reckon we've got a mite bit of time left."
"Lord willing and the creek don't rise."

Gumbo Mundee

Arkansas MacTerpin

River mist rose from reeds like earth-breath. Everybody'd gussied up, shoes shined, ribbons pressed. No one had to dress fancy for the event; it wasn't like we hadn't all seen each other whooping and dancing in our barn clothes. But it wasn't often that we all got together for parties where the whiskey wasn't served in tubs, and on those occasions we dressed high even though no one said we had to, like at wakes where we had to show the dead we cared enough to scrub between our toes. But on this night, for my cousin's wedding to the girl from town, in the argentine moonlight we all shone, even the wapiti bikers—oiled-down, waxed-up, and turned-out in their best leathers and nobody caring if they weren't. Granny would have called it a Saturdee soiree.

We'd parked at the edge of the chokecherries and followed a path of river-grind toward the house, the high spirits of distant fiddle strings beckoning the way, promising revelry. Spoons, jugs, and tubs came each at a time, with a harp finally joining the saw to deliver the peculiar melodic riddle of harmony that isn't.

A trail of fist-sized pebbles barred our footprints from sinking into the silt-washed loam beneath, earth that would undertake to dry and set up like concrete until the river swelled again, melting mud and rinsing rocks back into its current. My feet itched to brush bare across the smooth rounded stones as they pressed into the mire that held them, but the bottletops I'd glued to my boot-bottoms to sound like the tap dancer I desperately wanted to be clicked and scraped my thoughts into a sprightly song that matched my clumsy clatter-prance across water pavement.

It'd been this jaunty jitterjig that had prompted Granny to suggest Tanglefoot Fancypants as my stage name, and it took me places. On this night I tapped right up the knees of the trees and danced with the breeze in the branches above. I followed the echo of a katydid cadence across the hogback bluffs that lined the bottomlands and into Indian-summer rainsheets that rippled in southwind curves across tall grasses, folding back into themselves in graceful retreat when they met the dipping currents obliging them aside for a season. Lost to time and place amid the kudzu-coated cypress, my thoughts snapped back into clear sense as we turned a crook and our vine-veiled view opened at once wide and close.

High up on stilts, the unfinished cabin looked like a blazing altar to the river gods Granny had told me existed only in the best books and imaginations. Lit by kerosene and coal, flinty fire pits climbed its walls, and tresses of smoke drifted gently aloft, hovering, lightly, like gallinippers through a screen. His bride was crazy about porches, so my cousin had put one on all sides and two cut right through the middle, dividing the cabin's four main rooms whose broad doors could be flung wide to trinity's breezeway. The storms that had swathed the gibbous barley moon this harvest had also kept the house from being completed in time for its occupants; but on a night filled with cicada spirits, a pedestaled dance floor with walls and windows open to way-up stars and the fiddle notes that floated there was the perfect place to be.

The brisk forecast had been fooled by the humid atmosphere that always hung heavy in the bottoms, low and weighty wind-whispers that would ignore seasons and sigh snow on even the driest day of our Decembers. I watched it tickle and curl the wispy parts of the bride's pinned-up hair, just in front of her ears, as she cried softly over the contents of a tiny box my mama had just handed to her. It was a gift my mama had been given by her mama, who would have been the bride's Granny-in-law.

I'd seen Mama take the necklace from our 'loom box a few days before. The 'loom box was where everybody's favorite stuff got placed after they died, which is why my red-haired brother called it the doom box. Granny said the stuff was meant for "passin' on when you did," which is why my sleepwalking sister cried out fierce when she saw Mama put our newest baby sister's fancy robe in the 'loom box the day after her baptism. For a while, no one could notion why she was crying, but then no one really bothered to puzzle her tears because she only ever took to them over senseless and half-witted things, like the smell of Mr. Dumont's hogs when we passed them on the way to town—an act my red-haired brother said was about as asinine as a migratory bird hitching the Serengeti on a rhino. Even though he read lots of books, he shared knowledge solely through insults, so no one paid him much mind, either.

On account of living way out beyond those hogs, we couldn't check things out of the town library, so we played library in secret, checking things out of the 'loom box and keeping them hidden from those who would wallop us if they found out. Instead of charging fines, we decided overdue items would cause the borrower to be haunted by the original owner of the item. For this reason I kept Granny's rosary, the one

Grandpa Jelly made for her out of creek gravel, for weeks after it was due, hoping she'd come visit me. I still had it the night of the wedding party, but she hadn't hollered at me over it yet.

Granny had almost made it to the wedding, but she left late in September with the cicadas, barely three weeks after she returned with Texas and me from the Ozarks, where we stayed with Grandpa Hopper and learned about Ms. God Bless Bonnie Grace while the rest of the family went to Nashville. We learned that our daddy's mama had gotten herself involved with a rambler when she was a girl and that it had haunted her days for the rest of them, finally driving her away to die in a place far removed from her heart.

When we returned, the apples had been harvested, but Henry and long-muscled Joseph, who had stayed only to see the last Jonathan plucked, were gone. Also upon our return, my red-haired brother presented me with bright red cowgirl boots to pair with his cowboy blue ones. Neither of us have worn another pair of shoes since. We even wore them to the funeral for Granny, who never caught eyes with us together in our boots without winking an I-love-you grin.

Granny was the one who had liked my cousin's bride from the start and, unlike some of the family, harbored no misgivings on account of my cousin's fiancée having grown up with library privileges and wall-to-wall carpet. I liked her because one day when they were dreaming and planning the details of their future home, she told my cousin that in their kitchen, she would prefer not to have a telephone unless it was not a non-cordless one, and nobody could figure out which kind she meant. Still couldn't.

It was apple-picking time two orchardfulls ago when she first came around with my cousin, and Grandpa Jelly was out at the burn barrel with my dad and me when he'd remarked that she could make a bobcat snap a log chain by-god, sending Granny off the porch and into the yard bellowing in tongues and waving a rake. He ran from her then. The cats fled too, like they always did when Granny catapulted into a foreign tirade, but the dogs just joined right in the chase. Our dogs were dumb like that.

I turned to my dad and asked what she was so mad about this time. He just prodded at the ashes and said Grandpa better hope Granny's legs weren't as good as her hearing. He wouldn't explain to me what Grandpa Jelly had meant, and I would have threatened to ask Mama, but Dad had already warned me to always check with him when I overheard Grandpa's riddletalk because Mama didn't handle the translation well.

But I'd learned not to repeat anything I overheard ever since my red-haired brother's friend asked him what the fuck a cowbell was for. I didn't stick around for the answer because you could never trust them from that brother. Instead, I went into where my dad was working on a motor twice my height, pulled strips of twine from the seed sacks and tied bows all over my hair, and then climbed the bush hog before putting the question to him. Verbatim.

For two whole days I thought cowbells must be the most wretched things on earth until Granny visited my prison room and explained what had made my daddy show his barmy side. When she sat down on my sister's side of the bed and explained what *that* word meant, I nearly fell off the end of mine. Mama had never mentioned that word when she'd told my sister and me the outrageous news about babies one day not long ago. Just thinking about it made me want to throw away all of my dolls all over again. I had no idea what to say, so I just stared until Granny left the room, hollering over her shoulder that cowbells were for football games.

The bride's own daddy, a county judge, had helped marry them on top of Pleasant Hill, deep in the Shawnee, the only church in our parts that had a paved road running to it. It'd been packed dirt and rock until a few mammoth trucks came through to cut something called an easement. Turned out there wasn't anything easy about it, and before they were done, part of Pleasant Cemetery slid down its hill, including my great-grandmother who had spoken French in her kitchen, in confession, and in her sleep. She ended up in Our Lady of Divine Mercy territory after that. Her little-girl life along the Loire must have tiptoed into her grown-up naps alongside the Mississippi shores that kept her so tired. She had been babysitting my red-haired brother the day she lay down for good, and he says that's how he knew she had fallen into the sleep without dreams, because all at once she'd broken off trancing aloud in her voodoo-gumbo-language. But he hardly ever knew what he was talking about. He was only eleven months when her footprints quit the soil.

There wasn't anything voodoo about the way my granny spoke her mama's French, though she mainly saved it up for when she was mad at Grandpa. No matter how mad she got, it still made her sound a heap prettier than her crumpled-up face looked on those occasions, yammering and chasing after him.

She spoke Gumbo French to me once when I was telling Mama over carrots at the sink about the Huge-knots that got kicked out of France. Granny sat me down straight and taught me plain how to say the word Mr. Crowell had made us read about but never pronounced for us, yet only after she blessed me out and walloped my backside with a sack of flour that left a big white poof mark on my pants for desecrating the language of the saints.

The last time I got to hear the sacred language was on the day she died, spoken in a hush to my grandpa, though I don't suspect she was mad because the tears puddling in his eyes ran down his face and bent up into the seams of a smile. Thinking about that made me want to climb into his lap, and I scouted the crosscut dancefloor for my grandpa, finding him recollecting the very moment that sent me searching, staring into an almost-empty sugar-whiskey, the glass reflecting his face the moment Granny last whispered in tongues. I watched as his fingers fiddled inside the pockets of his suit coat, the same one he wore when they put Granny in the ground next to her reburied mama.

I had seen him digging in the pockets of his dusty denim jacket a thousand times before, and whenever I'd ask him what was in there, he'd tell me that's where he kept all his yesterdays. I liked hearing that so I asked him all the time. But this time I just wished I could pull one out for him.

A few days before when I'd asked what he missed most about Granny, Grandpa told me it was how she could mix into a sentence soup words like *magnifique* and *Mundee*, making them sound together as perfect as the poetry of pigeons, plainly familiar but lovely, like the kiss of a well-worn memory. Most people I knew couldn't stand pigeons, and after Grandpa Jelly's words, I knew I would consider this detestment about them for as long as I would know them, that they would wear it like a scar of suspicion.

"Looks like you're on the deep end of a drunk again!" hollered Cockeye Murk as he slapped my grandpa's back, smacking him back to the party and cheering him with stories of his mule-trading neighbor, Stretch. Stretch Waters—who hated town and treed coons and loved mama, all in equal measure like a country boy should—had apparently just swapped wads of cash for a prize-winning Portuguese hybrid whose name translated to "Buckethead." While Cockeye and Grandpa Jelly cut up over the expensive and ugly beast, I trotted off to cram buttermints in my cheeks and dance the wooly-booly boogie just like Mama taught me.

I must have fallen asleep on the rag rugs piled up by the fireplace sometime after Uncle Hap and Squint DeWitt quieted the fiddle playing to sing their homemade duet about "living south of the paddleboat shores where Tom kissed Becky on a summer morn and north of the delta shores where Tutwiler's water tower claims 'the blues was born.'" It didn't have a title so that's what they called it. My mama called it crap, and I didn't get to see her hush them up like she usually did because I fell into a dream where I lay belly-up on a sunny sandbar while river gods fanned me and the voice of heaven flowed to me in a language that made me shudder all the way down to my tips of my tapping toes, and in that moment I understood completely.

I didn't know what time it was when I opened my eyes to leftover grown-ups sobering up over the last case of beer. I just knew I had borrowed treasure to return.

Riprap

Clare and Tim MacTerptin

His thoughts meandered to Old Doc Harbar as he steered pontoons past buoys warning shallow shores, and for a moment they lingered on the curiosity of a body's decomposition in tepid waters. That his wife delighted in telling the grisly story disturbed him only slightly less than imagining the old doctor's remains. Surely the carcass was bare by now, fish having picked clean charred flesh. Drifting, on the brink of speculating whether he and his father-in-law, Jelly, had cleaned and fried any of those fish, his youngest screamed and thoughts converged to generate immediate action. The motor choked by the kill switch, his finger still pressed the toggle as he discovered with relief and annoyance Michigan had only dropped her Twinkie. He moved his hand from toggle to ignition while Clare moved to wipe tears and splattered spongecake.

She'd say all she wanted this, last, any weekend, was to wish the house silent, hexing a freeze on the tireless clatterracket of its small bodies while she enjoyed a coma on the couch with fans on high and tea in hand. But instead she'd pluck from midair the humidity-saturated little bodies of her youngest three, wondering what age sweat stops smelling like vanilla and fresh-cut wood, and toss them into the rear-facing wagon seat behind her oldest three, wondering when their hands and feet had stopped looking childlike. Squeezed next to each other and everything else needed to sustain six stair-step kids throughout a weekend at the lake, the kids would sing and slap-up while she and Tim listened to the same Patsy Cline eight-track they always did in the car ever since it'd gotten stuck there seven years prior.

Indian summer was in full blaze upon them, and Clare was as anxious as her children for the cove toward which they steered. She too had once been plucked from swing sets and blistery ball courts and then plunged into the initial chill of lake water on sunny skin. A handful of miles distant was a world where the full round moon competed with only campfires and fireflies, and she and her siblings and cousins had welcomed its liquid radiance, pouring into youthful imaginations, stirring up hours of sleepless whispers and hushed laughter. On those scorching weekends, they left the splinters of her backyard porch for wide spaces where breezes are born, for tall weeds peppered with ticks, for forested hills carpeted with desiccated leaves, for the waters of a lake that would lap through memories when time distanced days.

They had seeped in long ago, pulsing through moments when thoughts washed against consciousness—floating, the canebrake cove behind the beach, bicycle-crash scraped limbs folded across a tire tube, eyes shut tight against white rays that freckled and would eventually wrinkle her skin, ears witness to her soul's own symphony of satience: the generous laughter of her baby-oiled mama and aunts, the splashes of endless cousins rippling against her, the hissed opening of frost-hazed Nehi bottles that stained lips and flavored sweltering afternoons . . . and when she dunked her head to cool the sun-bleached straw hat across her brow, the underwater din of boat engines, passing the tiny cove and the perfect ease of its paradise accompaniment.

She was licking residual Twinkie goo from between her fingers when they pulled into the cove, and her surprise at finding it empty startled her. She'd half expected to see her scratched-up legs and her slender young mama and shiny aunts dangling from inner tubes. The cove was silent. Inside it, swelling underneath a gentle wake, were the breaking wails of a grown-up little girl, aching for her mama's smooth tanned arms about her, their damp fossa-sides hugging her everywhere, the cool-lipped cherry kiss to her forehead, the feel and smell of love and summer. And love and love and love.

On one of those bygone days, she'd opened the metal cooler and discovered a lissome wisp of her mama's locks shimmering across the reach inside, sparkling, tangled, and iridescent in the damp above purple and red bottles beneath—like a sunskein morning cobweb amid dawnsoft dewdrops undissolved. She thought of her mama's lip print on the glass in her girls' room, left from the kiss she'd pressed to the spider they'd adopted last spring. The spider and its web were gone, but her mama's lips remained.

When she turned to open the cooler this day, she discovered only boxes of juice. Letting go a few sunsquint tears, she said a prayer to St. Ambrose and to her mama. Looking up, her eyes pleaded with the sky for an evening shower to break this day's heat and leave in its wake a quenched heart.

Tim noticed her tears and when he asked she answered that this was the cove where it'd happened to Dr. Harbar. He knew better. This was the cove, but her tears weren't for the old man. Still, her lie relieved him. He wondered if his wife blamed him at all for her mama's death. His own mama and Ms. Hazel had been friends their whole lives, even after his mama and dad moved away. It was their falling out over Sister Aquiline's treatment of a watercolor Sass had painted that removed them some, and his mama died before the distance between she and Ms. Hazel could be closed.

He reckoned Ms. Hazel closed it right when she took the two oldest girls to see their Grandpa Hopper and learn about their Grandma Bonnie Grace, although he worried over how Texas kept close to herself ever since the visit. But then the whole house had been heavy since Ms. Hazel's departure from it. Only Sass, who'd been the closest to her granny, and whom he'd expected to be hardest hit among the kids, still pranced about the place as before. He smiled toward his twins in their swim gear and garish boots. Sass asked to hear again about Harbar.

Tim wasn't sure it was a good idea for the kids to hear such a macabre tale retold so soon after the passing of their granny. But death was death, Clare had insisted, and there's no sense hiding its whos and whats all of a sudden just because it had hit close to home.

Seventy-eight, still practicing medicine, and twice widowed, Harbar had grown up in the very bluffs blasted to create the lake. He'd never complained about the exile but returned often to the waters enveloping his childhood. His third wife, the one he teased was his trophy wife, sixty-five-year-old Frieda, savored the trips with her husband.

A hippie of a human long before the term was coined, Frieda liked to comb the shoreline while her husband fished and floated, watching herons skim the water and his wife skim the shore. Tall and reedy Frieda moved like the running gears of a katydid, he thought. He liked to search her mechanics for fluidity, finding comfort there, like in his favorite cove. Far up the lake, feeding it, the creek waters he bathed in as a boy poured into a small cove near a thin band of riprap along its south side. Here, with Frieda, his soul was saturated. Satiated. Baptized. It was this cove, not the one behind the beach, where it happened.

Collecting lacewings for her garden, Frieda, stunned by the light, couldn't recall what she'd seen first—the boat, severed engine, fishing pole, turbulent waters, or her husband, standing, palms turned outward. She only remembered that right after she saw these things, they disappeared except for the boat.

She swam out, knowing she wouldn't find him but feeling she should try. With difficulty, she gripped the sides of the boat, catching her breath before swimming back to shore. Two hours passed before another boat pulled into the cove, a conservation officer checking the riprap. He saw the boat first, then Frieda. Mistaking her shivering for chills, he wrapped her in an emergency blanket, warming her with his thermos of coffee, which he apologized, had a splash of whiskey in it.

She asked if there'd been a storm. His answer convinced her she'd witnessed rapture, and she shocked Harbar's children by insisting his body be left to the lake. Nevertheless, the cove was searched. The engine was found. Later, when people stopped swimming the shallow waters above the spillway for fear of their foot crashing through the cavity of a cadaver, a full-scale search was carried out. The lake was dragged. Harbar stayed put.

He has since turned into myth, skinny-dipping teenagers swearing they saw Old Doc Harbar walk the waters at midnight or when the moon waxes full or like times when it seems such things could happen. And then there are the mutant fish, descendants of the one Harbar had hooked when lightning struck.

Tim noticed clouds piling up in the west and that his wife had Twinkie in her hair as he listened to her tell the kids about these fish and the sunscreen that repelled them, so make sure to have it on thick.

He decided not to tell her about the Twinkie in her hair, preferring instead to savor the feeling it gave him each time it caught his eye. The Twinkie reminded him that he adored his wife. That he adored her delighted him. That he needed to be reminded saddened him. And as he watched the tiny dollop of sugary fluff slowly dry in her hair, then flake, then dissolve into the water as she dipped her head backwards on the inner tube beside him, he teetered forth and back on a bittersweet edge.

When nightsong's cicadence began, they headed back to the docks, watching the sky around them flicker with the day's heat. She heard thunder before he did, and each and all smelled the water on the wind before they heard and saw it falling behind them, the rainsheet creeping quickly upon them, traveling faster than their engine, passing its first gentle drops through Clare, noiselessly, perfectly, kissing her forehead with cool lips.

The rain had come and gone by the time they moored to the planks, and as she walked the dock toward the car, a sleeping daughter in each arm, she could hear the gentle splash against the posts below, sweet licks from the skinny-dip waters of youth; and it was only she who saw the spiderweb's stretch across their humid moonlit path, its gossamer night-tide constellation lissome and elusive as fossa-vein wisps, fleeting as a specter, full of grace and shadow, shimmering, tangled, and sparkling.

Strays

Maisala Dentleman

The tension that had been bubbling for some time finally broke the surface after Sarah froze the cat. Ranger, Eliza's cat, met his end while my sister was away protesting deforestation in the Shawnee. Eliza—five years older than me and ten younger than Sarah, our stepmom—was only a few miles down the road at the time, but she could have been a few thousand.

For several weeks, we only saw Eliza on the local news station and in the paper. She was camped out on a bluff just south of Lefebryon Orchards, where the MacTerptins lived. Eliza wielded no signs and chained herself to no trees but, instead, spoke eloquently into the microphones like a tanned fairy-of-the-forest statesman whose waist-long hair had been kissed by the sun and curled by the rain. The cameras loved her. I loved watching her effortless articulation and how it contrasted with the interviewer's formulaic and forced presence. I loved my sister exquisitely. But I also loved Sarah. And there was nothing eloquent in the potent words communicated to Sarah by Eliza the night she found Ranger.

The clear-cutting dispute was eventually solved by compromise at a meeting held in the dead of dark, while cameras and concerned-looking news anchors were sleeping. The protesters left quietly and peacefully, and Eliza returned home at four in the morning with a hankering for a popsicle.

At least I think it was four in the morning when I heard the scream. Time doesn't really fit in numbers for me but in shades. Yet that particular night, a new moon ordained that the shadows in my bedroom remain fixed, penetrated only by the streetlamp, which meant that it could have been four o'clock, or five, or three—all night long.

The nights have since grown shorter and now longer again. In the sky, a harvest moon wanes but the friction here below keeps waxing. It's never again flowed as unrestrained as that night's screaming, accusations, and tears. Instead it now surges like an undertow through our conversations, in the tenor of spoken words but mostly in the words that aren't.

For that reason, I have begun to prefer the early part of the day—when the tide of tension has been calm for several hours. I usually rise before everyone else, just when the birds begin to tune up, and I sit enclosed behind the screens of our back porch, my mind floating on smooth waters. On this particular morning, I watch time as it begins to blush the ground with strokes of sunrise. The swathes of color intensify and are on the edge of glare when a mist suddenly settles in to soften the dawn. Through it, I stare at the path that slices the backyard down its middle.

To the right of the path is The Mange, the bare patch of ground where a sandbox used to be—the bald spot where vegetation wholly refuses to go forth and multiply, no matter what miracles we attempt to conjure. We've tried to plant just about everything there, even kudzu. Hap McGann once told Sarah that the best way to grow kudzu was to throw it over your shoulder and run like hell and so we did. Nothing happened.

To the right of The Mange is Ranger's grave. Despite the protestations of my dad, Sarah had insisted that we freeze the cat-corpse until Eliza came home and could attend the burial. My only suggestion was that we bury Ranger beneath The Mange for fertilizer. Sarah wanted to know how I could be so callous about my sister's treasured pet, but I knew that Ranger had really been dead for some years but was just too mean to lie down until now. That's how Dad put it anyhow.

Ranger—the result of Sarah's uncanny ability to locate all strays-in-need within a ten-mile radius, most of them pregnant—was the single, bright-orange son of a streetwise and scraggy tabby. His seven siblings were distinguishable from him in gender only. The entire litter was identical in mark and meow to the Marscump's Mungo Jerry, but when we pointed this out to Mrs. Marjorie J. Marscump with hopes of kindling her possible interest in a loving-home-type placement, she just shrugged over a shoulder, "So sue him."

About two minutes after opening his eyes, Ranger found a permanent home in Eliza's smile. And about two days later, while Texas and I were digging underneath the front porch to create a protected spot for an extended doodlebug family to stay alive over fireplace season when their present woodpile dwelling would get whittled down, we overheard Sarah in outright defiance of Dad's no-more-critters-dammit decree, daring him to find anything *since then* that had made Eliza's eyes shine half as much.

It worked. The doodlebugs survived through the frost and hail of winter, and Ranger thrived in the arms and lap of Eliza. I got to keep the tabby, who loves insects as much as I do, but unfortunately in a different way. Her less feral son knew neither prey nor enemy until nearly a year later, while doing laundry, Sarah had accidentally sent a sleeping Ranger through a few revolutions in the dryer before checking to see what was causing the rhythmic kathumps that kept resounding from its drum. Ranger survived the ordeal but exhibited spontaneous and savage mood swings ever after, causing moments of perfect complacency to be interrupted without warning by claws, fangs, and, a couple of times, stitches.

A visit to our beloved and accomplished town vet confirmed that Ranger had been traumatized by the tumble-dry. But the only remedy offered was that Ranger should be put down before he put out someone's eye. Eliza hadn't yet finished her horrified scream when a revolted Sarah picked up the distempered and equally startled cat who raked skin from her arms as she asked the esteemed doctor, genuinely, if the size of his brain had perhaps constricted the volume of his compassion. We left the battle embittered and bewildered, arm in bloody arm, stopping on the way home for triple scoops of ice cream plus a sundae for Ranger. Strawberry-pineapple. The town had talked about it for weeks. But Sarah was used to them talking.

About twenty streets long, four churches wide, and eight taverns deep, my town is exactly the kind that knows what a person's been out doing before they get home from doing it. We hold parades for everything, and in addition to every holiday known to the Western calendar, we celebrate at least four harvest festivals a year, and two founder's days. Two.

Despite its own peculiarities, the town treats Sarah as though she is its most curious specimen, collecting stray animals and cursing their pedigreed doctors, and receiving more mail each day than the courthouse. She diligently completes every survey and comment card requested of her and as a result is on every mailing list known to the DMA. She is the only person I know who actually calls the 1-800 numbers on the backs of semitrucks to supply a cheerful and encouraging answer to the *How's my driving?* query.

My dad had initially contracted Sarah to help him with his survey business after our mother died. I don't remember my mother, and I feel guilty sometimes for not missing her. Eliza says I do miss her, in those moments when I cry but can't really figure out why I'm crying; but I don't miss her with the detail that Eliza does, remembering how she laughed and the way her right eyelid always closed just before the left one when she blinked. People say I have her eyes, and I do see my own in the eyes that smile back at me from her picture on the piano, but sometimes I'm thankful I don't have more to make me sad and angry—like my sister.

A while after Sarah's arrival, she resigned her survey position with my dad and took up a wholly different position sharing his room at our house. And even though it happened long after it should have started the town talking, the town talked anyway. And it continued to talk even after my dad and Sarah married.

The sun, no longer seated on the cusp of the horizon, now enters the sky to burn the mist and sharpen the focus of the day. I can hear Sarah's just-awake fumbling in the kitchen as she fills a tall glass of water. She unfailingly drinks a gallon of water a day to combat whatever she imagines will happen if she doesn't, and as a result is on a perpetual journey to the bathroom. A few minutes after the toilet flushes, the screen door squeals open to broadcast Sarah's arrival on the porch with the sunlight contributing to the debut by setting ablaze her messy morning hair.

She stretches slowly, "I swear it feels like someone has taken my bones apart and then re-pieced them backwards." Her breath is tinged with the smell of mint toothpaste, which makes me aware of my own unbrushed mouth. I watch as she takes a moment to pop most of her body's major joints before beginning a brief tap dance to limber up for the day.

"Sarah, where in the world do you come from?"

Taking me seriously, she sits down and tucks a frizzy tangle behind a pale ear. "Well, my mom says we're related to the Carlisles of Cumberland, but my dad always told me we just sprouted up one day from the Kentucky dirt." Both of our glances wander to The Mange and I wonder if, like me, she's wondering if the Carlisles could sprout there.

The kettle whistle interrupts our thoughts and soon Eliza joins us with a huge mug of steeping tea in hand and our dog Turbo, another stray, trailing at her heels.

Eliza has smiles and good-morning greetings for both of us, but even though she tries hard for them to be polite, the ones directed toward Sarah are rippled with conflict.

She stirs her tea, and trying again, she speaks softly to Sarah, "Hey, don't forget you didn't want to miss the sea-otter special tonight."

"Oh, yes!" Sarah enthusiastically receives the peace offering. "Thank you. That's right. I got to see the date change on my watch last night."

"What?" The disjointed way that Sarah weaves in and out of conversations produces a genuine reaction from my sister.

"Well, you see, I had my watch on at midnight last night, and I happened to be looking at it at the very moment the date flipped from the nineteenth to the twentieth." When both Eliza and I still look flummoxed, Sarah continues as though her last sentence hadn't ended,

"...which is a good thing, you see, because it reminded me about the sea otters on PBS tonight. Have you ever noticed that the music they play to go along with each of the animal shows suits that animal perfectly? I just can't wait to hear sea-otter music." The sea otter is Sarah's favorite animal, and I am surprised that we don't have one or two of them around the house.

She keeps going, "...which also reminds me: I haven't seen Mac Mackinaw on the news lately, have you?" Sarah developed an attachment to Mac Mackinaw—the regional fish, wildlife, and game expert who is also featured as a guest news correspondent from time to time on the local channel—during the bottomland flood coverage two years ago and still writes him frequently to let him know how much she enjoys his reporting. I'm sure the Mackinaw people have her name on a list too, but I doubt it's a mailing list.

"You are a case, Sarah," I tease when I see that Eliza is at a loss. "Actually, I saw the old furball on yesterday afternoon." Turbo's ears perk up at the word *furball*. The dog is forever mistaking for his name every phonetical sound close to the word *turbo*.

Sarah kicks toward my leg with a bare foot, "Mr. Mackinaw is not a furball."

Turbo starts, again on edge. "He is so! The man has hair sprouting from all angles."

"Well, he's a nice man and an excellent reporter, so let's not refer to him as a furball." Agitated afresh, Turbo shifts and looks befuddled.

Eliza tries to soothe him, and I wonder aloud what music they would play if PBS did a documentary on Turbo. Sarah laughs, the dog moans, and then there is quiet.

I close my eyes to it and try to ignore its underlying current. But I can't—just like Eliza and Sarah can't enjoy the silence, either. Trapped by it, each feels as though something should be said but neither knows what. Eliza said too much that night and Sarah didn't say enough. And it had as little to do with Ranger's cryogenic remains as do most catalysts with the arguments that ensue.

I open my eyes to find Eliza's and Sarah's immediately upon mine, waiting hopefully for me to cheerily dive into the deep end of their silence. I wish I had a glass of water or a tea mug to stare into, but I don't. The dog solves my dilemma when I realize that he's trembling. Their eyes following mine, Eliza and Sarah notice it too.

But before Eliza can shift to soothe him, sixty-five pounds of black fluff shakes to its feet and begins frantically pacing the porch and howling. As the volume increases, we sit transfixed, watching his entire body undulate with each wail.

Turning from us and toward the neighbor's house, he fixes his eyes on their driveway, never ceasing the cadence of caterwauls. Surreally, we witness as he winds up and then hurls himself mercilessly through the screen, across the yard, beyond The Mange, past the grave, and over the fence, plunging full-force and sidelong into the neighbor's car.

His body collapses and I turn to see Sarah and Eliza, mouths open and brows crumpled. We look at each other but cannot speak or move. Eliza finally stirs when Sarah begins to tear, repositioning to stand quietly next to her; and though she doesn't reach out to physically touch Sarah, her action is devoid of awkwardness or anger.

I gasp when I see the black tangle of fur twitch, certain that I am observing the final spasms of our anguished pet. Uncertain as to what I'll do once I get there, I start toward Turbo and then stop as he rises slowly from the driveway and hobbles, hindquarters sagging, back to where we stand.

Disheveled, he topples to the ground as we rush to pet and examine him, smothering him with affection and theory. "Poor thing must have been confused," surmises Sarah.

"Suicide attempt," I speculate, and then change my mind as I notice the car's dent. "Holy martyrs. Look at that. He must have been striking a blow for dogs everywhere."

Nodding agreement, Sarah walks to the gaping hole in the screen and traces it with her finger, her sympathy extending, as it often does, into the inanimate realm. "My, he certainly damaged you," she tells the screen.

"What the hell!?" Just awake, Dad scratches his matted hair and then moves to examine the screen. He looks to the dog, assuming his guilt. "Couldn't you have simply used the door?" No one mentions the neighbor's car.

"Damn mutt. What the hell is the matter with him? Sarah, the animals you bring around this place." He moves toward her and ruffles her hair. "With you around, there's no telling what needy miserable creature will appear on the doorstep next begging food."

Eliza breaks her silence with a playful smile meant for one of us, "As I recall, Dad, you show up there every evening about five-thirty."

A Sacred Heart

Texas MacTerplin

The red light above the confessional booth makes me think of the red candle at the altar, announcing Jesus to the room. Its glow makes me think of Toddy's grandmother, who affixed an electric Heart of Jesus to the kitchen wall that his mama recently coated with sugar. The Sacred plastic plaque plugs into an outlet above the cats' food and water dishes, its heart a roiling red of fluid fire. The cord is frayed from the cats' pawing and chewing, ragged threads of hotwire dangling just above their water, water Sass reckons must be holy, seeing as the cats are still alive. Just in case, she moves the dishes each time she's over there.

But I trust the fulsome Sacred Heart of Jesus on the wall, although the waves inside his chest have started to flicker and spark of late. The sugar glistens the wall from about two feet up where the animals can't lap it off, and combined with the fluid sparkle of God's heart, it's enough to remind a person that the bone center of everything is liquid.

Toddy's grandmother calls it a miracle. I know it to be one—not the electrical heart-current's smoldering churn but the pulse that courses beneath its meaning.

Sass has been in the confessional with Father Manzelough and God for so long that Montana and I start to argue over who gets to go next. If Sass's litany of sins is that long, the one of us to walk in the booth after is bound to appear saintly by contrast. We have just started to 'shambo to settle on whose turn would follow Sass's when we hear the unmistakable rumble of Father Manzelough's disgruntlement.

It gets louder.

Louder still.

Then Sass's.

Father Manzelough's again.

Sass's back.

We change our minds about the fortunate position of the subsequent confessor and re-shambo to determine who won't have to go next. When the tumult inside escalates further, Montana leaves the line to go get Mama, who is penitent in the side chapel underneath Saints Teresa and Agatha.

Montana's charge in leaving the line is misinterpreted by other individuals behind us, who assume that since she has been privy to a better auditory vantage point during the commotion, it's best to follow her lead and abandon ship.

Father and Sass feud fervently and out loud for twenty-eight whole seconds longer. I have never known anyone except my sister who riled a priest to the point of curtain-parting. But she did. And he did. Yanked the drape straight back and commanded she beg God's pardon.

Me? I would have been offering to crucify my own self to the wall right there, begging divine intercession and indulgence from every saint and seraphim I could conjure. But leave it to Sass to quarrel sin.

And quarrel mighty she did.

Afterward, Sass's tears flowed into Mama's quiet lap behind the church in the stoop off the vestibule. When finally they stopped, Mama's nonstop Rosaries started, because what followed the tears was an announcement that Reconciliation henceforth would be sworn off by Sass.

I'm not sure exactly what incited the tussle between my sister and the Almighty, but I aim to find out, and while Mama's Hailing Mary and beseeching Our Father for some Glory Be, I secretly decide to become Sass's surrogate confessor until that day when the Decades and the Mysteries start to work on her.

When next we visit Toddy's house, I hotfoot to the sparkling, flaming Heart of Jesus to spill my petition.

I reach it too late.

The smell of melted plastic slams into my sinuses, penetrating thought and impaling it mercilessly against the task-at-plan. The turn of a cog whines softly in my ears, winding futilely against a molten clog. Fluffalo circles anxiously around Rumpus and Pumpkin, who lie lifeless and sprawling in a puddle of water next to Jesus.

His cracked plaque has been sprung from its nail, having splash-landed in the gutter where linoleum meets sugar-lapped wall. I enfold the remaining warmth of Rumpus and Pumpkin into the bends of my arms and look to Jesus. The thorn-crown encircles his heart, engorged by the electric torrent that has spilled over, dripping red and molten onto its plastic frame. The cog turns still, and embers flicker and glow as the splattered water trails down his face and into the smoldering core.

Gently placing his siblings alongside the Heart on the floor, I scoop Fluffalo to my own churning core, and in that moment, I glimpse that I know why He did it, how His Heart could stand the fall.

The revelation is gone as soon as it's got, but still I can trace its affect and hope that someday Sass might glimpse it too.

Until then, all prayers for my sister will be directed to the sparking, shining, knowing, bleeding Heart of Jesus.

Bounty

Texas MacJerplin

Must have been the honeysuckle, ruffled by the breeze, surrounding the empty playground just around the corner from Brae Hill, that brought it all rushing back in a single, deep breath. Chain links on the climbing tower clinked against each other, and ghosts of memories dangled the swings. I stared out over the unchanged layout of metal activity equipment with names the youngest among us are best at bestowing, floating there on a tiny ocean of matted grass and trampled dirt that marked a separate world. And I could remember. Like no other combination of the senses, it was the sounds and smells of my childhood that poured into my malleable young mold and forged the die that journeys through the grown-up years of my life.

For a moment the air around me held its breath, but the honeysuckle still lingered. Then it was lavender, and the dots of lotion my mama would rub into my hands and feet when we played Princess Pamper; and then the smells that can only be described by memory—the tips of Sass's jumbled curls jutting from the folds of her pillow and tickling my cheek, flickers of lightning verifying the hint of her presence through the shadows of the storm; and powdery pink wads of tissue pulled from Granny's wide pockets moments before I would need them, as if she could anticipate every wrinkle in the fabric of my childhood needs.

And Maisala, who smelled like the heat of sunshine on wet hair. At ten years old, and for six years on either side of it, my truest friend was Maisala. I loved everything about her except where she lived. Her house rose above a giant magnolia at the intersection of Fifth and Elm Streets, at the crest of Brae Hill, a subdivision whose name suffered the exact kind of duplicit ignorance that most subdivisions do in towns too small to have any business subdividing themselves in the first place. But apparently giving neighborhoods a title became stylish at some period during my youth, and it seemed every cluster of streets had chosen one.

Most of the subdivision names didn't stick, and their wooden signs have rotted and faded with age and dog urine. Maisala's subdivision's name stuck fast. It was my Gaelic-speaking grandpa who was first to point out that the intersection of Fifth and Elm had just been rather absurdly renamed Hill Hill, and most likely its residents have yet to forgive him.

Hill Hill was the kind of neighborhood where, despite the depth of your character, you'd be loathed in any case for the trivial things: name the family cat something standard and you'd be repudiated for being a dullard; give the cat a clever name and you'd be despised for being a wiseacre. In Hill Hill, no matter what, you'd always be punished for being who you were.

Except for Myrna. No one bothered Myrna. For as long as I could remember, Myrna had been sitting on her unshaded front stoop yelling incoherencies at passersby. No one—even out-of-towners visiting for the annual Big Muddy Apple Stomp—paid her any heed. And perhaps that was precisely Myrna's punishment for being who she was: thorough isolation.

Maisala possessed all the right reasons to be a target of Hill Hill's contempt. For starters, there was the transgression of her name. How I got away with *Texas* and *Maisala* was deemed an infraction seems a crime against sanity, but according to Hill Hill, *Maisala* was too difficult to remember, to spell, to pronounce. Too lovely. But for the offenses to stop there would be too apparent. The scorn toward people like Maisala was acute and had roots in notions far more entrenched.

Maisala was the second child of parents who'd never married, perhaps the first infringement. The greatest was that her parents didn't care that it was one. Before they were our dads, Maisala's and my own came home from a war they barely survived, when Dog Dentleman made the acquaintance of Treesong Tillyard. Treesong was the best college friend of my dad's sweetheart, my own mama. Originally from where she never knew, Treesong was raised in a camper-van and had lived in every state that touched an ocean, most recently Oregon. She'd come inland to Shawnee hill country on her own. Planting herself in the fertile land amid two wide rivers, she set out to study its past. Fascinated by its place in time, she immersed herself in its artifacts. The one she liked most was Dog.

They built a ramshackle cabin in the heart of the Shawnee and called their first child Eliza Skyshine, after both parents' mamas. But Treesong's parents had long since faded from contact, and Dog's mama could barely hold her granddaughter in uncertain arms without cringing from the disgrace the other half of her namesake evoked. By the time Maisala was born, Mrs. Dentleman rarely held either child except in contempt. Yet for all that the older Eliza felt her granddaughters out of grace, they were in fact filled with it.

Mrs. Dentleman left life one year after Maisala entered it, and Treesong lived only three months after she and Dog moved their girls from the drafty cabin into Dog's mama's huge and unhappy house in Hill Hill. Treesong lived long enough to sow enough generosity into the bounty of her daughters to redress the absence of the other, grander mothers they might otherwise have known. But she couldn't make up for her own absence. Despite her harvest, Eliza was Dog's daughter, and likewise, she held every speck of resentment for the missing parts of her life. And though she hardly knew her, Maisala was Treesong's. Both girls were free-minded, but because Eliza suffered the loss of her mama out loud, Hill Hill afforded the older sister a measure of mercy they could not offer the younger. Unlike Eliza, Maisala was carefree in a way no human ought to be and get away with. She hadn't any right to her blitheness without having suffered aloud the hardships that earned the badge of unforced flippancy.

By some glorious accident of nature, Maisala's contentment in life was both casual and unmitigated. Genuinely happy people aren't supposed to exist. Maisala was not only an aberration but unsettling flesh-and-blood proof that the version of misery on which most of us depend was a choice.

Honeysuckle again. I opened my eyes to the spot of ground where Twinkie had taken his punishment. It was Halloween, so we'd dressed up for the school's annual costume parade even though Toddy Milby said it was stupid because he had friends in seventh grade and in seventh grade they didn't do that. We ignored him. Fifth grade wasn't seventh grade; any first-grader could tell you that. But Toddy was like that. Forever reaching somewhere else for his own affirmation.

We had just turned in our latest poem assignments to Sister Celeste. This one had to have ten lines, no rhymes, regular beats, with the topic (Sister was big on topics) "The Abundance of Autumn." She'd been on about poetry for a whole month now, charging us to hatch heaps of lines, stanzas, shapes, and sounds of every sort. Turned out, Maisala and I were naturals at weaving the words together, but we could no more untangle them to suit Sister's rules than my brother can read minds like he's always claiming. It was uphill sledding for Toddy too, whose mind worked best in terms of numbers. He could figure anything as long as it was in digits.

So the three of us had gotten together to swap our knacks. Maisala and I made up line after line, and Toddy worked them into patterns for us. Together, we hadn't mustered a poem yet that didn't make it to the bulletin board. We let Sass in on our secret because she was as yippety over poetry as Sister. One night, when she asked me if it might could be cheating, I answered that I liked to think of it as sharing blessings. And I did.

When the three of us worked on our poetry, we each seemed to change a little to the betterment of the other. Toddy let loose the tight rein he held on the world's every move; Maisala tightened her rein on words, pouring to the page in a higher form all those flung against her; and I learned how to laugh from the bottom of my belly. The three of us together felt like a poem that maybe God would write about a blessed friendship.

I had read about the Seven Wonders in the *Britannica Concise Encyclopedia* guarded expertly by Frieda Harbar at the library, and I wanted to go dressed as an Egyptian pyramid and had already talked Maisala into going as the Hanging Gardens of Babylon, but somehow Maisala's stepmama, Sarah, got it in her head that we would be positively adorable and just as original dressed as twin plastic sacks of leaves—clear, she insisted, so people could see we weren't garbage. I was tugging at the leaf crumbles that were invading my leotard when Twinkie the Kid got off the bus and was immediately surrounded by a swarm of screaming second-graders. Miniature goblins and tiny witches wanted to know if he was real, could they have a bite, and would he let them see his lasso.

Toddy Milby parted the petite crowd of worshippers and approached his friend, telling him he was going to beat him up for dressing up and that JesusChristAlmighty, if he had to wear a costume, why couldn't he have picked something better than junk food because what kind of daintytippytoedpansyass dressed like a snack cake. He got sent to the office for cussing. The sixth-graders told us Sister Aquiline paddled him for saying a bad word in the same sentence as Jesus, but the sixth-graders were always saying things. At last year's parade, they spread it that Benjamin Bowers got sent home for showing up in his Superman Underoos. Turned out he'd only had bronchitis. That's what happened when you stayed home sick.

Mother Cosma did send Toddy home later that morning after he made good on his promise. I don't think Toddy really hurt Twinkie through all that padding, but he did tear up his costume in a dreadful scene, horrified little goblins and witches crying and dodging into the fray, picking up pieces of snack-cake foam and then darting to the safety of the battle's edge, but not before attempting a swift kick or heartfelt shove at the ankles and knees of the enemy who was destroying their Twinkie.

Toddy's dad, Slug, picked him up from school that morning, and when two days later Toddy showed up in class with bruises, we knew they hadn't been delivered on the playground. When Sass asked Granny why he was harsh-headed, she told us Slug had gone across the sea to the same war so many of our daddies had gone to before they were our daddies, but that for Slug, things got so awful his mind fell in on itself. I supposed time must have stopped for him over there too, because he only ever told stories from before.

Anymore they mostly bored me, but Maisala couldn't get enough of them. She used to sneak down to Tump's and squeeze behind the bushes under the awning of the busted-out window just so she might hear Slug's hog-voice inside recounting stories about her mama and dad. Her favorite was the one where before her parents met, Dog had promised Slug to strip to socks and climb the coal hopper if he could ever be proven to have lost his senses to a girl. Dog Dentleman never made it up that train funnel, but he did turn black and break a collarbone trying. That was two weeks before Mrs. Martin Marscump, Sr., reported that Treesong Tillyard was beginning to look exceptionally bulky.

She eventually returned to willowy after Eliza, but both Mrs. Marscump and Hill Hill would refuse to get over the event. So would Dog's mama. Even and especially when it happened a second time. When they named Maisala, Mrs. Dentleman said it sounded like a name for a girl living near the Taj Mahal, not in the armpit of the Mississippi bottomlands. (Maisala had eavesdropped that story under the window too, but it was Stretch Waters who'd told it, not Slug.) When we finally figured out how to spell *Taj Mahal*, we looked it up under Frieda's watchful eye. The entry led us to India, Art and Culture, which led us to words that raised Frieda's brow when we asked how to pronounce them. It was then that we knew we'd all-out stumbled onto something and there was no stopping us from that point on.

After Frieda banned us for dog-earing most of the section on India, we played Taj Mahal almost every day for two weeks, lifting silky half-slips and beaded jewelry from adult drawers and turning them into elaborate costumes. When Emily Marscump blabbed to her mama, who was raising money toward a larger Hill Hill sign, that Maisala had let her join our secret concubine club, Mrs. Marjorie J. Marscump marched straight up to the Dentlemans' to say that Emily wasn't allowed to come over anymore. I told Emily that that's what she got for being such a yammersnitch, but Maisala just told her that she should have reassured her mama that boys weren't allowed. Emily swore she had, and that that was precisely when her mama had gone off her onion.

My own mama just shrugged her shoulders about the whole thing until a set of beads slipped from Maisala's brow and into the toilet bowl from where she stood on top of the tank—the perfect location for practicing the supreme balance needed for our harem dance. After that, we weren't allowed to play with the jewelry and slips anymore, so we gave up our Eastern treasures and moved on to other things. But we swore we'd see the Taj Mahal together someday, hand-in-hand, wearing beads and slips.

And we might have. I was in Chemistry II class, braiding Evie Trotter's hair and rolling my eyes at Toddy's plan to lure unsuspecting freshmen into some kind of ambush he'd orchestrated in the honeysuckle when Maisala died. It was Monday. Dog had just left the house, late for work after employing Stretch's guaranteed solution for clearing the slow drain in the upstairs bathroom sink. While Maisala slept off a fever, Sarah, her stepmama, had quickly run to Eagerton's to pick up Maisala's new prescription. Both she and Toddy had been out of school most of the week before with strep, but he hadn't been allergic to the medicine like she'd been and had recovered just in time to score the winning touchdown at Friday night's homecoming.

Sarah could smell the fumes as soon as she stepped from the car, clutching the small white paper sack that was too late to fulfill its purpose. Immediately realizing what was causing the terrible smell, she hurried to Maisala through an invisible, burning haze. Though Sarah swore there had been one, by the time the ambulance got to the house at the top of Hill Hill, there was no pulse. And by the time Toddy and I got there, there was no Maisala.

The next time we saw her was at the funeral where Father Manzelough talked a lot about her and told us it was a blessing she had gone so quickly. But it was obvious he didn't know a speck—he'd never mentioned her acorn collection or her kindness to the crickets her cat routinely captured, and he hadn't looked up sulfuric acid in *Funk and Wagnalls* like I had or he'd know that twenty-four-and-a-half parts per million is lethal to freshwater bluegill but nobody knows what concentrations of it kill a human or exactly how because they don't do studies like that.

People called her peaceful in death who'd never called her anything in life. Most folks started with words of comfort and then went on about how bizarre it was. I learned that day that her death would be remembered, not her life.

Stretch's method may have been fail-safe, but it was hardly harmless. Stretch had told Dog and Dog had told Sarah not to run water for at least half an hour after filling the pipe and then plugging the drain. But nobody had told a sleeping Maisala, who'd awakened from a fever dream to splash cool water across her brow.

And right after the part about how in high concentrations, the mist from its reaction with water can be so corrosive that breathing it can eat away enamel on teeth, was a sentence describing sulfuric acid as a common additive in snack foods—for preservation. I tried to picture Maisala's smile, but all that kept coming up was Twinkie the Kid.

Cheated that way, I knew she'd be remembered only during safety lectures in chemistry lab, and even then they'd probably mispronounce her name. I couldn't cry. I waited for my mind to fall in on itself.

After the funeral, as I sat on the stoop of our front porch, Michigan tried to cheer me with the most recent spoils from the batter bowl. Without looking, I knew the cake was chocolate and that Sass had made it for me with extra buttermilk, the way Granny had taught us. When Michigan handed me the bowl, I could see that my sisters and my brother had left their shares for me. I had to smile at the single spoonful Michigan had obviously nipped on her way out to the porch, a smear of it gluing curly wisps flat against the corner of her mouth. I looked into the bowl and could see how she'd tried to cover over the telltale spoon scrape. I used to do that too, back when it had been my job to carry the bowl from Granny's hands to those of my siblings. It struck me then that I'd never nabbed any of the batter when I shared with Maisala.

Suddenly it was Granny's hands I missed above all else. I closed my eyes and saw them wrapped around the bowl. They smelled like cocoa and Kleenex. Opening my eyes, I saw in the leftover batter abundant and unspoken generosity. Michigan handed me two spoons and walked away.

I thought of missing Maisala, wondering how the doodlebug family would survive the winter without her, where all our cornsilk had gotten away to, the shoebox of it we saved from August's shuck, carefully combed, plaited, and barretted for the braids we planned to give February's snowmen. I thought of the long Indian summer the year Granny told me about Grandma Bonnie Grace and then left, when the end of everyday smelled like dirt and sunshine and we wrote the "f" word in the dust beneath the magnolia—its low limbs embracing our shaded innocence, sheltering our misspelling from the street—just to know what it felt like. I thought of the spillway a few Septembers later, its boulders unwashed and pebbles parched to a sunrayed sparkle, when we barefooted the beachbald break rounding up rippled rocks and fossilled testaments to bygone waters. And how without a budge in the weather since that harvest hard and fast, most of December felt just like October, the year nothing changed before everything did. I still wonder what happened to that cornsilk and if doodlebugs roll up sometimes not in dismay, fear, or alarm but just for fun.

I thought of missing Maisala. Again.

Always. I tried to hear her voice, but I only heard Myrna and the whimsical sound of playground chimes, passing through the quiet on a whisper of wind, carrying the memory of cornsilk and honeysuckle.

Curtain Call

Toddy Milby

Poor and happy was what he'd told us to say if she asked and so that's how I answered our mom when she posed, "And how is your father?"

Lucas just rolled his eyes, "*Dad*, Mom. He's always been *Dad*, not *Father*." I felt Texas squeeze my hand. Thank All she was here. Desideration had saturated my understanding so long ago I couldn't recall a time when she wasn't passing through every part of me.

A heavy sun clung above the horizon and cast the muted autumn oak to fiery brilliance, perfecting the Indian-summer evening, and I knew Texas was thinking about her granny. Mom's last wedding had been at noon midsummer, and the one before that on a spring morning. Lucas had recognized the pattern and won a bet with Dad over the timing of this latest one. Both were eager to ante up for the next, but I wanted no part. The tale was a weary one and the characters too familiar, supported by a chorus that offered little more than *Life's a bitch and then you marry one* coffee-mug consolation prizes. I had been relieved when college cued my exit, but still searched for ways to change the script.

Lucas and I were the product of Mom's first and longest marriage. Money came out of the second one, as well as our sister, Cara. The third provided the house whose backyard garden I sat in now. I'd arrived home for the wedding just this morning, spending it and most of the day at the MacTerptins', where Texas and Sass had arrived separately the night before, with Sass chatting the whole house up 'til dawn. We'd arrived late to the wedding after finding a snapper upturned in the road. When his jaws locked on our stick, we turned him a-flip, revealing a hairline-cracked shell, then dragged him to the grass, aimed toward the swamp-bottoms. Two miles later we had to turn around when Sass became convinced we'd headed him in the wrong direction and he'd have to cross the road again.

"Sass, this is going to make us late."

"It's got to be done, Tex. We can't aim him off-beam and then leave him to suss the whompasaddle, only to die making the road-cross again. Can you imagine how steamed he is right now? He was nearly across when he got walloped, and then we came along and plopped him back at square one."

"Did you just call me Tex?"

"I think I did."

"Have you done that before? Have you?"

"Easy, Sis, I'm mulling it."

"I mean, you just lopped off the part of my name that we share."

"Yeah, I reckon I did. And no, I don't reckon I've ever done that before."

"Well, don't do it again."

"Fine."

Texas sighed. "At least it was a turtle. I just hope we don't pass any kill." It was true, and I hoped it too. Sass insisted on checking all road-dead to ensure deadness. It was frequently a gruesome business, but every often or so something would either be clinging to life or begging for it to end more quickly. Sass was adept in either situation, and I have to admit I'd learned through her example, never realizing how utterly protected a possum pouch could be. The three of us, each and together, had found entire litters alive and well, tucked safely within the devastated remains of a mom. Sass and Texas's grandpa had constructed countless makeshift habitats for Sass's recovering critters, by-godding and goddamming his way through each ordeal, and the MacTerptin hounds had gotten used to sharing their grounds without quarrel.

As predicted, the turtle was in the road again, headed in the direction opposite we'd aimed him, incensed by our mistake and even more enraged by our return. He clamped hard on the stick and fought it harder all the way across the pavement. We arrived just as the ceremony finished, but Mom wasn't upset by this. She was simply relieved to see us, as my presence had lifted the burden from her of explaining my absence to the vultures. Huddled by the gate, they had assigned themselves the duty of greeting and assessing each person who walked through it.

They'd made a keen ruckus over Texas, who'd smiled and abided with patience their inquisitive flurry about her grown-upness. But Sass had completely flummoxed them. She was all bliss and action to their hiss and reaction. They weren't accustomed to such Ain'tLifeGrand-JustAsBig-AsYouPlease waving about and decided quickly it was offensive. What they understood—less than that all proceedings in life were about them—was that Sass's feet had hit life's ground full bore and bare, refusing to let up until they discovered its measure, moving out from under her by a force she didn't whatever-once question. Coming face-to-face with that kind of quiddity clutched most folks in the grips of a stumble. The carrion magnets simply couldn't recover from the introduction and instinctively turned to preening and cooing sycophantically about their attire and how it blended perfectly with the gerbera daisies and mums.

Sass hardly noticed, shrugging and making a beeline for Mr. McCord, who recently swore up and down the Kinkaid hills that he and his lifelong friend, Old Doc Harbar, held regular conversation and Pitch games out beyond the canebrake. While most dismissed McCord's claims as the impossible ramblings of an addled cortex, Sass had been intrigued by the notion that the two old friends must have been joined by other company. At least three are needed to play the card game proper, and Pitch was her granny's favorite deal.

Sass passed excitedly through Mom's fancy new garden, which poured from the fence and splashed right up to the house, where a few of the vultures were now busy recanting the events of the ceremony— who was unacceptable and who was intolerable. The cluster consisted mainly of my aunts, wives of Mom's brothers, who, unlike their sister, had managed to stay married, plus a handful of Mom's friends who really weren't. It struck me for the first time how old they appeared. Tiny creek-beds of sweat and foundation pronounced cobwebs of fine wrinkles, and the dry lips of working mouths flaked bleeding creases of color, the deep pencil outlines accentuating their own absurdity. I assumed they each still elicited the services of my two Avon-calling aunts since the palettes adorning their faces blended and merged as though they had all played dress-up with the same make-up samples.

One of the Avon aunts had been flaunting her brand-new hair combobulation all day as if it were a rare sculpture. She had explained to us earlier just how difficult it was to wind all of the curls into one smooth roll and how only a skilled and trained hand, like that of "Kelae—spelled with a single 'l' and an 'ae' instead of a 'y'—an *elite* professional stylist, from the *exclusive* new salon in the city," I was bursting to a gag inside, "could possibly attempt such a technique." I guessed by her mannerisms that she was explaining the procedure in as much orthographic detail to a few fellow vultures who seemed genuinely interested—captivated actually—when their circle was abruptly severed by the wielding cane attached to Mr. McCord, who, upon being greeted by Sass, demanded to know what had taken place during the ceremony since he hadn't been able to find his *damned hearing aid for weeks* and thus hadn't heard a *damned speck of the service.*

Deaf from the clang and bang of archaic farm equipment and off-kilter from birth, Mr. McCord's behavior was usually met with unequal parts confusion and pity, the scale tipping either way depending on the situation. I didn't pity Mr. McCord. I adored Mr. McCord, who was convinced it was the peach pit he swallowed as a teenager and not all the fried potatoes and ham hocks he'd eaten in his lifetime that was causing the blockage in his arteries.

Mr. McCord refused to use the walker that was prescribed after the surgery to "remove the peach pit," and as a result his arrivals and departures to and from the most simple destinations were executed with the aid of a hawthorn cane and any unfortunate soul that lined his path, which had always been somewhat tremulous but since the surgery had become downright wobbly. Anything but tranquil episodes, the nature of each journey fixed eyes upon him when he rose for such an occasion. Seated people braced themselves and hands clutched tensely to the nearest stable objects, preparing to anchor as the old man teetered by, grabbing for support.

Mr. McCord lurched on, Sass at his side and dodging the cane, while Mom floated around the reception in a blue dress, drifting, flattering, and charming her guests. Her easy laugh balanced dark eyes, heavy lashes, and an even heavier heart. Though her own mind was far from it, crazy had hung on the threshold of her doorstep for too long, demanding remedy, smothering sense, evading cure, refusing exit.

Long learned in the steady of pain's pulse, when the situation within threatened crumble, Mom would buckle under, rebounding with a spruce-up of sorts. Walls would be repainted, wardrobes updated, houses upgraded. Like most preoccupations with appearances, hers had little to do with external conditions.

Texas and I went inside to look for my grandma. We found her in the family room, dozing to a *Hogan's Heroes* rerun. The semi-smile she usually wore turned into a broad one upon seeing us. "Why, Lucas and Sass!"

"Toddy and Texas," I returned her open-armed invitation to hug.

"Of course. What are y'all doing here in this gussied-up house?"

"Mom's wedding," I explained.

"I'll be! Is your mother getting married again? I just can't keep up with her. Sass, when is that mother of yours going to get married again?"

"Well, I suppose she'll wait until she's not married to my dad any-more," smiled Texas.

"That would be the thing to do," my grandma assured her.

We ambled through several more minutes of talk, leapfrogging with her thoughts as best we could before she fell asleep mid-sentence, and we rejoined Lucas and Cara outside after adjusting the pillow beneath her fractured dreams.

Mom had joined their table too, and she turned to me as we sat. "I haven't gotten to spend much time with you all today." Cara was smiling hopefully and pleadingly towards me, letting me know at a glance how strained the conversation had been in my absence. Mom fluttered on, "You're planning to stay for the weekend, right? Texas, where's Sass? Toddy tells me you're thinking about applying to grad school." Texas took over for her as I watched Cara, struck by the way Mom's prettiest features had marked my heavily accessorized little sister. Ribbons sprouted from the dark tangle of not-natural curls piled atop her round face, and frosty pink lips matched exactly the paint on her fingernails. I wondered if Kelae spelled with an *ae* had gotten to her too. Cara's hands fidgeted in her lap as she breathed the fractious atmosphere between Lucas and Mom.

Texas was explaining her plan to study cicada larvae when Lucas cut her short, "Mom, your new hubby is beckoning." The Piersons were leaving.

Mom rose, apologetically promising that she wanted to be filled in on everything that was going on with us, adding quickly as she moved away, "Don't forget to say hello to the Marscumps; they've asked about you several times." Then, straightening her hat and discreetly rubbing a finger along her front teeth, she must still have been running through the inventory of our assigned agenda, "Oh! And be sure to congratulate Emily on her new little one."

"That's all the world needs is Emily Marscump proliferating."

I interrupted my brother, "Will do, Mom. You look great." And she did, floating off to the Piersons, the star attraction on display through reds and oranges and yellows, the perfect autumn backdrop to an imperfect scene.

"Couldn't you just say something nice to her, Lucas?" came downy words from soft pink lips. As she began twisting curls around painted fingers, I searched Cara's face for the tears I thought I heard in her voice.

Lucas seemed to soften for a moment, then hardened again. "Just stay out of it, okay? You don't understand Mom the way I do, and if I broke it down for you, you'd feel the same way. But you're serving five more years here, and I'd rather you enjoy them in the relative bliss you've insulated your world with than be all pissed off like me. You live in your world with Mom, and I'll live in mine."

Texas shinned me, my cue to enter the argument. "Look, Lucas, we've all got issues with Mom, alright? But we have no control over the situation, so we might as well accept it instead of wallow in it, okay?" But I knew all about the silent anger I was asking my brother to embrace.

It burned when it didn't get out, and I knew it would do the same to Cara until the sweet frosting she coated her world with would scald to a blistering tinge.

"Hey, who wants cake?" Texas singsonged, trying to deflect the breeze of hostility that swirled around us. But Cara's look confirmed that the offer was bootless, and I braced for the battle to continue.

"It wasn't Mom who suggested splitting up, in case you don't remember."

"Which time?"

"Shut it."

I looked around and noticed that our table had begun to receive the stare of the vultures. Determined to avoid my siblings becoming their next victim, I preyed back, concentrating my gaze on my aunt's nose. Examining it from afar, I deliberately rubbed my own nose, not taking my eyes from hers, and watched with pleasure the search that followed, producing an Avon hand mirror from her purse while the rest of the flock reassured her that there was absolutely nothing on, in, or wrong with her nose.

Lucas continued, "Jesus, your world is so simple, Cara. He had the sense to get the hell out before it destroyed him. I'm sure he thanks God every day that she drained his bank account before she drained his spirit. Marriage to our mother is nothing more than a bad business move."

The echo of tears finally ricocheted. My sister's lips tightened, squeezing away their soft pink yet unable to smother the words that flamed against them, that came blazing from a white-hot mouth, that distorted Cara's face as she yelled them, producing a rage that even Mr. McCord could hear.

The whole garden tensed. Mom's stricken look was no match for Cara's—a compression of hate, horror, and helplessness. Eyes penetrated the scene, spotlighting our table.

Guests froze, rigid in their chairs, clinging for dear life to stability. It was then that I saw Mr. McCord's silhouette totter in front of the dazzling disc cusping the horizon. He was being led briskly and awkwardly on the arm of Sarah Dentleman. And knowing Sarah, I would bet divinity to doodlebugs she was winking at us from the shadows of the glaring sun as she swayed Mr. McCord toward the vultures, his cane aimed directly for my aunt's enormous dark twist.

Hangdog

Texas MacJerptin

Heat rises heavy from blacktopped intersections and pushes through the screen like fading breaths of notion tendered a trillion gusts ago in cooler places on warmer days. Memory whispers to me of these places, where Mississippi currents stir breezes from valleys, brushing reeds, sweeping shores, and singing up the sides of cliffs, drafting toward the tops of trees to fan far across flatter parts where small arms, spread wide, welcome the hint of its chill against skin damp with sunshine. Drifting with the vigor of childhood, it soars atop hills and then spills back down them to stir curtains and pass through the heat of an afternoon kitchen where it teases corners of buttered oven-paper and tickles wisps that fall from pins over food hard-won and skillets filled with devotion.

I reach back to knot my hair from my shoulders, and for one fine moment this zephyr recollection lingers like snow's breath on a sun-stung nape—a kiss from the hunger moon—unseasonal, unbidden, divine.

Eclipsed.

A horn blares, brakes squeal, but the impact never arrives. The woman seated across from me lets her cringe of anticipation fade as the wind withers through the window beside her. Thoughts born on breezes die here. Tender, gentle days are never one away when concrete lines a river, when a zillion footprints press hard the blacktop that has stolen from summer every swallow and cast the sun back her shadow, when windy-hot days stir only city dust like powder bones, combusted bits of desiccated marrow.

It's been a longsome month of Sundays since I've awakened to nature's nightrays pouring through my dreams. Lying wakeful to midnight thoughts, I pretend the moon for the streetlamp outside my window, stumbling on sleep somewhere among the notions it summons.

One of them is my ten-year-old self, and I remember well the grateful kisses Sass braided into my hair on nights when the dumpling moon floated in its starry stew, spilling like warm broth across our skin. Sass would press her face into the curls across my pillow and tell me it was like breathing petals. Her curls smelled like rainclouds. I don't think I've ever told her. On those nights, we conjured questions and apprehended answers. We swam in a soup of sacred solutions, sopping them up, side by side, sisters, surrounded by skyshadow, saturated in welkin shine.

Moonwash drifted through our nighttides in a window-shaped silhouette that passed leisurely across the walls of our awareness.

These nights, the light moves fleetingly across the enclosures of my wakefulness, headlamps racing obliquely through the night.

It was Granny who called them hangdog days, and her rules for dispensing the mope were plainsung: Bless It and Move On. Grandpa Jelly added to the policy his own Rule of Gold for hangdog dispensation: Toast It. Hard and Well. Then bless it and move on.

Sister Aquila used to prattleyak unending about the Golden Rule, and until the fated fourth-grade day I was called to task on it, I'd never reckoned that her bullion legislation was any different than Grandpa Jelly's, which got me excommunicated to the hall as I dutifully stood and tried to explain what hangdog days were. Afterward Sister told me that Grandpa's golden shine was an elixir leading straight to the devil himself; and when I reported this to Granny, the word *malédictions* sprung at once from her mouth with the exclamation point so furiously attached I knew not to question meaning.

Later, during Toddy's Japanese nunchaku demonstration for Show and Tell, which occurred after what should not have been an utterly terrifying class discussion concerning St. John's *Noche Oscura*, I put it to Maisala and wondered if we should try out Granny's word on Sister so we could discover surefire what it meant, but Maisala said it probably meant swats and that we should hush up talking because we were well on our way. Right after that, one of Toddy's martial-arts maneuvers malfunctioned, smacking him flat to the floor and sailing his weapon through the window above Sister's roost. Toddy's mishap left him unconscious for seven whole minutes and made me forget all about Granny's word, as that kind of excitement at St. Brendan's happened only once in a barn rot.

In the end, it was Sass who ultimately cleared things up for me, after coming home with an essay stamped INSOLENCE for choosing mystic as her future occupation. Granny used the foreign word on that occasion too, and the more recognizable words that followed took away all uncertainty as to meaning. I took Granny's tirade to mean she was as rattlesnazzed at my sister as Mama was. It was only after she had the original essay laminated, presenting it to Sass alongside a copy of *Misunderstood Dissenters*, that I realized Granny's words were intended for the other Sister.

That was the last thing Sass packed when she took off for college in a pancake part of the state, becoming fascinated at how rain rippled across blacktop stretches and storm-gusts swept corn flat. She saw it as divine inspiration and chose meteorology as a major. My brother was more reluctant to leave, but Grandpa Jelly encouraged him, saying he could always come back, but if he stayed in the armpit of the Mississippi bottomlands his whole life, he'd either become bubba or subversive.

Like Toddy's dad, who ever-after his accident took simple pleasure in the complicated, concentrating for years on the construction of an ornate, concrete slatted fence around his heirloom tomato patch. Whenever anyone asked him why, he said it was "to keep out the goddam hybrids." It was as though the accident had splintered his reckoning into a jillion and six pieces, and a certain few of them never found their way back together, perpetually floating in a bumfuzzle of thought-gumbo.

Slug enrolled my help with his tomato garden one spring—not on the fence, but to pull up volunteers. I thought it was a shame to yank out of the ground a plant that had liked life so much the first time around it was willing to give it another go, but Slug insisted in his reasoning with the same determined adamancy he'd apparently employed in his fervent justification to the county officer who'd pulled him over for running a stop sign. He first mistook her for a nurse, thanking her kindly for flagging him down and assuring her he was hale as a mule, so she could get back into her ambulance without worry.

She handcuffed him.

Slug had never fought another day in his life after meeting his air-intake pipe head-on years ago, yet he still took to trouble over things that warranted none—like stop signs. He insisted they should read *pause* instead. Said it was more accurate. After all, if people really did take stop signs at their word, they'd all be stuck forever at the first one they came to. He bothered over it unending, unable to suss how folks could abide a world with such inconsistencies.

Sass thought Slug lived life in a brilliantly strange way that suggested holiness. I only wish I'd been there when he explained his moving violation at court, watching how his characteristic off-putting sideward coal-miner glance—essential for any type of tête-à-tête deep in the earth's dark—must have disquieted the judge, who threw out Slug's ticket along with Slug.

What convinced me to leave wasn't Slug but the threat of turning out time-warped—like my technology-thwarted mama, who was always hanging up on people as a result of operating her cell phone like a CB, and who twice on a single trip to pick up Sass pulled into a drive-through and ordered into the gaping opening of a hooded trashcan. Twice. I drove after that.

Sass had gone north; my brother chose south, and I had already crossed the Cumberland on a visit to the Carolinas, so I'd chosen west. I'd known it was all wrong when I saw captive gardens planted without any thought to keeping them in due-south sunshade at summer's high noon. They were ornaments without function, but without the originality of Slug's fence. Sass thought the same thing of her move at first too, especially when she'd discovered that no one baked with buttermilk and found out people used serrated utensils to cut peaches out of necessity.

Our first forays away from home, from each other, were uphill sledding. We all missed our orchards with their honey-skinned blossoms and peaches that split wide at the mere suggestion of a butterknife. We missed exhaling frosty fogfulls of strawberry breath on milkshake Fridays with Grandpa Jelly at Dorothy's—established in 1934 and filled with coffee-sipping regulars, most of whom were established only a year or few on either side. We missed shifting in sync to the cool parts of the sheets during sweltering summer darkness that melted into morning light.

I didn't know those swamp days would become the cool shadows of long muggy days to come. I didn't know that Sass would leave college for the rest of the world, conjure me to do the same, and then leave again. I didn't know I'd get stuck forever just inside the yonder edge of memory.

If Granny were here, she would tell me it was high time to light a shuck. But all I hear is the hard-road sigh.

Roamin' Catholic

Arkansas MacJerptin

Hollowed by several long and cave-dark mountain tunnels, the hallowed roads that lead to Rome are clearly meant for Ferraris, Alfa Romeos, and various other rockets similar to the blurry ones blazing past my sad specimen at speeds that shear wax from their shiny coats. In my rearview mirror, they appear like dots on the horizon then moments later scream past like warhorses on amphetamines. I can hear all 1.3 liters—*Do they even sell milk in containers that small?*—under the hood, huffing and puffing to choke out all they've got. It's downright religion-inducing, and I force from my mind its picture of the frenzied goings-on under there at 140 kph—a speed my car strains to produce, and one the cars around me were designed to mock.

Purchased used a few countries ago—and a thousand times as many miles as months past, from Harold, a retired mime and veteran of Her Majesty's Royal Army—the compact, right-drive jalopy bore the battle scars that marked its own service in several road wars. Purchased new my whole lifetime ago by the eccentric, sparkly-eyed pensioner who stood in front of me, constantly losing hold of his dentures but not his pipe and periodically breaking into vigorous song and dance; the old soldier pronounced the little car a bloody demon on the motorway, and upon my entering for a test drive, reminded me as his teeth shifted that he was asking seventy-five quid.

I'd followed him home from the National Gallery in London for reasons that are still unclear to me, the same reasons that made me see the "For Sale" sign on his car as a sign of another sort—a divine signal from another place I understood about as much as where I stood.

The old man showed me how to turn the key without screwing the ignition into the gaping nether regions of the steering column. Explosive sounds emanated from the dented hood, accompanied by great plumes of black particulate from where the muffler used to be, greeting my turn of the key and daring me to shift into first. Before pulling the alleged safety harness across my chest, I leaned in to investigate the dash and the red fluid it leaked. Though curious, I deferred to the voice of my mama that always percolated its way into my thoughts at moments just like this one, and I refrained from touching it. Leaning over to close the glovebox, I learned that it didn't.

I drove until I lost my nerve.

Stuffing fell from my seat as I pulled over to consider that a sane person wouldn't pay seventy-five cents for this car, much less seventy-five pounds. I decided to offer him fifty.

Upon my return, the old veteran waved exuberantly toward his little Cromwell as it entered the drive, engine hammering. After great difficulty and lurching, I was able to force the tiny tank into halting the forward motion of its death march, wondering where its owner had disappeared so suddenly. Exiting the ever-excreting vehicle, I watched in horror as he unfolded his old bones from the ground in front of the right tire, walloping the hood on his way up.

I scrambled to his side, not having any real idea what to do when I got there.

"No worries. I was just having a look at the indicator there. The shell had only slipped from its proper position. All better now. Right, then. Tea?"

I tried to thank him anyway for the offer, but he persisted so I accepted, and he reacted with an enthusiastic whack to the long-suffering vehicle again, this time on the fender. The turn signal responded by popping out of place again. We ignored it and turned toward the cottage.

I followed him into a dark, red living room filled with dark red furniture crawling with cats. He introduced me to his cats first, then his wife, who seemed sullen in comparison to her spouse, but then so did most mortals. As he danced off to prepare tea, she ate biscuits, recounted denture mishaps, and openly despised the car, agreeing that I was right to pass it up.

"But I want the car," I corrected, and even the cats looked stunned.

She choked on part of a biscuit before dislodging the offending crumb and feeding it to the nearest cat, afterward yelling the news of the car and the choking to her husband in the kitchen who was stirring and singing sea shanties, making me happy that the purchase of this car would tie me in some way to them.

He accepted my offer, filled me with tea, and sent me on my way with a sticky sack of candy that was meant to be crunchy when it was manufactured around the time Jesus could be found cooing and drooling on his Blessed Mama's shoulder, but had since fallen into a sad state of gummy.

Having proved its worth over several thousand miles and made up for its lack of luster, my mini assault-vehicle must now struggle to maintain its go-cart dignity in the midst of these jet-engine wakes. Earlier, while plucking threadbare but clean and dry laundry from the branches of the olive tree under which I'd camped, and then cramming it into the pack that held my every earthly belonging aside from the car, I had wondered what Rome would be like this time of year, and just like that my next destination was born. The last sock stuffed, I was soon on the road, blissfully charging into another day and country.

The lack of speed indicators provokes a check of the guidebook, which advises simply that I make it up as I go along. Overflowing with renewed vigor at the prospect of freedom of adventure, destination, *and* velocity, my mind begins the satisfied and arrogant mental noodlings akin to one recently presented with the idea of manifest destiny.

Holy Mary, Mother of God. I am promptly humbled. The beasts that breathe down my neck rock the car violently each time they overtake it, forcing up through the tailpipe one last noxious assault as they pass. *Pray for us sinners now.* The little engine keeps increasing in volume and roar, and the only remedy is to sing show tunes in the hopes of pacifying my nerves and fooling my brain into thinking that the buckets of adrenaline it's encouraging my body to produce are entirely unnecessary.

A check of the atlas confirms that I am hurtling fast and furious away from countries that end in *ia* and toward a stretch of Italian highway punctuated by mountain slopes perforated with tunnels.

In one of these, three lanes of traffic are reduced to one in what must be the most half-witted road-construction decision since the human stop sign. True to form, every single car and truck starts blaring maniacally and incessantly, confirming that Italians should probably be prohibited the possession of honking implements in addition to the vehicles in which they can be found.

Soon, no one is moving at all but the horns are still screaming, ricocheting off the tunnel walls. I laugh until it's not funny anymore, and then I comfort myself with the thought that soon, one by one, the horns will all stop sounding as their possessors slowly succumb to carbonmonoxide poisoning in this ventless tomb, regretting that I will be the innocent honkless victim of this roadworks road-rage one-way deathcave fiasco—but at least I will enjoy peace. *And at the hour of our death.*

Toward morning, something happens that I thought I'd not live to see: I arrive in Rome. Packed with stand-up coffee bars, there is literally one around every corner of the city, and bolstering the supply-feeds-demand premise, at six-thirty in the morning they are frenetic places. As I sip my cappuccino, I consider how Italy has brought to light previous indifferences of mine surrounding the miracles of the coffee bean, my thoughts a-swirl at the madness surrounding me.

The man on my right, who I eventually discover is a local business-man, is also the only other human not operating on fast-forward. He initiates conversation, and I work hard to communicate with him, but he doesn't speak bad Italian, so we supplement with charades. I explain to him as best I can my observations regarding the brilliant chaos that ensues when Italians gather en masse. He laughs and nods, confiding that he shares my Group Theory, telling me he's lived, loved, and loathed it all his life, agreeing that it manifests itself here inside the coffee bar in the most enjoyable way. Full of riotous energy, hollering, clinking of saucers and cups, patrons jostle for room to stand and slurp amid the ever-increasing pour of caffeine-craving humanity that keeps bursting through the door, adding street noise to the robust blend.

After about seven minutes of this, I understand why there are no chairs. Since I've been here slurping on the equivalent of frothed ecstasy and smacking on pastries that would create a doughnut revolution in the States, at least two separate crowds have swooped in, slammed down their addiction with a swift, determined ferocity like I've witnessed before only in bars on college campuses, and then scattered out into the bluish-white haze that is Rome when the sun is low in the sky. Another caffeinated crowd later, I join the haze and hotfoot the streets.

Early morning traffic corroborates my notion about what might occur when caffeine gets added to the Group Theory. To the combustibly-geared, I am not an obstruction: I am a target. Stepping off the first curb, a man in front of me is nearly mowed down by a petite blonde on a petite scooter. Despite her size, her speed would have taken him out for sure. He barely notices.

At the next corner, a scooter pulls up on the sidewalk, steers around, backs up to change direction and, in doing so, plows right into a parked car, and then without so much as a backward glance, speeds off. I lean over to survey the damage and discover that the scooter has critically gouged the car. Though other witnesses to this collision stride past, no one seems to be giving it a thought. And so, with the only smattering of moral regret to be found in a one-block radius, I try without success to comfort myself with excuses for neglecting my civic duty in failing to report the accident—after all, I'm not a Roman citizen. I haven't even been here a day and already my integrity is falling apart. No wonder Rome fell.

Valuing my perpendicular relationship with the ground, I decide to forgo the real-life video game and instead try the subway, discovering that the Group Theory applies underneath Italy too. A sign announces the arrival of the next train in two minutes. Six minutes pass, and the assembled crowd swells.

Finally, the graffiti-covered train squeals to a halt at the platform brimming with people, and the doors slide open, revealing compartments completely chockablock with wall-to-wall passengers. But instead of accepting their fate and waiting for the next train, the crowd on the platform starts shoving forward like an impregnable wall. I look at the sea of people ahead and behind me, and suddenly realize with alarm that I am part of this wall and there is no retreat.

No one is moving independently anymore. We are compacted together like Roman bricks, without mortar. We in this crowd have ceased to exist as separate entities and have become something scary that is about to wage battle with an electrified underground locomotive.

The army advances. Physics tells me that there is no way we will fit onto the train. Common sense tells me that, sardined and distracted as I am at this very moment, I am probably being pickpocketed. Survival instincts tell me to get the hell out of here any way I can, and notions of Granny tell me this is cloud-cuckoo rich and to laugh heartily.

With these thoughts in my head, my body finds itself suspended over that perilous gap between platform and tracks. The only thing holding me up is the pressure of bodies. One fault in this wall and I'm a goner for sure. *And at the hour of our death.*

The wall lurches; I'm in the train. It falters; I'm back on the platform. This pattern continues, and as the ataxic throng keeps me teetering precipitously on the edge of life, I consider how public transportation has the ability to speak volumes about a country: In London the metro kindly calls to one's attention to "Mind the gap," while in Rome one is dangled over the gap. My lungs collapsed minutes ago, so crying *uncle* is not an option.

Bells clang, signaling that the doors are closing no matter who's in them, and this is apparently the encouragement needed to send a final crushing wave of bruised bodies, including my own, surging through the portal. The doors slam shut, cutting off our wall, but not without casualties. Two trapped bodies squirm and try in vain to twist themselves from the unforgiving metal jaws. As the train lurches forward, I realize that nothing in my life has prepared me for the kind of bloodshed I will be witnessing moments from now.

Thankfully, the train stops and the doors slide open. But instead of stepping back out onto the platform, the liberated men start bodyslamming the occupants of the train's compartment in the hopes of fitting themselves fully inside when the doors close again. One of them is successful. The other's shoulder is mercilessly clamped upon by door jaws moments later.

The train lurches, then stops. The doors automatically open to free the human obstruction. More bodyslamming. Doors close, free of limbs this time. Train lurches. Train stops. Doors automatically open (must be a bodily obstruction in another compartment). Repeat last scenario once more. Train finally advances.

I suddenly realize that I have someone's hand in a death-grip. I let go casually, trying not to make eye contact with anyone in the near vicinity.

Happily ascending from the depths into present-day, street-level Rome once again, it's a full thirty seconds before my desensitized brain notices the monsterpiece that looms large just across the street—the Colosseum.

The subway experience has given me added incentive to tackle the frenetic streets of Rome, so with conviction born of necessity, I march deliberately out onto the striped pedestrian crossing and stare down four lanes of traffic. They stop. They stop! For me! They stop! I feel like doing some kind of victory wiggle-dance, but decide that the best course of action is to skedaddle on across before their patience wears thin.

Entering the superdome of the ancient world, I stare toward the labyrinth of passages underneath the long-gone floor of wood and blood-soaking sand, fascinated and repulsed by what these walls have witnessed. Standing amid the ever-changing shadows of the superstructure, I overhear an English couple discussing the comparisons between modern-day media and ancient-Roman violence. They conclude that Hollywood will prove the end of polite society. Though a personal fan of neither, the only conclusions I draw as I weigh *Terminator 2* against the systematic real-life, real-time slaughter of literally hundreds of thousands of animals and men combined—nine thousand and two thousand, respectively, in the first hundred-day opening festival alone—is that human nature is a peculiar beast, and ancient Romans must have had access to caffeine too.

Weaving through the outer arches, I come across a stray-cat colony that lives and darts among the stretched-out shadows, present-day felines freely wandering the grounds where their larger versions used to be held captive and fought to their deaths. Digging into the stash of snacks that I keep on hand at all times expressly for stray-animal consumption, the large crowd of cats I attract is matched only by the crowd of people who gather to watch me feed the pride. When some of them start taking pictures, I snicker, noting that the Roman Colosseum is a far more interesting attraction than one of its visitors smashing up stale biscuits for cats, but to each his own. Then again, that's probably their point exactly.

Though I'd prefer to, it's too far to walk, so I take the deathway to St. Peter's Square, which really isn't. It's a semicircle, and from my vantage point it emerges like the arced, 284-columned equivalent of a welcome hug. I reach to the tarnished chain around my neck, touching Granny's medallion. So devoted to the Mysteries that as a very young child I used to mistake her for the Blessed Mother, Granny had handed the necklace over to me for safe-keeping (my own) one morning two oceans and countless sunrises ago. Prior to my possession of it, the medallion had been around her neck for more years than I've been alive, and since my possession of it, it hasn't departed a single Old World destination without having been blessed beneath a belfry that reaches toward the god it knows.

The divine world inside St. Peter's is so vast I can barely wrap my mind around it. Unlike its Gothic cousins that use visual tricks to make them appear larger, the Baroque megalith uses architectural deceptions to make it feel smaller and more intimate, making me wonder if it might otherwise open up and swallow perspective altogether in one gigantic celestial confirmation of eternity.

As I marvel at the mountain of marble and the illusions it embodies, I sacrifice perception and become a blessed victim to the mathematical harmony put to task by the hands of each and every craftsman in planning and creating this heavenly optical funhouse. The length of the nave encompasses more than two football fields, yet it seems I could sprint to the opposite end in twenty-two heartbeats and five windless breaths. The ground-level granitic cherubs holding the holy-water dippers appear deceptively small until I walk past, allowing my brain to consider that the statues are eight feet tall and one might actually enjoy a bath in sacramental waters were it not for the fact that baby angels can be frightening at that size.

As I walk toward the Holy Spirit's doven perch high in the apse, statues rising on either side of me increase in actual but not perceived size as their niches climb to somewhere near the stratosphere. The seven-story altar canopy towers, but is still dwarfed by the famous dome soaring above it. I reach toward the Third Person in the Trinity, blocking its luminous seven-foot wingspan by my outstretched palm, recalling Granny's instructions for the Sign of the Cross—that I should call upon not only the God in my mind and heart, but the Spirit perched upon my shoulders as well.

I take a seat in the quiet expanse to ponder the perspective and spiritual genius at work until before long, the scad-heaps of pilgrims the Basilica was built to hold arrive, testing its limits—snapping pictures, shoving, talking. My silent seat is soon surrounded by two orders of monks and a mess of large pilgrimages from southern Italy. Contrary to hackneyed image, most monks do talk. A lot. And being many times guilty of liturgical jabber, I really can't fault them for conversing as the High Mass begins, but I'm surprised when they don't stop. Yet nothing prepares me for the Communion mob as the Italians demonstrate once again how they feel about the rest of the world's tendency to line up and take turns.

They zoom in on the host from all angles like enemy planes vying for target positions. No line, no order. My entire section just mobs together, pushing priestward in a giant Eucharistic blob. A small, rosaried woman surges from the back, climbing over chairs and knocking people to the side, including me. She plows through eleven more, many of whom fight back, before crossing the Eucharistic finish line. I'm assaulted several more times, which makes me giggle; and I've never seen anyone laugh at Communion before, which makes me think it's probably one of those Cardinal Sins, meaning now I shouldn't take Communion because I'm damned.

Defying my probable status as an eternal roaster, I stand amid Holy Mother Church and all her Robed Brethren and decide to stick it out in the sacramental mob fiasco, looking hard for that feeling I'd had the day of my First-ever Communion, when Father Manzelough had smiled at me, *smiled*, and God landed himself in my palm and on my heart. But when it's over and final blessings are bestowed, I still feel unsettled.

I start to wander toward the *Pietà* when I notice several confessional booths roosting in a row near the left shoulder of the cross's blueprint. I shudder, thinking of Father Manzelough not smiling and yanking back the curtain. I start to walk away and then look again toward the *Pietà*. Mary looks like she will not survive this, and I wonder if she's trying to rewind their lives back to when he was a whole, fat, goofy giggling baby in her arms and not a broken man, back to when he was maybe twelve and they shared jokes. If, in that moment holding him broken there, it had been written in her impeccable soul to hate us, no one ever could blame her. It makes my tussle with Father Manzelough seem dunderheaded.

I think again about Answers and the one I got that day long ago inside the booth. The English-language line is conspicuously empty, inviting my sinning self to step right up.

As soon as I take one breath of close confessional air, I completely lose my nerve and contemplate the loss of my senses—who in her right mind, after all, chooses Vatican City of all places to perform a sacramental rite she hasn't practiced in her own hometown for quite some time? My throat swells all up into the roof of my mouth, and when a disembodied voice from the other side questions "Hello," it takes a few moments to muster my response.

"Hi."

Nothing. Then, "How long has it been since your last confession?"

Oh, yes! It all comes back in a rush that way. I'm supposed to say what he just said for me.

Swept up by recollection, I begin, "Bless me, Father. I have sinned. A heap I think. It's been . . ."

Great, long silence.

Quietly, " . . . seven years since my last confession."

"Uh-huh. And have you strayed from the Church in other ways as well, child?"

Shit.

"Well, yes. Lots, in fact. But I have tried not to stray from God." Good answer.

"Tell me what you mean by that." And when I do, he decides that we need to go through the Ten Commandments together, one by one.

As we discuss their litany of interpretations as well as the litany of Saints that might help me apply them in my original-sinning life, I am shocked to grasp that, given their subtler meanings, I have broken all but two of the Commandments. No idol worship. No murders. Brother Brodie would have a heyday.

I am not only a curser, a liar, a cheater (just one paper I borrowed from Texas in college), an unfit daughter, a thief (that college-paper thing), but a polytheist too—apparently my interpretation of the Trinity is more than modestly off.

But despite the fact that I am a wretch, this priest doesn't call me one like Father Manzelough did the last time I attempted Reconciliation. This priest is very kind and patient with me. We end up having a mighty but mannered catechismic debate that he wins, and I am inspired to do better and nobler things with my life when it's time to wrap up our visit with one another and God. But I'm nervous again when it comes time for him to assign my penance, and I expect him to tell me to pray the Rosary nonstop for the next twelve years. Instead he asks me if I remember the Act of Contrition.

"Yes."

"Very well. Go ahead and recite it." That's it? That's all I have to do? I thank him for his time and am about to make a move when he adds, "Now."

Shit. Shit. I remember it, but I can't recite it on demand anymore. That hasn't happened since grade-school religion classes with Sister Aquila the Hun. Now he's going to think that I lied to him. Oh my God, I did! I lied in confession! *And* I just used the Lord's name again. All a mere stone-chucking distance from the Rock of the Faith. This is bad. Very, very bad. Not to mention a catastrophic launch into my better/ nobler intentions.

"Um, can we say it together?" is the best and most moronic response I can muster.

"Alright." And we do. When he starts reciting, the words do come back to me, but his version and mine aren't perfectly congruous, and I run from the confessional when it's over, hiding out in the middle of a passing crowd of tweed-jacketed, pasty specimens from an antediluvian age. They smell like pipe tobacco and are too distracted with higher-minded endeavors to notice my presence, muttering among themselves in many languages, including English.

This alone is enough to entice me to follow them wherever in the world their attentions may lead, which happens to be down a marble spiral and into the slick cool air of the Basilica's crypt. Other small crowds are gathered here and there around various polished monuments, but ours doesn't stop to contemplate these memorials from a time too recent to pique our interest. We are headed into deeper parts of the realm, and as the air gets damper, I realize that we are descending toward an off-limits area of the church's underground. An apparent guide emerges from the circle of scholarly jackets, producing from his a ring of gigantic keys.

The door groans as he pulls it wide, and he starts as my dubious presence in the privileged group is finally noticed by a legitimate member of it. I am evidently still invisible to everyone else, so I nod seriously as I pass by the guide's questioning eyes and through the doorway, pretending to examine thoughtfully the dark and dirt-packed surroundings that mark my passage and make me wonder what part of hell I'm moving toward.

Forced into single-file by the mud walls that now envelop us, I'm thankful that the arrangement makes it impossible for the guide to pluck me back to another existence. The sagely gentlemen from an age gone by continue to conspire mindfully with one another in multiple tongues, and I struggle to piece understanding from the few English fragments I catch until the man behind me catches the front of his footstep on the back of mine.

"Many pardons, my dear," he says with soft "r"s before asking me if I'm with the university dig. Deciding that nobler, better intentions can wait just a little longer, I tell him yes, thinking it might have been wiser to pretend I didn't understand English very well, but he'd probably know the language of any country I feigned to be from, including ancient Greece and probably Lydia too.

He seems on the verge of asking me a question I'll never be able to comprehend much less answer when the earth opens up to reveal a mini-city of tomb-like structures with the last flecks of frescoes clinging to them in the humid air. Attention is shifted, and the guide moves front-and-center to weave together an archaeological and historical storyweb that keeps me captivated start-to-finish, enhancing exponentially my understanding of the multiple layers of significance amid which I stand.

We have reached the ancient necropolis beneath the Basilica, which is only the most recent of the grand monuments conceived on this spot of earth. The centuries of construction that have taken place here have preserved each successive layer of treasures beneath, and thanks to a recent archaeological expedition of which my erudite companion believes me to be a part, we literally walk the intact layers of history.

Originally constructed aboveground, this mini-city of the dead was actually a happy place where ancient Roman friends and family of the deceased would gather and celebrate the memory of the entombed. The buildings, which housed the remains of first- and second-century loved ones, were lavishly decorated inside and out—frescoes, mosaics, sculptures. A few even had rooftop balconies for picnic feasts and wine parties, leading me to believe that the Irish didn't invent wakes after all, they merely made them more dramatic.

As we walk freely and contemplate the dim, humid underground along these streets next to these buildings, I try to imagine them in their original setting on the side of a hill in the sunshine, with flower gardens cascading from the rooftops, and people happily prancing about with baskets of food and wine for themselves and libations for Great-aunt Lyvia. What a bang-up place.

The great big grin on my face contrasted with the cerebral contemplations of my comrades convinces the guide of my illegitimacy, and he joins my side to whisper the pedigree of a few of the savants among whom I stand—a group who completed a petition two years prior in order to be placed on a waiting list for the opportunity to visit these hallowed grounds. I ask him how much trouble I am in, hoping that Roman Law has softened in the years since crucifixion.

He just smiles and moves off to my right to engage in a conversation about the controversy surrounding the most recent excavation to claim that these same public cemetery grounds were in fact the burial place of the Peter for whom the Basilica is named. He turns back momentarily to notice my wide-eyed stupor, nodding me toward a simple pit with a seemingly hastily-scratched inscription scrawled across the small slab lying atop it.

Standing next to the alleged bones of this icon in evangelism, perhaps second only to Paul in terms of zeal, I try to have profound thoughts but can only wonder what the world would have been like had those two had access to television. The plainness of this pauper's tomb stands in stark contrast to the building above, which must be one of the largest and most lavish monuments ever attributed to anyone—a notion in which Peter and his martyr-pals in Saintdom, especially the persistent Paul, would likely disapprove, making me glad I wasn't in charge of its construction. I'd hate to be on the bad side of one of the most inexhaustible corresponders in history.

Loud voices jerk me from quiet thoughts, and I realize that our time here is finished as a boisterous official, who looks so unofficial that had he approached more quietly I'd have presumed him a haunt, begins shooing us back toward the gated and locked entry point and berating the guide for having allowed us to linger so long.

As soon as the turbulent tirader notices my presence, he begins to venomously spit Italian words that must rarely be used in polite company because the tweed jackets are stumped. When he's finished, he walks over to inform me that my tour will end as soon as we reach the upper crypt. I'm so relieved that he employed the word *tour* instead of *life*, I have to stop myself from hugging him.

Once free, I leave one underground and head for another, where a shrill voice over the metro-station loudspeaker is, judging by the reactions of the Italian-speaking population surrounding me, announcing the Second Coming. People begin elaborate lamentations, tossing up their arms in despair. *And at the hour of our death.*

I consider for a brief moment that what is unfolding before me, like so many other ponderous Italianisms, might be entirely normal. But the piercing voice and crowd mannerisms only get more urgent, and I begin to fear the possibility of Armageddon.

I add my voice to the ruckus and start repeatedly clucking *Parla inglese?* until my chirps are noticed by a kind man who tells me simply but efficiently, "Accident. Man down on tracks. Trains no more today. Bus number *settanta*."

So it does happen. The metro has claimed a victim that the communion line missed, making it a far more serious threat than I had previously given credit.

Having no real idea where bus *settanta* will take me, I follow the crowd and hop on. The bus fills quickly to capacity and beyond while still more bodies try without success to glom on before the doors close. Sandwiched snugly in the armpits of others, I become convinced that a bus this full must be violating some kind of international human-rights legislation.

We cruise past pick-up/drop-off points without stopping and I watch the Italians waiting there to board wildly curse the bulging doors of the bus as it blithely sails past, obscuring their flailings in a fog of particulate matter.

I'm definitely ready for a change of scenery when it stops near the Trevi Fountain, dazzling in Baroque splendor. I purchase a cup of sweet creamy coolness from a gelatto vendor and sit on the steps of the fountain to slurp it down. Many Italians, young and old, all surrounding me, are also heavily involved in some slurping. Only it doesn't involve ice cream and it would be censored on the Disney Channel. Previously, when I've witnessed Italians operating in tandem their voices and appendages with this much gusto, they appear to be in passionate disputes over pastries or bodyslamming each other into suffocating metal boxes, but while there is indeed a great deal of passion here, there are clearly no disputes. I toss a few coins over my shoulder and make a wish having to do with moments just like this one.

Aimlessly wandering back in the direction of the Colosseum, I reach the Arch of Constantine and then pass through the Arch of Titus, descending into the Forum, plodding downward through literal layers of time and spilling out onto the pavement of history. Despite its fall, Rome has since risen several feet through centuries of history, paving-stone by paving-stone.

Footstepping through the Forum on the now-uncovered original stones of the Via Sacra, I imagine toga-clad emperors, senators, citizens, vestal virgins, civil engineers, and ancient souvenir peddlers trodding the same stones, making the ancient hip hangout an intellectual and cultural bazaar. The senate building still stands, as do the walls of Julius Caesar's temple, where his assassinated ashes were venerated—and still are. On this day there are three fresh flower bouquets scattered amidst its ruins. Several columns soar skyward, hinting at the grandeur of past lives.

Towering over these tall witnesses is Palatine Hill, site of Rome's very first mud-hut squatters, the Romulus and Remus myth, and eventually the opulent dwellings of emperors, now in ruin, overlooking the Circus Maximus track, itself nothing more than an antiquated outline ringed by a modern busy road—the present-day, fuel-born chariots skirting the ghost-chariots of old. High above the bowels of the city, I spend sunset watching Forum shadows lengthen in the quiet beyond metropolitan din, the ancient scene below serene in the fading light. I close my eyes to two thousand years past, when the stones below me pulsed with the feverish energy that beats beneath the city today, and I become quite fond of the bizarre bazaar that has always been Rome.

S.P.Q.R. is everywhere below me. And rising above is the Basilica, as though declaring on top of all the fray, *God was here*.

Latitude

Texas MacJerplin

"I often forget where I live."

The day had only started and already the latitude was closing in on her. All week she'd been craving pickled okra. Her stomach persistently at odds with her geography, she often forgot where she lived.

It was this figurative state of affairs she'd been attempting to communicate after scouring the aisles in search of pickled anything-but-cucumbers, except her response to the stockboy's not just helpful but also cheerful, "The pickles are right here, Ma'am," left the young man puzzled, as is wont to occur when sixteen years are confronted with sarcasm ten years their senior. "Um, well, maybe you remember your name?" he tried, reaching out and gently placing four fingers on the fossa side of her elbow. He was skinny and smelled like her first kiss.

"Oh, for the love of Pete, I am not cold-duck cockamamie." She threw off his hand, "I just want some pickled effing okra!" The outburst surprised them both. Of the boisterous brood with whom she shared childhood and kinship, she was the least-so, and unlike more than most of them, she could physically count using only three fingers each and once the number of times she had cursed—to her, *effing* counted—out loud, though in her head it happened more frequently, and when it did, it did not sound like a second-language speaker trying out a new word, as her friend Evie had teased on those occasions. In fact, the cursing that remained inside her didn't sound at all but rather was felt.

And it felt nothing like the rig-driving champ-of-a-mouth Evie challenged her to aspire to; it felt like release, like plunging from the bluffs above the rivers' mixing point, bare-feet first and screaming into the kudzu-choked swamp-bottom sludge-waters, mindless of copper-heads and cottonmouths and all such, knowing only the nothing and everything contained in the viscous blackness below, filling her slowly, snaking its way through her veins, its thickness halting her heart for a single, stretched-out beat just as the whole world starts to make sense, slowing time to turn a waterbug's single skim across the slime above her into an impossible infinite moment in which she dies, dies to the beat of her heart and wakes to the rhythm of earth's pulse, wakes seeing and knowing the all and mighty of the world through a hairline insect slit in the earth's scum, wakes inside its guts, its richest and most blessed treasure where the whole of life seeks purification but somehow mistakes it, by fallenness perhaps—that most sacred of original excuses—as nothing more than a cesspool of watershed hopes.

Security came swiftly and rotundly, so swiftly that later she marveled the suddenness, their round, unexpected, and abrupt appearance, as though spying through jars of capers from the next aisle over, a bizarre undercover design that might explain their disguise as giant roly-polies with badges. Had they manhandled her when they showed her to the automatic door, what had they said as they escorted her out of Dominick's, were those guns in holsters at their sides or just walkie-talkies, and holy rollers had she really been kicked out of a grocery store?

"No. It's okay." The stockboy swooped to her defense. "She just doesn't know who she is. She didn't cuss at me or anything. She only . . . like . . . spelled it out. *For crying out loud* was the worst thing she said. Well, maybe *cock*. But she's just looking for pickles."

Even though in later moments she would change her mind, in that one—in that particular moment, standing amid condiments and things that passed for hors d'oeuvres on lesser tables than her mama's—she was convinced this feral teenaged boy, looking slight and ridiculous in a logoed cap and smock—was the kindest person she'd ever met. She opened her mouth to tell him, but "I didn't say *for crying out loud* and I am not looking for fucking—yes, *fucking*—" she felt it: they all felt it; and she stopped to savor the moment, "pickles," was what came out instead.

Between the security meatballs and before the scrawny stockboy she stood, stunned, pleased, pitied, and held in contempt, making a mental note to call both Evie and her red-haired brother and relay the incident to them, verbatim.

Evie would be so excited, she'd spend the whole day driving up with as many of the girls as she could assemble on no moment's notice, just to toast the occasion in the flesh. This thought convinced Texas not to call, for when Evie learned of the curse's true impetus, it would be all Texas could do to keep her friend from seditious acts in the city streets on Texas's behalf.

Her brother would laugh with her, buoy her, and then tell her what he always told her: *Come home.* Unlike other members of her family, he was keenly disturbed by her stories about the oddities of life where she chose to live it. If cities were supposed to be so full of opportunity and choice, then why was his soft, gentle, beautiful sister living in one of the hardest, meanest, and ugliest areas he'd ever seen—and without access to pickled brussel sprouts at that?

It was her dissertation on cicada mutations and ground contaminants that landed her the job in the city, which he thought ironic considering there was precious little ground left in a city from which a cicada could emerge, and it was the last place you'd expect to hear one. Cities had long ago made themselves deaf and blind to the nighttide, shutting out the timbre of nature, even extinguishing the stars.

When folks asked after his sister, he'd reply that she was still working to make the world a safe place for loud night critters, but what he kept silent was how it saddened him to think she never heard them anymore, that she was left only with their lifeless, altered forms, to examine and explain the spectacle, hoping to help plead their case to chemical-company ringleaders who cared only that the big-tent operation was profitable to them, minding very little the cost to the circus's freak-shows.

He would certainly share her indignation about a place where the word *pickle* existed solely as a noun. Like beets—which she thought mildly ironic, considering one could only get beets north of the thirty-eighth parallel if they *were* pickled—but no one called them pickled because pickled things didn't exist at this latitude. Buttermilk suffered the same obscure reality.

There had always been those fleeting glimmers of hope—like the cashier who'd recalled stories of his great-grandfather having a glass of buttermilk every evening with a cupcake, or was it every morning with a muffin? And the well-manicured woman, buying well-groomed stuffed shrimp, who'd definitely and distastefully heard of pickled pig's feet and other unspeakable animal-part varieties.

What bumfuzzled her most about these episodes was the reminiscent manner in which the information was delivered: countless people had "recalled" and "heard of" such things—as though buttermilk belonged to the collective consciousness and the term *pickled* as a modifier existed solely in books featuring croppers with tumbledown shacks and bad manners who played poker and never won, or charming women with lacy parts and high boots who played whist and never lost.

More than most of the time these recollections, volunteered in response to her overheard queries, were accompanied by a phrase like *Where're you from, Honey?* As with most twangs, hers tended to swindle the good sense of many good people into assuming her IQ was significantly lower than theirs.

And as with most twangs, hers carried that mysterious element of inclination that caused these same good people to suddenly adopt a twang upon encountering one. Whether or not she realized this, the involuntary twangers usually did, right after committing their artificial twang, almost always eliciting from them an immediate measure of residual awkwardness that kept them from continuing familiarity. This was perhaps the reason she'd reflexively grown to temper her twang, forcing the fullness of sound from the back of her mouth to its front, flattening the exquisitely rounded vowels of her hills beyond indigenous recognition.

This was probably also the reason why—during her year-long graduate internship at the lab, which had been continuously renewed to total four years of servitude in the city—the only genuine, twang-true interaction she allowed occurred on the final day of her life north of thirty-eight degrees and with her mailman, a circumstance her neighbors would wonder at but a subject they would never broach (with her).

So while she took pleasure in relationships with coworkers and friends she genuinely enjoyed, even a love interest or two, she never truly let anyone inside, into the fullness of her silence. Instead she silenced only her accent and left them to wonder, shrug, or smile at the odd-sounding elongated phonemes that every so often inadvertently found their way into her conversation. Except with the mailman.

The mailman knew where she worked, since he delivered her paychecks and had smiled on more than one occasion at Apartment C's apparent resistance to direct deposit. What he didn't know was the hope held close by the occupant of that apartment—a belief that her work would make a difference, that the underfunded lab's research would prove invaluable even though the perforated print-out she cashed every two weeks indicated precisely the opposite. She knew the fruit of her four years' devotion well-surpassed the value of any salary she might ever and would never attain there.

Until the morning she said *fucking pickles* and got kicked out of Dominick's.

It was the same morning she'd received news that the senior researchers had decided to redirect the focus of the operations on account of "unsettling results." She realized straight away what this meant, for the results were indeed disturbing. And if those who controlled the purse strings considered this threat enough to end the project, then she had been indentured to the antithesis of her ethos.

"Just bring your six-eyed frogs home to take 'em apart," her brother had told her after she'd climbed out the window and onto the apartment house's roof with her static-afflicted tag-sale phone to relay the morning's events. "I'll build you a nice operating room in the cellar for all your little Frankensteins."

"Punk, I don't dissect frogs. I develop alternatives to the chemicals that are threatening the habitats of particular amphibian species." She smiled along about the word *habitats* as he chimed in and finished the oft-repeated sentence with her. And then frowned, realizing that was only what she'd been made to believe.

"By-god, I don't see anything wrong with frogs having extra legs. I'm telling you, bring 'em on down here and we'll have us a helluva fry-up with those bastards. And I'm not talking about the frogs. Goddam politician bastards. Hell, bring the frogs too and we'll fry 'em up along-side the bastards." He listened for her reply and read the silence. "Jesus H., Tex, get rid of that half-ass phone. Sounds like I'm hearing your end of things through a goddam gramophone on a thirty-three." He sounded just like Grandpa Jelly, and she smiled at his grown-up voice, searching her memory for the sound of their youth and longing for the smell of her sister's hair across the pillow they'd shared for the first half of life.

Measured in miles, her present residence wasn't that far from her home-soil, but measured in things like cortège-courtesy and porch-swings, the two places were too far apart to share map-pages. On her visits down home, the grief her red-haired brother gave about her apparent citification intensified. He blamed her watered-down accent for any misunderstandings they held between them, spoken or not. And even though he was sure he'd forgiven her for encouraging their sister Sass's cockamamie idea to purchase a one-way ticket to Europe instead of moving home after graduation to run the orchard with him—a plan the twins had made long before the day they set it down in a pact before setting out in separate directions for college, a plan he had counted on, needed, yet a plan Sass hadn't counted on him needing so soon—it was a loss his siamese heart could never make whole. So when he mocked and called his big sister *citified*, probably neither of them realized the extent of its cut.

"Sis, you know the only thing you liked about up there was that damn job. Bastards. Now I know there's no such jobs like that here, but maybe you could make one up for yourself. You know all about what you're doing, and we got amphibians out the ass down here. Chemicals, too. I just sprayed the orchard this week."

She cringed, trying to reconcile the glorious taste of July peaches with the hideous effects of compounds that kept bugs and disease from tree-ripe bounty so it could get to that point. She was glad he'd taken charge of the orchard alongside their dad and pictured him now, taking a break to receive her phone call, shading himself on the slatted back porch.

He reached a tanned muscular arm to receive a jar of tea from the ever-patient Kathleen, his college sweetheart who didn't mind that he still hadn't told her his real name. She had a laugh as big and piercing as she was small and soft, and she playfully ruffed his wild curls with one hand and tickled his taut belly with the other, winking to let him know what was in store after tea.

Turning from him, before Kathleen could swing the summer door to enter, his mama came through it with an exit that made both lovers sure she'd seen their wink, and the daily Rosary she was off to say beside Granny's grave was sure to hear about it. Although his mama hadn't raised an eyebrow about the way Kathleen's post-graduation visit had turned into a season-long residency with no signs of fading alongside its cicada-song, he knew she consulted the beads about it daily. He blushed as Kathleen winked toward him again, but not at all because his mama had seen the first one.

Kathleen had grown up in a three-storey, wood-framed house in the Vermont countryside. Knowing naught about how a bona fide farmhouse actually operated, she was enthralled by the MacTerptin homestead and had entered it with her heart wide open. Grandpa Jelly took an instant liking to the "slip of a girl with a slap of a laugh," recognizing her ignorance for what it was instead of mistaking it for condescension as most of Sharp Rock seemed intent on.

Texas was saying something about returning to grad school in Arizona, finishing the two semesters she'd had left before accepting the ill-fated four-year servitude in the city, when he interrupted, "You could bring all your greenhouse smarts down here and maybe do some good for all those bullfrogs this hayseed is causing to glow and whatnot."

His sister knew the tease well—the weed was always accusing the wildflower of hothouse notions—but she also heard the underneath parts of his words and cautioned them. Hothouses were lovely places but so closed, their air so thick with scent as to dizzy everything inside into forgetting the winds that once carried their seed and the waters that grew their buds to a blossom. Greenhouse soil was rich and the showers temperate, dependable. But there was no earth-breath, no freeze, no flood, no life not regulated or contained. The sun's rays, allowed, but only obliquely. Moonshine neither gleamed nor intoxicated. Hothouse honeysuckle could out-glam grain sorghum every day the weeklong, but the former survived no tempest, didn't even know it from a breeze—and the latter was sweeter besides. Her mama's own fence depended on its roots to hold sway.

"Just think, Miss Citydrawers, you could make me organic." She heard ice cubes and then his swallow. "Hell, you've got a monthly lease for that booth you call an apartment. Call it up and load down that rattletrap of yours with all your earthly belongings like I know you can do in six seconds flat and drive down home for a spell. Damnsure you won't make any money down here but you don't make any money now." He took another drink. "And by-god, maybe you just might could make some money after all. We could test out some of your highfalutin ideas on some of the older trees, and then whatever seems to be working best, well then, we'll just use it on 'em all and become a model for the rest of the bushel-pushers around here."

She could hear Montana, Alabama, Michigan, Delaware, and Nevada in the background, all suddenly having a come-apart over something or other. With Montana home for the summer and Alabama leaving at its end, her red-haired brother had insisted on a road-trip a few weeks past, the whole sibling tribe, plus Kathleen and minus Sass, sleeping on the floor of her studio, using the length of her air mattress as a single, colossal pillow. Delaware, with Michigan's experienced assistance, was finally old enough to notice the city as an entity and had been fascinated by its pulse—not just the El trains and impossible height of the buildings downtown like on her first trip a few years back. Nevada just wondered aloud where all the grass was.

Texas knew then she didn't want greenhouse-grown kids, wanted them born in breezes, knowing a zephyr from a bluster and feeling everything in between. They could plow all they wanted into the ways of conservatory concepts and sprinkler sentiments, but she wanted them to feel inside their bones the very wilds of the winds and waters that made them whole.

She knew it would be this feeling that would make her return for good someday, despite her passion for the work she might do here if she could, despite the thrill of the city that burned bright all night, successfully competing with every single star except the one that hailed dawn. Whether standing in her mama's wide and full-to-bursting kitchen or at the hotpot that passed for a stove in her studio, her feet would forever be firmly planted in the bluff-edged footprints of generations amid the swell of a river where she would hold close a mess of their secrets, listen in between the space of wind and breath for their songs, feel in her blood the wake of their memories, and know in her heart the all of their might.

"What do you think, Sis?"

"I think an idea like that just might could run the orchard to ruin."

"Better it than you. Come home."

The mailman knew almost every song that ever once had echoed from the Cumberland to the Ozarks. She'd discovered this following the conversation with her brother, after she'd climbed down to swap the tag-sale phone for her Grandpa Jelly's mandolin along with a trash bag filled with ice and four of the Stechers her brother had brought from home on his visit. She aimed not to come down until she'd drunk them all.

She climbed atop the dormer and straddled the apartment's roof with the mandolin responding well to her calloused fingertips. When the mailman recognized the tune, she started at the unexpected voice below and accidentally knocked over the side the Stechers she'd wedged into the cross-hip behind her. She lunged impulsively forward in a futile attempt to catch the fugitive bottle and caught sight of the mailman below.

"I'm so sorry," she vowelled with the fullness of her roots. Upon hearing her voice, he nearly ran off without his skin—not because she'd spoken but because the tune had been so at home in his heart yet out of place in his environment, he'd assumed it was playing through the speakers of a radio show or television documentary somewhere inside the apartment house's open windows. The last thing he expected when he started singing the tune out loud was to be accosted by a beer bottle from above.

He quickly collected himself and the bottle, recognizing the label. Stunning herself, she responded by inviting him up for one.

He told her that accepting the offer was like to get him fired, and the twang with which he replied was bona fide. The freckles on the tops of her cheeks rose closer to her lower lashes in a playful smile. She scooted forward to swing her bare feet over the eave, and he understood at once the challenge beneath the gesture.

He'd lived on the edge a time or two hundred, but the girl with the big freckles and small ankles dangling above him made him want to stay far from the edge of everything and anything that might keep him from her. It was a foreign feeling for a man who on several occasions had double-dog-dared life to kill him. He wanted to ask permission to sit beside her wherever she chose to dangle herself for the rest of her life. "Where'd you learn to play like that?" was what he asked instead.

"I have a grandpa named Jelly," as though that explained it.

"That so? What's Jelly's granddaughter's name?"

"Which one?"

"The one I aim to come sit beside."

"Thought that meant a firing."

"I've been thinking I ought to quit."

"Me too. Why you?"

"I'd rather trim trees. Why do you think I ought to quit?"

"I meant that *I* should quit *my*—" and then she smiled, realizing he'd known what she meant. She drew up one eyebrow and both ankles, moving toward the window. "Go on in. Head up the stairs. First door on your right. I'll meet you on the other side of its lock."

He had only a moment to notice the "C" adhered to the door before it swung open. "So you're Texas," he grinned widely. "I had you pictured . . . well . . . differently." He tried his best not to up-and-down her and hoped she hadn't noticed if he had. He had.

She noticed. "My parents had a cockamamie notion to name all of us after states."

"How many are you?"

"Too. And I don't mean the numeral. But not enough to run out of choices, unfortunately. If it'd been the days of the week they'd taken a shine to, we'd be all out by now. As it goes, I think Rhode Island and Utah are still up for grabs."

He considered the apparent attraction between her mother and father, and it caught him off guard as he began pondering how sublime the thought of spending the rest of his years continuing the tradition with the next generation before him. It was alien territory for a man who'd spent nine years finishing college in four different places. That he'd spent the next three in a single location owed only to the grad school he'd devoted them to, turning over most of his paycheck to the university for tuition and housing, and spending the rest on books, booze, and failed relationships, searching each for a feeling whose existence he'd always suspected—the very feeling that had delivered itself moments ago when he'd looked up to discover a pair of ankles and a spray of freckles, and inherently the woman to whom they belonged was embraced by his heart, as though the reason for its original beat, the motive for its last, and the celebration of each in between.

She moved toward the window and gestured him to follow. He noticed the room for the first time. The space was tiny, and as he glimpsed the air mattress in the corner, he couldn't help picturing himself there, next to her, naked; and then, strangely, he felt an overwhelming urge to pummel himself just like he'd want to pummel any man who might picture himself like that with her. Befuddled, he went back to the daydream, placing his lips gently upon her flesh, working his way from one end of her body to the other, unsure if he should start with her freckles or her ankles.

That day, he did neither. He sat on her roof instead, leaning his back against a gable's slope, listening to her, watching her mouth as she spoke, grateful to be breathing in the same space with her, hoping it would always be so. She was leaving, she'd decided. His heart willingly gave over to her desire and panicked just the same.

When they'd each finished a bottle, she handed him the one remaining and rose to retrieve another for herself. He stopped her, taking her hand and calling her to him. She sat beside him, the gentle pitch of the roof inclining her against him. He started by asking permission to die with her when she did, in case he hadn't already done so, then asked if she might also acquiesce to him sharing space with her while they lived.

After taking his eyes into hers for a long while she replied, "You should know that I've been barred from a reputable grocery-store chain."

"Then you should know that I hope you always will be, and that I'll never do anything to sully your good name."

"Well, alright then. But you should know that if ever I reckon we might could try sharing a piece of this life, I don't want to be held accountable for yours ending."

"That would be impossible, considering you just saved it."

She smiled and leaned past him to tame the vine behind his ear. He turned, plucked a leaf, and placed it in her hand. "Have you ever seen it flower?"

"You know kudzu?"

"Enough to know its presence here is unlikely, that cultivated kudzu will mind its place for only so long, that its northernmost reported stretch is just a few miles from here, and that the best way to plant it is to throw it over your shoulder and run like hell."

"Have you ever seen it smother a whole field—house, barn, and trees included?"

"Never."

"Ever seen it choke a swamp?"

He shook his head. "But I'd like to." He placed his hand over the leaf in hers.

She removed her hand from his and with index finger and thumb spun the leaf by its stem. "I'm leaving tomorrow. I aim to have everything packed tonight."

"As soon as possible is precisely what I was thinking."

"If we leave in the morning we can be there by sundown, but you'll have to follow. I'm not coming back."

"My God, am I in love with you." He was floored, and wondered if he'd really just spoken the words aloud.

Her brows were furrowed. "What about the mail?"

She hadn't jumped when he'd last spoken so he felt safe to continue, "Texas, I don't love the mail. It means nothing to me," on a lighter note this time.

"I'm serious."

"So am I. Rain, sleet, or snow has nothing on the hurricane right here," he gestured toward his heart with the hand that had been holding hers.

"Do you even have a car?"

They shared the remaining bottle and then set the sun in perfect silence, each a part of the other's shifting latitude.

A Woman's Place

Texas MacJerptin

The table adjacent remains uncleared for the twenty-three seconds it has taken us to decide on ordering two of each appetizer as well as a mess of entrées from tonight's menu and sharing until we are glutted, then divvying up the leavings (except for Colleen, who despises leftovers to a degree that prohibits even bottled condiments from occupying her fridge) for tomorrow afternoon when we'll laze around in pajamas, worn t-shirts, and happy-pants and have lunch together without each other being there.

I know it was a woman, not by the lipstick on the empty wine glass, but by the way the raspberry-vinaigrette-dotted napkin has been folded and placed atop the empty plate in the shape of a Pilgrim's hat. I don't know a single male at a table for two who has ever executed the jaunty post-meal inclination to fold a cloth napkin into a minor work of banal art. Much less a Pilgrim's hat. Sass would do that, I consider.

The gladhatter is gone when we come in and take up residence at a table for eight, shedding custody of covers, carryings, and concerns and piling them into the extra chair. Without thought attached, the four chairs on one side of the table are scooted closer to embrace naturally the same sum of space as the three on the other.

But I'm not paying attention to this detail when we sit. The eyes of my awareness are focused on where she'd been sitting. I see her hands as they gently, deliberately crease the folds of the napkin she'd used to dab the corners of her mouth after mixed greens had grazed them on their way inside. See the corners of that mouth bend up into a private smile as she places the napkin on top of the place where garden leaves had been presented as though they were worth the money charged to arrange them. See her fluff the hat in the middle toward the back, where it sags.

A lovely smile. A satisfied self.

A damn fine Pilgrim's hat.

A busboy crushes the creation as he stacks the table's china.

My focus shifts back to our table where a clutch of girlfriends who skipped and bounced through childhood, then gangled and ripened through adolescence, is still gracing and stumbling through life's choreograph, understanding little of it apart from the role of champion for the other. I watch them now, their animated dance, celebrating my return to Sharp Rock with a much-needed departure from it to the mini-metropolis nearest, a college town enrolled primarily with city-ites, some so taken by the hills surrounding them that topographical dividends trumped tuition debt, causing many to add at least two semesters to their study.

A little over a week ago, after I'd incited Sharp Rock to a lather by returning abruptly and with a stranger at that, the girls had rallied to my side in a rare mission of detection and devastation. After a thorough discovery process, they approved of the mailman, thereby sparing his destruction, and set about to demolish any loose prattle on the subject by announcing, with wrecking-ball subtlety, that the U.S. Government had taken a keen interest in part of the MacTerptin property, had been sent away to fulfill the rain-sleet-snow obligation, but would be returning in time so the two parties could explore the matter further.

He would return tomorrow if given the go-ahead, but I'd refused to allow him to drop a 36-month degree in pursuit of a 36-hour relationship. We both teared when he left, but I didn't show him mine. They came again after that, for different reasons, as my friends helped me unload the last four years of my life, which had taken far longer than unpacking the car. They huddled with me in the center of my old shared room at the house, holding together my heart's many pieces, drawing theirs close to mine as we sat clustered, legs akimbo and tangled, mixing flesh, laughter, and tears.

I watch them now, festive and vivified, commanding jubilation, daring discontent to find the mettle to match, much less rout, this moment. Joy pulses doggedly into throbbing wounds, and my heart joins a rhythm rapturous, defiant, steadfast, incarnate: the salvific grit of friendship. There is a helluva hallelujah in my heart as I become aware of myriad snippets of conversation happening all at once, part of a larger, au fait design that I too would grasp if I'd been listening.

"Evie, what in the name of my ass is going on with your hair?"

"Buddhist, hell. You can't candy-wrap the Dalai Lama, suck on a few sweet platitudes, and then call yourself a Buddhist."

"Yep. Five hundred forty-two of them. Right there. Just like that. I nearly wet my pants."

I look toward Evie. There is something going on with her hair.

She reads my look. "I visited Sexy's hairdresser."

"Professional Stylist," Alexi corrects.

"Oh, Christ. I suppose that makes me a Human Resourcist and Texas a Froggist."

"I don't dissect . . . ," I start and then remember I don't do anything at present, preventing me from completing the familiar sentence.

Evie recognizes this and stands immediately to make a dramatic toast to Maggie, knighting her with a butterknife. "I hereby dub thee, Ms. Maggie the Magnificent Multiplier, Professional Momist!" We clap and clink. Evie. The first and middle initials *E* and *V* spelled out to harmonize their union. Coalesced, just like the words each letter stood for had merged into the person they branded: Élan Vital Trotter, whose parents had named her with the hope she might live up to the christening in the face of the five boisterous brothers preceding her. It was their singular gift to their only daughter. And it had taken root.

Evie's most recent love interest had told her Élan Trotter sounded like a Derby horse. But that was only part of the reason we now referred to him as her ex, even though they were still dating. (Sass thought this deeply unfair; she alleged there was something inherently worthy about any man who claimed, without irony or subterfuge, the Buick Somerset as his favorite car.) She suffered no pedigrees. But she was world-class.

Rinker's cheeks are filled with laughter, and they flush as Evie finishes the story I'd been listening to as well, but without paying attention. I doubt I would have blushed, though. Evie had sunk in years ago. Rinker Wave Tatum, so-named for the runabout her parents had been rolling around the ski-slogged bottom of the night she was conceived, was prone to redden at any mention of sex, so I assume that had been the subject of Evie's tale. The boat was an outboard. Mr. and Mrs. Tatum now own an inboard and a pontoon. And three more children with less-inspired names.

Having grown up surrounded by several states, I'd bonded upon acquaintance with Rinker and Evie in the unconventional-name category that had landed each of us, alongside Maisala, immediately on the "Somewhat Questionable" roster that all first-graders on playgrounds everywhere carry in their pockets. It had also landed us automatically on Sister Aquiline's "Bound-for-the-Middling-Place" list. We were never sure if the purgatorial list truly existed, but because rumors planted by sixth-graders held a sort of mystical incontrovertible sway, we were not at liberty to challenge our semi-damned status and each wisely chose Mary Teresa Elizabeth Anne for our confirmation names after scouring Sass's *Funk and Wagnalls* for days in search of the most thoroughly redemptive combination.

"Texas, you should visit my professional stylist," Alexi determines. "Not that you need an overhaul or anything, but the salon can be so relaxing."

"Thanks," I look over toward Evie's hair, "but no." She flips me the finger.

Appetizers had arrived so long ago that in any other company, the gap of time elapsed since physical proof of our waiter's existence within this lifetime would feel stagnate. Instead it's entertaining. There are rumors of his materialization at tables near ours, but to us, he remains a shade.

Alexi—who Evie had renamed *Sexy* upon their introduction to one another in fourth grade by Rinker, who had blushed then too—claims his disappearance stemmed from my use of the word *vagina* just as he'd placed in front of me a plateful of petite puffy creations I vaguely recalled should erupt with pulverized falafel beans and puréed sprouts when prodded to do so.

Not that this was a declaration I typically employed upon the arrival of hors d'oeuvres. It was merely a mid-sentence manifestation that happened to coincide with his approach from behind announcing "*Rotolo!*" at the exact moment the other three-syllable word left my mouth with more crescendo than I would direct had I the opportunity to reorchestrate the brief duet.

Our eyes had met. Mine grateful and thrilled at the arrival of my spriggy-looking stuffed masterpiece. His, repulsed at the evident shock of confrontation with an unanticipated body part. The rest of the appetizers were delivered without introduction and the intensity of his disregard since that time has shown no signs of tapering.

At first I felt bad for having accidentally thrust the word upon him, as it seems to have apparently been a terrible distress to him. But it's only a word, after all. And it was professional conversation at that. I'd been describing a recent theory concerning the rising numbers in wetland tree-frog infertility. Perhaps not typical dinner conversation, but not *so* exceptional. It's not like it's one of the four-letter transgressions. We decide he must have issues.

"Just think if you'd used the *p* word instead."

"Are you kidding?" asks Maggie. "He'd be all over us right now. Why do they all love the *p* word?"

True to form, Evie trumps Maggie, "Just imagine if you'd said *c*—" but the table drowns out the rest of her sentence with a burst of protestations against the word that prompted it. As the table erupts, concerned patrons lean and crane to determine the source of the flare-up.

We immediately capitalize on the opportunity to disguise our disgust as pretend, redirecting it from a word to our plates. The tables nearby easily fall victim to our game as they begin surmising the possibility of a stray, baked-in hair and then become alive with stories of unidentifiables discovered in cuisines du jour across the city, country, ocean.

Our waiter remains in shadow, as I suspect would stay the case were a three-toed sloth to burst from my rotolo and wrestle me to the floor. Satiated by the first round of food, no one is in too much of a hurry for the second, but when Maggie starts sweating gin, Sophie moves toward the bar to collect another double martini with a side of cranberry juice, bottle of wine, and three margaritas, extra salt.

"What gives? What the hell does waitboy think we're going to do, whip out our—"

"Evie, don't say the *c* word," Colleen interjects.

"I'm not, Coyster," acting annoyed but not really. "What I wonder is why he has to act like we have the clap just because Texas said *vagina*."

"Not so loud. My grandparents eat here. It's just not right."

"See? That's exactly what I mean. What's not right about it? Why does it cause everyone but your gynecologist to flip when you say anything like that? Like you're some kind of militant she-ra blazing sex maniac or something."

"But they *do* love the *p* word," reminds Maggie and then adds that there's nothing wrong with blazing sex maniacs or militant she-ras, thinking of her experimental college years. "By the way, were you going to say *whip out our fallopian tubes and start waving them around?*"

"Yeah, why? Have I used that one before?"

"Yep. Pitch night at the Legion last Thursday."

"Damn."

"You said that in front of *veterans*? In front of Maggie's dad?" Alexi's head is in her palm. Rinker is saturated crimson. Colleen is thinking about germs.

"That's why he insists I bring her along."

"Unbelievable."

Sophie returns bearing drinks and a large platter of artichoke tapas as well, compliments of the bartender. Sophie is a magnet for freebies—one of the reasons she has become the official candidate for these types of tasks, and the reason Evie calls her *So-free*. Colleen calls things like this brazen, which is why Evie has dubbed her *Coyleen*.

Later, after we've officially given up on the arrival of our entrées, and after another round of drinks is delivered from the bar, this time with three bowls of garlic-, gorgonzola-, jalapeno-stuffed olives in addition to a plate of dolmas, it has become far too late to ignore that we are probably going to be late for the performance of *Summer and Smoke* to which Sophie had been bestowed seven free seats three days after they sold out.

There are several appetizers left, but since our waiter has officially vanished from our sphere of existence, we forgo any expectations of a respectable wrap-up and instead swathe what food we can into the paper napkins that came with our drinks. We're not at all hungry now, but no one will feel like cooking tomorrow. Colleen excuses herself from the table briefly. Tomorrow, she'll have crackers and individually wrapped slices of cheese for lunch after a breakfast of fruit salad, freshly-sliced, and two granola bars.

She'll spend part of the morning scrubbing microbial bacteria from all surface areas occupying her kitchen, including the neck of the milk bottle inside her fridge—the one and only item aside from a jar of French mustard (somehow, that condiment received a bye) allowed to be reconsumed after its initial visit upon the premises. Though she's not necessarily comfortable with the milk reuse, she hasn't found another way around it aside from pint-size cartons, but milk stored in paper repulses her more than milk stored in large quantities over time, so she's just accepted it. No other way around it. Nature of the beast and all. No one had asked about the mustard yet, though its retention was seen as a breakthrough.

Then, for the rest of the morning and most of the afternoon, Colleen will study for the PPE. Evie will sleep late to fantastic dreams. Rinker will stuff various junk-mail return-envelopes with the junk-mail of other companies in the hopes of *sending a stern but smile-filled message*. Maggie will spoon mashed foodstuffs into her very loud and pink child's mouth, then clean them up as they run their course. Sophie will contemplate listening to R.L. Burnside while she takes her mammoth hounds to the park, where she'll probably come across a twenty-dollar bill lying in the grass; but instead she'll just put the dogs out in the yard for a while and find the twenty there. Sexy Lexi will do yoga and then call her mother, aunts, grandparents, and sister-in-law while she works on crosswords. None of us will want to cook.

Around noon, each of us will still be wearing whatever pajama-type attire we slept in, and minus one, we'll rummage around for last night's stash of leftovers, unwrapping and reheating tamale cakes, spring rolls, strombolinis, and whatever else could escape neatly enough in a cocktail napkin.

We're out of the paper coasters, but there are still several breaded raviolis and seasonal wraps left unclaimed, not to mention honey rolls and parmesan pepper bread. Sophie is about to make a trip to the bar when I suggest a Pilgrim's hat as the perfect take-away container, especially for olives.

Evie calls it a capital idea, bugger-all, which offhandedly reminds me how she despises the British for no real reason. Alexi's wrap and Maggie's mom-purse are almost large enough to contain our spoils. Rinker places the remaining two napkin hats inside her wide-brimmed blue one she carries all summer, everywhere. Colleen is back. She has the hiccups and tallies what we owe for what was delivered, plus a sizable tip for the bartenders. She collects and places a pile of money on the table for the bill and hands the rest to Sophie for transport to the bar.

Just as we are leaving, invisiwaiter makes a surprise appearance, ignoring us still, but hovering nearby to fill the water glasses of our neighbors, his eyes glancing toward the wad of cash on our table. We stare at his lack of acknowledgement that we are doing so. Evie smells fear and swoops in to execute the coup de grâce. He places the silver pitcher of water in front of his chest, like a shield. Smiling the words, Evie tells him, slowly and deliberately, that the service was . . . well . . . less than inspired. He stays fixed and silent.

She winks then turns toward the door, predicting the precise moment he will move uneasily to count the money we've left behind, then looks back over our shoulder with a casual "Oh. But I nearly forgot to mention, the cervix was divine."

Alexi guffaws and hiccups at the same time, a sudden sound that makes our waiter start and people turn. Rinker has totally missed the exchange and is trying to figure out what was said because Colleen is melting into the floor. Maggie grabs Evie's hand in hers and then pulls toward the door while I tug Sophie away from the bar and its tenders.

In the crammed car we blaze through yellow lights, and five separate packs of gum are passed among bodies piled on top of one another— cinnamon, bubble, something fruity, spearmint, and mouthwash-smelling sugarless purposeful gum. I choose bubble. We're late and have to wait to be seated until after the prologue about eternity, which lasts about as long.

Tomorrow I will ignore laundry so I can finish three books begun four years ago upon Mama's recommendation, still waiting patiently on my nightstand, free of dust and judgment. And call Toddy. Twice. At lunch I'll find the playbill on the counter where I left it. Thumbing through, I'll discover it's not mine. The wad of gum pressed into the center folds of a two-page advertisement isn't bubble. I'll smell its spiciness as I flip through last night's unread pages, and I'll know exactly whose program I have.

Sand and Rice

Texas MacJerplin

"Okay. Put all the money on the counter now."

People shouldn't joke about that, she thought.

She knew, had worked in this very bank during summers from college. Small town. No worries.

Hardly.

Still, the little jokes here and there were never laughed at. Only given glances. A sign posted on the doors during the annual July Gangster Days Parade insisted toy guns be removed from costumes before entering.

It was the same small-town bank she sat in now. Except this time she was a customer. She and the jokester on her left, two windows away.

He stood. She sat in a mahogany-stained, cracked-leather-padded chair. Its rounded arms encircled her halfway, allowing her just enough room to lean forward and confer with Rinker, seated on the other side of the low cashier's window. The other three windows were standing windows, but Rinker had chosen this one as the best option for helping her friend pour over Grandpa Jelly's checkbook records, which hadn't been balanced since Granny passed away. Texas had volunteered to straighten them out.

The friends smiled as they'd come across the place in the register denoting Grandpa Jelly's bail check for Texas, written the day she and Eliza Dentleman had been arrested for protesting the development of the wetlands below Devil's Backbone. Dog had paid in cash, but Grandpa Jelly wanted a documented record of the event, and had written below the line denoting the County Clerk's receipt of his seventy-five dollars, "toward abetting my granddaughter's criminal and correct actions." The charges had been dropped and the plans to develop abandoned after the drainage scheme proved ridiculously flawed. To Grandpa the arrests were a joke, but the million-dollar homes that threatened to topple tupelo and stand atop the heron refuge and old-growth cypress swamp south of Rattlesnake Ferry had been no laughing matter. Like the customer two windows away.

But as she looked up from the register, it was the eyes sitting across from her that told her this wasn't a joke.

She blinked once, without moving the position of her eyes. No one moved. There was no sound.

Not even breath.

"I said put the money on the counter. Now."

Just like that. Calm. No yelling. No swear words. Unruffled.

She didn't move. Didn't dare gaze toward the voice. Only stared into the liquid parts of Rinker's eyes that were pulling her across the counter. And it was that which told her how vulnerable she was. It hadn't occurred to her before that instant.

Her mind hadn't been ready for it to be real, but it was. Except still no breath. No movement. She wrapped her legs around the legs of the chair. Silently. Slowly. Without even knowing it. Arms around the arms too.

Mind singular of thought, a person could be dragged from the building hostage. Right through the door. But not a person and a chair both. Not easily.

She didn't look, but she knew there was a gun. Knew it wasn't pointed at her. Probably wouldn't be. She thought that was strange, then. The rush of objective realization. Awareness of the moment and the next one too. Maybe it meant she was going to die.

Maybe it meant she was living on the edge of her senses. For the first time in a long time. Perhaps ever.

Maybe it meant time had stopped. Was never real.

Then he spoke again. This time swore. Fucking money. Goddamned counter. And that's how time began again. It was real. Breath was real.

The shot propelled stomachs through hearts, and she was surprised to find her limbs still wrapped snakelike to the chair. Surprised to notice the cracks in the leather. This is what she said to the federal investigators after the agents had finally shown up and divided all the witnesses from one another, sequestering them in separate offices inside the bank, keeping them away from the crowd outside, cut off from one another, from the local police, from the body, from suggestion, from anything but a purely detached retelling of the events before the bullet pierced objectivity and mixed reactions with reality, passion with blood.

"What was the second suspect wearing?"

"I don't know. It's kind of strange. I didn't even know there were two until afterward. I only heard one voice—the voice of the gunman."

"Did you see a gun?"

"No, I didn't."

"So how do you know there was a gun?"

"Well, from one of the tellers, I guess. They said he had a gun."

"Which one?"

"I think it was Susan. Or maybe Rinker."

"I meant which suspect."

"Oh. Sorry. The one who asked for the money, I guess."

"But you never saw a gun?"

"No. But it felt like there was one. If that makes any sense. Never mind."

"It's alright. It's good that you're trying to remember with all of your senses."

"It's just that sight stands up better in court, huh?"

He smiled. "That's why we call them eyewitnesses."

"I'm sorry I'm not one. It's so strange. I felt like I saw everything. I mean, I smelled it and heard it."

"Tell me more about what you heard. Would you recognize the voice?"

"I think so. Sand. His voice sounded like sand. Ever-so-slightly gravelly. Of course, I guess I don't know which one, since I didn't even know there were two. Oh, and rice. He smelled like wet rice. Like when you first lift the lid and all the steam escapes." She was surprised to see him writing this down. Or perhaps he was just drawing squiggles. "I'm sorry. I know you need visual details."

"You've done a fine job. I'm going to send in someone else with some contact information for you if you need to get in touch with us. Someone will probably follow-up with a phone call in the next day or so as well."

After he left the room, she remembered that the second suspect—the one who ran as soon as the first went down holding his throat, sliced through the neck with a tiny metal missile fired from the gun of a policeman, one of many who had been signaled by the silent button on the floor in the vice-president's office, pushed when Mr. Martin Marscump, Jr., saw what was taking place in his small lobby—was wearing a red flannel.

Excited at this snippet of memory, she thought to make sure and tell the person who would come in next. The one who would finally release her to go home, asking her not to speak to the media. But by the time he finally came and did all of this, she realized that the fragment of recall wasn't her own. She'd been told the man was wearing a red flannel. If it had even been a man. It could have been a boy. Or not even male.

All she had to offer the agents were grains.

They let her leave through a side door that she didn't even know had existed, but she looked into the lobby on her way and saw that the body had been covered. She heard that the red-flannelled one had been caught too. Shot once, but not killed. She recalled precisely the sound of the bullet searing flesh, knew it would brand itself in her ears, blister her memory, and scald her blood heart, which had rippled, had not beat, when the shot found its target.

The cameras had been pushed back to the other side of the street, and no one rushed up to her as she was escorted to her car. She heard shouts. She felt sure there were flashes. She turned so she could witness them.

In the car she noticed that a spider had cast a single thread from the steering wheel to the gear shift. She thought about this as she pulled away and headed toward the hard road. The only road in the county with two stoplights.

The lights were on at the crossing, and she could see across a bottomland field of flattened husks the long chain of freight cars that would make the highway section of her journey home longer than usual.

A bird soared above the earth that stretched flat to the horizon, flying, then gliding, curving toward her away from the train's wide bend. As she watched and slowed, an unexpected impression surged up from someplace longsome undisturbed. At once she saw everything. Saw how she'd held her eyes closed wide open.

She cried after that. Hard.

Cried like life was new.

The Drop Edge of Yonder

Arkansas MacTerptin

I am checking the map when the man next to me is abruptly swallowed by a flurry of hair. As he wrestles the shrieking female, I suss that they must be acquainted. Their phrases are unrecognizable, but familiar gestures and intonation reveal a friendship lost to time, one that will be enthusiastically recollected during two minutes on a busy street-side, only to fade into memory when destinations direct them hastily around corners and into separate-time once again.

Damming the traffic-tide, a light signals the pedestrian pool into the crossway, washing a wave of walkers past the pair who embrace amid the swell. And when traffic is beckoned once again to spill its racket-cluster of imperceptible progress into the street, the two are fixed in a kiss that transcends the stop-and-flow of here-and-now, confirming that my foreign-language skills are lacking in at least two of the five senses. I don't know how many lights have changed when time starts again and they turn toward me, and I smile warmly at them before realizing the reason for their stare is that I started it.

"*Lo siento*" is all I can mutter before remembering that the language doesn't match the country. "No-no! Um, uh . . ." I move toward them, wanting to make it right, but the words coming out of my mouth form a strange protolanguage, and the couple lists backwards against it.

Frantically trying to conjure alien terms from my mental phrasebook, all I seem able to summon in moments such as this is *My name is*. And judging from the looks on their faces, I have just employed the phrase, followed by the words *Bubonic* and *Plague*. I am moving toward them like some sort of monosyllabic Cro-Magnon monster, and he is practically shielding her from me when I finally recall that I'm supposed to say *Désolé*.

Instead, I run.

Fast.

But I can't even get that right, careening first into a mammoth purse and then the petite blonde attached to it. "Sorry!" is what springs out this time, exposing the Ugly American.

"It is nothing." She touches my arm with a gracefulness that matches her accent at the same time the sun ricochets from the polish of her purse and into my eyes, resulting in a glare I'm sure can be seen from space. I reel and blink, struggling to see around floating black holes and into her face. She steadies me, "Can I help you with some matter?"

The affection in her voice is so genuine I want to spill my whole heart in a Niagara-sized woe-wave, but I'd already alarmed a stranger a few countries ago in Rome with my details. And that was in a confessional, a place with few surprises.

If Granny were still talking to me, she'd tell me exactly how this should go, but she'd stopped her impromptu visits with my thoughts a long time ago. The last thing she said to me in one of them—the spring after she left, on a drizzly, shut-up afternoon I was imagining away in Sister Aquiline's math class—was how much I was going to love visiting in person the river gods who'd swapped places with word problems in my concentration. I took that to mean my days were numbered; but after a few years when I still wasn't dead, I realized that Granny must have been speaking Gumbo French, and if I could only work through what she meant, she'd start visiting me again.

I still hadn't sussed it out when she started whispering into my mind's ear once more, speaking this time in coincidences—what she'd told me in life was the language of mystics. I'd liked that outright as soon as she'd said it, wholly because the word started in mystery and ended in poetics. But my first inkling that mystics were a misunderstood lot came the day Mother Cosma agreed with Sister Aquiline and sent me home with a behavior note stamped in capital *INSOLENCE* attached to my "What I Want To Be When I Grow Up" essay.

Even though I'd collywobbled and stomped against the world's unfairness, Mama made it clear that short of a special dispensation from the Pope, I would be rewriting the essay and suggested a career in theatrics as a topic. When I glared at her and made the mistake of putting forth the Dalai Lama as a more impartial consult, she added a letter of apology to the written punishment. And no pecan pie.

Later that night, Granny hugged me with her whole lap as I cried about my hand aching from all the writing. But she knew the real source of my tears, whispering to me that not all vision problems were the kind glasses could correct, and it was curled into the apron-folds of love that I learned I didn't have to be a mystic to understand secret languages. Granny had given us one of our own, and ever after that I would listen hard for all the underneath parts of her words.

Both Granny and Mother Cosma smiled and nodded at my revised essay, telling me what a wise choice ophthalmologist was. It was probably the only time those two agreed on anything, for though not a day passed when one of the Mysteries didn't play itself out across the misshapen beads of Granny's creek-gravel rosary, it was she who taught me that my fascination with learning about the gods who don't use capital letters isn't the same as sinning. That was when the itch must have started. But it wasn't until five Julys after her death that I became infected, like a dermatitis of the mind, by the places we'd visited in *Funk and Wagnalls*, stories, and conversation, and I knew I'd go in search of our gods.

Granny must have understood this the same way she'd known every ripple of joy and pain that waved within me. Like the shreds of tissue she'd shuck from her purse pocket exactly when I needed them, she knew that one day long after, I'd open the 'loom box, searching for the smell of that purse, and find within it several crisp bills with a handwritten note attached, scripted in the language of her saints: *Pour mon ange des dieux—à coup sûr voyage.*

I'd set off with a sure stroke, just as she'd directed. Determined to locate in ancient effigy the gods of our lore, I'd begun my calamitous quest in London at the British Museum, among the pilfered and catalogued ruins of an Empire that had chosen to exchange all its deities for one—which in Catholic math calculated three. But there had been no epiphanies. No Kerouacian moments. The only thing that hit me over the head was the upper set of dentures belonging to a pensioner at the National Gallery, when his mouth accidentally dropped them from a floor above and then fussed me into such a bumfuzzle (of which I grasped nothing until the teeth had been replaced, and then only every sixth word), I somehow ended up following him home for a cup of tea that was supposed to make it all better when nothing was really the matter in the first place.

Along the way, his dentures shifted position continuously as his mouth shaped words around recurrent draws on an unlit pipe, clacking against it in a tap-dance of extra syllables. A retired mime, his old profession was alive and well in the whole-body symphonic tableau that harmonized, inextricably, phrase and gesture and expression. And above it all, rattling steadily, was the staccato-without-end of his dentures.

After stepping from a train in the outer stretches of London where the Underground isn't underground anymore, and shortly after making the acquaintance of the dentured man's wife and cats, I left with his car and moved south, slowly, canvassing kingdom and country, rise and fall. Ending up in Rome, I pondered wide and deep the paths that placed me there. Still no epiphanies. The revelations discovered were the ones spelled with an upper-case *r*—the ones that recalled the dregs of my Cardinal-sinning self. So I'd gotten out fast, moving without awareness toward the capital city of Granny's sacred language—only to be pitied by a small and sleek mega-pursed Parisian.

Combining equal parts compassion and concern, she takes my hand in hers and looks softly at me, so very out of my element amid Place St. Michel, which I can only assume must be the genesis of all catwalks, the tiny world-within-a-world behind the shimmery curtain, swaggering off the pages of magazines chockablock with odorous cardstock tear-outs, parading into the streets of Cosmopolita punctuated by accessories with barely pronounceable brand names—like the shiny, deep-red purse monstrosities, pervasive and pomp exclamation points with two large pewterish baubles hanging from the oversnap. No zippers. One strap. Fads of such specific nature, they are doomed by saturation to replace themselves indefinitely.

Surrounded by this populace of chic makes me suddenly aware of my own presence. My backpack is purple. Bright purple. With a Lorax patch stitched across the worn spot in the back. I recall sitting on the stoop with Mama when she stitched it there, a thought that floods with a desire for home and a stem-bowl of orchard salad with mouth-size chunks of fresh peaches tasting just like August sunshine.

My hand-holder asks again how she may help. Her insistent compassion completely convinces me that I need condolence, and I have to choke back tears when I thank her anyway, trying to use her language in saying how much I appreciate the kindness, but the pop quiz on her face tells me I've screwed that up too. I think for a moment about trying to fix whatever I've said but am so upended I accidentally start to cry. In English.

At this she guides me toward a seat at a nearby table, manhandling a waiter who swiftly produces a carafe of wine and a box of tissues. They seem to know each other, yet I refuse to trust the all-systems-failure of my interpretive skills that landed me here. She hands him something, which I'm struggling to see when a baguette passes by, followed in quick succession by cheese. When the view clears, it reveals only one person remaining. I stand to look for the woman, but am abruptly shooed into my seat by the waiter.

He stops by three times during my carafe, asking me a few basic questions in French and pretending to understand when I pretend I can answer. The wine slowly erases vocabulary and by the time I request the bill, it's all I can do not to trip over my native tongue. He shakes his head and smiles, closing my fist over the cash while saying something about grace, hearts, France, and mending. I want to tell him he read my mind.

My head a gumbo of language and notion, for a moment I mistake the clouds for the way they looked the day Granny took me to town to buy tap shoes—real ones—until I remember that she never did. I'd fever-dreamed it two flu seasons after she left, and it had put a smile all the way across the rest of wide-awake that night. When I look up, the sky is changed; the waiter has moved on.

Despite the fact that the red-bagged people of Paris have just shown considerate hospitality to me and the Lorax, we wander to the Louvre to get lost among fellow foreigners. Discovering a line of them with socks as white as mine used to look as they wait to check their guidebook-filled backpacks, I tackle the first few galleries with giddy and tipsy fervor, seeking out Venus and finding her surrounded by a thick swarm of worshippers. Down one palatial hall, Mona is similarly occupied, so I aim downstairs toward the Phoenicians, trusting their pantheon to be well represented in a world-class museum.

The twisted-upright bodies of stony Etruscans greet me along the way, smiling into the afterlife from atop their sarcophagi. According to Granny, the demonic and fascinating Xaru peeled right off the Etruscan tomb frescoes and into the hands of the Greeks, who revised the god's image and updated his name. Charon thus became assigned to ferry a dead river into the perpetuity of prose, with only a two-headed dog for a consolation prize.

I had always trusted the tales Granny told, even though she'd always insisted on including the Big Muddy Monster in her crowded temple of divinities. I certainly trusted I'd find no trace of him here, as he lives outside the canons in the murky bottomlands of my youth. At least that's how Granny told it. And there are t-shirts to back up the claim too. New ones are printed each year for the Big Muddy Apple Stomp Fest. The festival used to be three distinct town celebrations—the Big Muddy River Festival, the Apple Harvest Gathering, and the Shawnee Wine Stomp—held one after the other for three straight and separate weeks.

But they were combined upon the mayor's insistence he couldn't run a town that shut down every September. And just like that, twenty-one glorious, parade-filled, Indian-summer days were combined and truncated along with their names, so now it just sounds like we celebrate giant bruised and soiled fruit.

This always makes me a little low when I get to thinking about it, but I don't have long to swell my woe-wave before I spot a series of low-ceilinged salons, openly joined and positively animate with the miles of tiles that used to mesmerize me from the black-and-white pages of *Funk and Wagnalls*. Far from the flat images that so enthralled me when life was still a decade new, these patterns leap from their exhibits in brilliant affect.

A crowd is gathered around a dazzling display at the center of the first room, and I close in swiftly for an eager look at the color-dance when my head is abruptly and cruelly met by an invisible wall of blunt pain. There are gasps. Horrified intakes of breath. I stagger, and for a second time I am steadied by the hands of a stranger, consequently preventing further damage to the glass cabinet that turns out to be far closer than what my eyes accepted as truth. Accursed astigmatism.

The man seems to be putting a question to me in code. I watch his mouth. It's a language I can only hazily discern. Might be English. I act as if I don't understand him and then realize it's not an act. Blast all; my head dizzies and throbs as I move toward a bench where I will sit and wait for the international incident to finish panning out. But no leather-trenchcoated guards show up to haul me away. Still, I decide to stay put until at least half the crowd is not staring at me. I close my eyes to will theirs away.

A short time later, when I fall both asleep and off the bench in consecutive moments, a terrific guttural noise reverberates through the gallery. Working my awareness slowly outside of confusion and pain, and then up to the enlarged whites of several pairs of stares, I comprehend from a prone position that the noise was mine, occurring when the air in my lungs forced itself backward through my whole self upon impact with the floor.

The same kind, questioning man hurries to my splayed-out side, wanting to know did I fall unconscious, faint, swoon, pass out . . . speaking English with an impressive array of modifiers given the foreign accent he is using to hurl them at me.

"Ahmerrykhan?" They always know.

Inadvertently, I play right into the hands of inspired stereotypes after I stumble over him as he helps me back into my seat where I vocally confirm the answer to his question—much too loudly, gathering from the renewed and repulsed glares from my gallery mates. "We can rest for a moment in this place," he assures me, and viscous syllables pour into my ears in no hurry to catch up with the consonant beauty that preceded them. A familiar inflection from years ago. Granny-sized tears start welling up, and I can't tell if it's them or the concussion causing walls to warp and staring faces to ripple.

Pressing my hands to my ears, from somewhere deep in the throb of my mind I hear the footsteps, and for reasons beyond response, I silently count them off like seconds, mississippi-style.

Wishing I could wad and stuff this entire episode deep into the lost folds of time's pockets, I watch as the Samaritan takes from his a neatly tucked, bleach-white handkerchief and places it tenderly against the paths my tears have traveled. It smells of pure tobacco, not cigarettes. His eyes wash over the crowd, and one by one my silent tormenters turn away.

He turns toward me, and for four mississippis I look into his eyes. I look into his eyes for four seconds, minutes, months, generations, and come back never all the same. Long eyelashes surround hazel irises as soft as his words, and I want to keep gazing right into them but instead my dilated pupils wander to his left earlobe. It, too, seems divine.

Divine. Holy martyrs, that's it! I'm passed. This is heaven. And he is God. My mind reels with the disjointed chatter of nonsensical panic as it reviews how my heart was three beats from going fluttery over the Our Father of fathers.

I'm positive this blunder is covered in the Commandments, and I'm about to reach into the catechism of my youth for a prayer I hope will save me and a saint that might possibly recognize me when reason steps in to calm the flurry—reassuring that the ever-after does not take place in a museum basement, and reminding me that in my eternity the Virgin and I are tap dancing hand-in-hand across the waters of the Pontchartrain Basin toward the wide-open arms of a rump-shaking Mahalia Jackson and the Jerusalem her song promises. At least that's what I'd told Mother Cosma when she'd asked me to interpret my watercolor of heaven.

My mind settles, measuring relief all the way up to my eyes, which my saving grace notices. The pump of my heart pulses against my ears, and blood footsteps fill my head. I close my eyes to imagine their path, and when again I open them, the Samaritan is gone, his handkerchief still bearing the faint impression of his palm against my cheek. Pressing his gift to my eyes, an embroidered corner tumbles from beneath folds, where answers lie. A yellow rose.

Gaelic Gales

Texas MacJerptin

When I'd gotten the call from Sass, I started gathering things to pack before she'd even asked me to join her. She and her Cromwell had boarded a cargo ferry at Cherbourg, thinking it was a passenger ferry headed to Portugal until landing in Portsmouth with a cow-filled hull. She decided she may as well continue on to Stranraer toward Glasgow. We met up in Scotland and then struck out for Ireland on my suggestion that we hunt down Grandpa Jelly's roots in Clare, hoping we'd find living proof of Quinn's Pub. It always bothered Sass that *Funk and Wagnalls* had no information on our aunt. Secretly, I was relieved we'd be traveling in countries that spoke our language. I'd never been good at charades.

Sass had copped Dad's army pack, so Dog loaned me his. I didn't discover until later that Maisala had stashed some of our harem beads in it, forgotten in a deep pocket of shadow—and suddenly I wanted to be heading somewhere far from the language I knew.

In the same pocket I found part of her voice—a poem we had created for Sister Celeste, who'd been obliged to cut short a very long poetry unit when Deacon Neaput disagreed with Mr. T.S. Eliot about our place in this world. That hadn't stopped Maisala, Toddy, and me from hatching poems together until long after the day Sister stood before us and Mr. Neaput, clarifying the error, explaining that his interpretation was full of criticism.

We knew whose she meant.

I held Maisala's words in my hand, reading them two times and again before tucking them back into the folds of time. I smiled and cried at the lines, recalling how thrilled we had been upon discovering that sentence fragments were acceptable, determining to work them in at every opportunity. Our poem's title had been smeared, but I remembered it. We'd called it "God's Gourds," thinking Sister would like that. She did.

Frost got the pumpkins up north this year.
Twice.

Mold got the ones down south.
Again.

At home, neighborhood vandals got theirs.
No matter.

The end of every autumn marks a season
of gourds gone by.

Flesh doesn't last.
Seeds do.

As soon as the plane had debarked—placing me wide-eyed and stock-still, lost in the middle of marvel while more seasoned travelers excused themselves around me—the airport's intercom began kindly calling my attention to instructions I could barely distinguish as my native tongue. I could feel my senses trying to terrorize me as they struggled to summon some semblance of acquaintance with my surroundings, but then a part of me I'd misplaced beat them back, thrilled to be separated from understanding by not only an ocean, but a common language too. And there I was in varying states of comprehension, as strange accents trickled information and pardoned me, when I heard the voice of Arkansas holler *Texas*.

A new country plus a sleepless night yields a blissful coma. Add to this jelloheaded state of sublime a ferry ride resplendent with sunshine, which carries us across a sea that last night threatened to consume us, and despite the clear skies, my thoughts remain partly cloudy. Closing the door to leave the noisy ferry deck behind me, I find a soft chair in the lounge next to my sleeping sister. Curling into well-worn tapestry, I notice that color is just beginning to seep through the edges of the enormous welts on my legs, floating my thoughts on a cloud of mental fog to arrive at the precise moment the thrashing began.

The tent had taken on a life of its own, its roof pinned flat against our bodies with an incessant pressure heretofore experienced only at extreme depths. Thus awakened from my dream-filled stupor, for more than a moment I actually held the idea that the tent was trying to swallow us, a reality far removed from the one in which I'd fallen asleep.

After a long drive from Loch Lomond, we'd pulled over and set up camp in a lonely spot on the very edge of Scotland. As the glow of a gentle sunset winked satisfaction over a perfect evening and tender waves teased the rocky shoreline just outside the cozy confines of our nomadic nylon home, we feasted on a supper of shortbread cookies and Carlsberg and congratulated ourselves on our choice of accommodations.

"I think we should hit some of the —*ia* countries next, don't you?" I smiled at Sass.

"Is Grandpa still in a swivet over that?"

"Oh yes, and he's added another category to the list. At the hog roast, he told me to make sure we stay away from countries that cure their meat 'with p-i-s-s.'"

"And what countries might those be?"

"I'm not sure. Mama choked at the four-letter word so we moved on to *that* matter."

"Kind of like someone else I know. Just say it, Texas. Piss piss piss."

"Shut it. Brother Brodie was there or I would have pushed the issue once Mama recouped."

I was about to tell Sass about Frieda Harbar attending the roast on Grandpa Jelly's arm, a subject the rest of my family was reluctant to introduce to Sass, especially during brief conversations across deep waters. Mama feared Sass's devotion to our Granny would shut out an acceptance of Frieda, so I'd promised her I would let it slow on my sister. It bothered me that I hadn't mentioned it yet, so I started to but then remembered the banjos and knew that if I got onto the subject of Frieda, we probably wouldn't get back to the banjos. I decided Frieda could wait five more minutes. "It was like nothing you've ever known. A four-string and a five-, tuned open, capoed crazy, and fretted without end. No one could figure out if they meant it or if they were just completely shine-sogged. I mean it was nuts, Sass. Like a sound that's impossible to fathom, much less to make."

"Like woodchucks doing math."

"Precisely."

"Texas, do you think that's why you sent the mailman back? Because it felt impossible?"

And with that my thoughts turned hard around a tall corner and without knowing a thing about its coming and even less about its why what-for and how-come, I slammed into a good sob. Just when I thought I'd found love's antidote and called it simple, memory smiled back and called my bluff.

Sass put her head in my lap and told me about meeting her mailman at the Louvre, about how she remembered only four things from her visit there: discovering the Etruscans were more exciting than Mona all day long, hitting her head hard against an invisible surface, letting walk out the man she thought she was born loving, and swearing she could see up Napoleon's nostril in the coronation painting.

"I don't know why I didn't say anything to him, Texas, why I let him walk away when I know he would have, and indeed wanted, to stay. He was my Joseph."

"What did you say?" I snapped to.

"My Joseph. He was my Joseph. Like Mary's. He stood by me through the thick."

"Not all Josephs are that way. Remember mine?"

"Of course."

"Well, he sure left in the thick of it, and even after I plumb directed him not to. Never came back, either."

"Duh, Texas. That's because he down-deep truly loved you."

"What are you talking about?"

"Duh more, Texas. You were there, remember? In the barn. So was Dad and Henry and Joseph. On the other side of the alfalfa."

"Joseph wasn't there."

"Yes, he was, Your Duhsome. I can't believe you don't remember. It wasn't even me he loved and still I'll never forget how he shed tears when Dad explained how the town talk could ruin you, cut you to pieces, like it cut his mama, and he just couldn't have that. Joseph vowed to Dad right then and there he would cut out if it meant you could be left whole."

"What! Sass, why didn't you tell me this?"

"You were there. Love-a-duck, do I have to say that again?"

"Yes, I was there, but with my ears smushed between your ankles and my view blocked by bales. I can't believe I'm just hearing all this."

"Yeah, Sis. Joseph totally unforsook you. That's what Josephs do. Remember? The main one even got sainted for it. Hey, isn't this backwards? Aren't you supposed to be instilling capital Catholicity in me?"

We both knew our hearts were thick with a bluster that refused to lie down. It was a giddy and tormented truth, the kind of happenstance love that sneaks up on your thoughts and stays for weeks at a stretch, then starts feeling like it's been there forever and you'd go cold-duck crazy without, the kind you mistake for everything you ever wanted and no one can tell you otherwise, because at the same time their mouths and heads call it silly, their lips and hearts beg to remember.

It had surged into both of our lives like a heavy rush of honeyed heat, heat that pushes the door wide and pours on in. It had singed sweet our skin to a luster glass burnish we would remember each taste after. It was pure but hardly simple, and it made me think of Eve unstained, how her lips must have swelled when she tasted the devil's own sugar, and Cain, how he felt its scald. It was the divine aspiration underneath sin kisses and original desires. It was the falling part of love, and it had dropped us hard.

After sussing hard, coming up without answers and bothered to a swivet, especially over the nostril trick, we settled in underneath an argentine moonsliver sparkling over the Irish Sea. Tugging at a shared sleep sack, we tried to find our way around thought to rest amid the imaginings of our planned ferry adventure to Ireland in the morning. We finally edged from the threshold of waking dreams to enter the world of REM sleep, only to be battered from it by gale-force winds bearing down on the walls of our consciousness.

The poles of the tent were warped hideously inward, continuing to smother us. Our sleep-sogged brains barely had time to register the nightmare before us when suddenly the walls snapped back to their typical dome-shape, but only for a deceptive second before the wind commanded them to relentlessly slap us prostrate. Overcome by visions of being tossed out to sea in our two-man-capsule-prison, I considered hopefully that instead of sinking into icy blackness, our tent might skip like a rock across the waves all the way to Ireland. Then, emerging more clearly from a dream-world where tents eat humans, I realized that the wind was coming from the direction of the sea.

Rolling over the pummeled body of my sister and hoosegowing my toe in her forever tangles, I managed to wrestle my way to the zippered portal and pull taut the screen to view an army of monstrous waves abusing the shore, which made me instantly wonder if tsunamis were a problem in Scotland. The wind raged on, intent on turning our tent inside-out.

Fighting back at the walls, we scrambled to a conjoined semi-squat, my toe still snarled in a mizmaze of locks. Sass's mouth opened and gestured words that were immediately carried away on a torrent of air. My own mouth moved to answer her, but the words were likewise stolen by a howling gust. In their stead, I simply nodded and crawled to the side for her to go ahead with the plan that I didn't hear at all, but nevertheless understood.

Sass freed my foot, and on hands and knees I followed her outside the tent to throw myself on top of flailing vinyl, guaranteeing its tangible relationship with the ground while Sass skittersprung headlong into the vicious air to pull up stakes that gamely struggled with the wind, dutifully vowing to rip seams before releasing an inch of ground to their furious opponent. Ominous black clouds tumbled just overhead, impossibly low and fast. Lacking rain, the breath of thunder soaked us with a sea flung ashore in bursts, surrounding us with a blusterstew of rolling currents bellowing into our heads, stirring our thoughts to an uproar.

As Sass pulled the second stake from the ground, a portion of the tent whipped over my body and I shuffled to contain it, shifting each of my moveable parts just in time and tandem for a blast of enraged air to scream my clothes straight off me. My eyes followed the invisible fury and caught sight of my pajamas in the distance, plastered to the trunk of a tree whose squat and stooped stature was a surefire clue we'd wholly missed of the circumstances unraveling before us. Barely able to hear my shriek above the roar, Sass glanced at my prone position and continued to frantically pry at stakes, puzzling at my nakedness but not stopping to ask. When finally my body became the tent's only anchor, we labored together to wad up walls that continued to fight against us.

Scooping the tent and its contents into a bundle, Sass tugged me up, and for a brief moment I leaned into the atmospheric crush, bare-chested against the tempest like a figurehead—though hardly on par with that kind of grace and bosom. Fumbling forward, I started to take a step toward rescuing my pajamas, consequently releasing the heavy plastic ground tarp I had forgotten about to rise like a wall and flat me smack.

I somehow regained a vertical connection with the ground, but not my self-control. Chased by screaming pockets of air that were being hurled at the rocky edge of a country, lifting waters from its shore, I utterly abandoned all semblance of a plan and began a beeheaded sprint toward Sass's Cromwell, not bothering to grapple with the plastic tarp that was adhered to my body by no intentional means. Sass must have watched the demented display of naked panic engulfed by a saran-wrap surrealism, forgetting momentarily about the tumultuous black sky that threatened to scoop us into its roiling fury, and wondering why she'd ever asked me to join her.

My momentum eventually propelled me faceward to the ground, surging Sass forward to assist the tangled mess of muddy tarp I had become. The wind bullyraged past, whipping plastic and stinging nylon across our skin as merciless as the shore-thrashing waves. Our bodies craved the shelter of the car, and when at last we reached it, we sat frozen to our seats, both unsure and unable to make a move in any one direction. Wide awake, we sat up all night in a car that was jolted, rocked, and swayed until morning, but divinely possessed walls that didn't warp inward.

By sunrise, calm had been restored and magic conjured—a magnificent rainbow greeted us, stretching across the horizon and over the Irish Sea, beckoning us to the Emerald Isle. It was as though the producers of Hallmark television specials had stepped in to direct our day.

Yet by nine o'clock, the smooth beginnings of my morning's television debut were being intruded upon by static and commercials. The sleep that my body was robbed of began stealing logic from my head. Reality became a series of disjointed thoughts that would never make sense no matter how they were strung together. Memories of last night's tumult were being tossed among daylight visions that presented a placid sea and a tranquil coast, all combined with dreamy impressions of the hours ahead and the new country they promised. While these notions may have appeared in order on the outside, they remained a jumble inside. And while I had never considered linear thought to be the corner-stone of existence, life without it seemed to drift on a haze of incongruity.

I float in this manner all the way to Ireland, not sleeping but nevertheless lazing in a nonsensical doze. "Perhaps arrival to a new country has this effect on everyone," I explain to Sass as we disembark the ferry, when out of nowhere, a thought captures me in totality: *This is Ireland, and everything here is Irish.* The unremarkable nature of my reflection is completely lost on me, as is the remarkable fact that my myriad divergent thoughts have managed to come together to form a singular notion.

The thought is insistent, repeating itself over and over, making me feel I have been gripped by the fingers of profundity. I speak it aloud to Sass, but she recognizes banality when confronted by it and is nonplussed by my repetitive marveling, "Wow, those are Irish houses. That's an Irish cat. There's an Irish tree. This is an Irish road. That must be an Irish bird." The mind-marvel continues all day until I've catalogued most of the commonplace objects around us. I even catch myself being utterly fascinated by an Irish school bus.

Deep in this ethereal zone I gaze quietly upon a hill speckled with equal parts sunshine and shade, considering that I've never set eyes on a more hue-saturated hillside with only a single color involved. I have the intention of making this thought aural, but when I try to speak, a strange word blend gets in my way. "Again and forever once," I tell Sass, and then stop immediately upon realizing that what is in my head and my mouth do not equate. This pattern repeats throughout the day, so I center my speech on the focus of my thoughts—an inventory of Ireland.

Even though Sass teases me about my displays of verbal ineptitude and the trancelike spell from which they effuse, I soon notice that she stops the pretense of trying to communicate with me using words and simply pulls me along at her side, feeding me when necessary. She tugs me to the apex of a bluff to sit on the stony ledge of the abandoned building atop it and look out over the sea it dangles precipitously above.

I follow her along a small road lined with fuchsia blooms and together we visit a beach that washes up new treasures with each breaking wave. I gather a handful of tiny shells that must boast the rest of the colors in Ireland's spectrum. Flanking either side of the beach are windswept and water-beaten ridges that glisten in the sunlight, as they must have since long before mankind determined the world had a measure called time. Surrounded by such enduring beauty, I am at once and for once able to feel the soul of verses constructed long ago by persons with names that stir the blood of scholars—and by so many others who might have, had history recorded their names as well.

Without calling to mind exact quotes, I recall the language of poets, in the voice of Sister Celeste, who insisted their words be heard aloud and often—words that were meant to capture the essence of beauty. Words she insisted should be committed to memory, precisely and faithfully. And even though I have failed her in this respect, I believe she'd be right-well pleased to learn that I've committed those words to my spirit in this very moment.

And while the words of the renowned have gone on to pepper speeches and pages, the words of the nameless remain here, washed into sparkles of sand each time they endeavor to rise and murmur on the breeze, yet still able to be heard by those who acquiesce to compose themselves and listen for that one fleeting moment between whisper and wash. A beauty so intense it must remain ephemeral.

Part of the sky is enveloped in a crinoline haze and begins a sporadic but gentle drizzle. My eyes are closed to the soft kisses of an invisible cloud when Sass hauls me to my feet and points over my shoulder toward a rainbow in the distant sky. It would emerge like a stunning jewel in any other setting, but remains merely an accessory to the beauty here.

Rain and sunshine seem to occur both simultaneously and in quick succession for the next few hours as we move along the coastline, and the prisms of Irish legend continue to appear as if to substantiate the existence of the cliché. I continue to catalog all things Irish, and I think Sass is grateful when nightfall cloaks needed sight and hushes my tireless inventory.

We settle into a drafty hostel, and just before descending into sleep, a whisper of last night's wind brushes against my ankles and I turn to adjust the coverlet, tucking the scratchy throw beneath my feet when the thought kicks in again—an Irish blanket!

I close my eyes to exhaustion but sleep is impossible. I remain on its cusp all night—along the very edge where dreams and reality get confused—sailing the crest of a cloudy current, and riding the novel intensity behind each ordinary wave of thought.

Vapors

Texas MacJerplin

Gentle breezes of summer struggling to settle are forced farther inland by a week of gales, descending thick and salty along the coast. Having won temporary hold on the fishing village, they gradually become less insistent, finally moving into the unnoticed parts of days like lingering echoes, ghosts of gusts, sighs, breaths. A cloudless sunset hovers over calm waters, paving the way for a starry path to streak the sky and disappear into a sable sea beyond an uneven shoreline where sheer drop-offs, twisted by time into metamorphic masterpieces, plunge into pounding Atlantic waves.

Stepping from Quinn's into the night, whistle notes and whiskey fumes endeavor to escape, muted by heavy air. With a faraway song on my mind, I breathe the familiar vapors of home. The third reel ends as the door swings closed, trapping the final fiddle fill inside where it fades into smoke and applause. Standing, facing the lower village, the pier, the cliffs, the blackness where sky meets sea-swell, road winding with river, even breath is forgotten—flow, water, and wisps of wind the only proof of time.

Leading from the pier, rising and falling, the narrow road weaves through the village and then separates from its river-path to pass in front of Quinn's, inviting us to join its journey over miles of bog and into the heart of the mainland. We meet the pavement, but our path's direction is that of the Aille's flow, and where the road splits from the river we join it, hop-wobbling from stone to stone to reach the farmhouse.

Treading carefully amid a sea of unfurled sleep sacks, half of them occupied, Lark stirs the peat fire as we enter and begins apologizing in a frantic whisper of a language I barely recognize as my own. Home-soiled in New Zealand, Lark left there one holiday weekend for a trip to Ireland that has since turned into something of a walkabout without end. When his boots wore holes, he took a seasonal stint as a dish scrubber, and twelve years later, he's an official transplant with an inimitable accent. This season's work involves managing the hostel where we are staying, and from the unique sound of things, it's all gone horribly wrong.

Sass insists Lark is a mystic and will swear on Granny's medallion she's seen him evaporate into mist on two occasions. I hate it when she does this, because then I have to confess it for her. She stopped going after Father Manzelough decided her notion to canonize Granny needed absolution. Called it sacrilege and her a wretch. Right there in the booth. *Dunderheaded* is what Sass called Father before renouncing Reconciliation and concluding that if canonizing Granny was a heresy against the Church, then the Catholicism she practiced from here on out would be the lowercased kind. Mama is still saying Rosaries.

Upstairs, in a room that can barely contain our bed and our packs, we find the backpacks of two strangers stacked on top of our own in the only available space not already occupied by the mattress and our standing bodies. Lark emerges from shadow to apologize once more in an impossible tongue before vaporizing with such ability and velocity I start to suspect Sass might be on to something. She demystifies his words for me, explaining the bus didn't come today and now the hostel is hopelessly overbooked. Shrugging our shoulders, we squeeze into the mattress and hope for the best.

Sunrise at the overbooked hostel affords me the unique experience of waking up next to the scrawny, naked, and hairy hind-end of a complete stranger. Opening my eyes to the day, I lift my head from the pillow and take a quick survey. Our bed. Our packs in the corner. My jacket hanging on the door. My sister sleeping on my right. Mysterious, undressed wooly man sleeping on my left.

Concluding that the best course of action is to return to sleep and suss it later, I do so, but am soon jolted from slumber by a penetrating brogue. "Foor fook's sayke, Swish, poot yar trousayrs on!"

The exposed man opens his eyes toward the voice. "Christ. Have you a volume save deafening, Love?" Then, noticing us, "Sorry, mates," and swiftly jumping up to replace trousers, "Who'll have eggs?" And that's how we met the rest of Swish, our new roommate and lifelong friend—of the latter I am certain because people who enter a person's life in this fashion are simply not allowed to gently fade from memory. His girlfriend's speech, thick as daub, is an absolute joy to the ears, but a whole other matter to the brain that must interpret it. So much conversational concentration is required, I'm actually thankful when she leaves after a few days to return to the Orkneys.

She and Swish met in Edinburgh during its annual festival, seated next to one another at "Puppetry of the Penis." She was at the Fringe to write an article, he to make some spare cash selling mushrooms. When Swish had initially explained this to us, I thought he meant the fried kind. Sass claims she knew better, but I doubt that.

Presently out of spare anything, Swish has returned once again to the little village as it gears up for its summertime swell of music aficionados and tourists. Last summer he lived in a deserted camper that had blown into a ditch and could only be entered or exited through its rear window, but his home has since been trampled by cattle and pummeled by a storm into a state of sad abandon. Lark has agreed to let Swish stay free at the hostel in exchange for cleaning its bathrooms. He's decided to look for work.

Originally from York, the freewheeling expatriate could be from anywhere. He has the feel of infinite possibility. Quinn's is hiring, so we follow him there.

Quinn's

Arkansas MacTerptin

The height of Quinn's lunch- and supper-crowd crush, the reason for our hire, is populated by tour-bus throngs who make the jaunt over to the little village from the nearby Cliffs of Moher, with the locals strategically filtering in and out for their midday meals between the bus crowds. The suppertime mob consists mainly of B&Bers and backpackers eager for a night of musical entertainment, the villagers settling in for their evening pints after the supper plates have been cleared.

Each day, when the busses open their doors and release herds of hungry sightseers, the lazy little pub swings into action, abuzz with the clatter of plates and languages—and usually the reverberating baritone voice of Peter Boyle hovering above it all, heaving in gulps of air and turning it into song, refusing to allow his melody to be drowned. As the crowds swell and roll about him, his slow ballads crest their surface, leisurely, staying their course through the full rush of the atmospheric tide. Were he here, Uncle Hap would be right rallystruck and join in, no doubt waiting for the inevitable intervention of Mama to tell him when he'd strayed the bounds. But the only other Americans here are strangers to Texas and me, wide-eyed and muppet-mouthed transients, eager to ingest the novelty around them, swarming amid stories carried aloft in measures layered and lasting.

Happily familiar with this reverential wonder, it is how I recognize my own countrymen before they speak; and for this reason I am reluctant to speak back to them, tossing handwritten, pint-stained menus into their snugs and skirting cheerily around them until the time comes when I must open my mouth and ask for their order. I hate witnessing even a sparkle of their notion extinguished, and I cringe each time I see the hangdog flash momentarily across their face when they discover my complete lack of Irish inflection.

A few times the intrusion from home remains resented, but often-times it engenders a peculiar mutual intimacy that hovers, tacit and palpable, just below the surface of conversations over menu items. This causes me to puzzle at length over the more befuddling communications, like the question I find myself repeatedly answering about a menu item I never would have predicted to be a bumfuzzler: "Does the Guinness stew *really* have *real* Guinness in it?"

But whenever I try to suss these things with Texas, she tells me to lighten up buttercup before my ramblings about connectivity plunge me creedless and drown me comatose into the deep and yonder end of my divineless communal consciousness where no measure of decades will be able to save me. I have no idea what that means.

Still, one afternoon I consider she may be right about cooling it when I am faced with the perplexing, "Irish coffee? I'd no idea they grew coffee beans here in Ireland;" I am bona fidely unsure if the Florida-tanned man asking the question is trying to be funny or not. I consider erring on the side of what Granny would call *savoir faire*, and Grandpa Jelly, *by-god half-assed moxie*. And I know exactly how my red-haired brother would answer. But in the end it is the plainsung voice of my ever tactful mama that intervenes just in time for me to answer him straightforwardly, realizing my mistake seconds later as I suffer through a sallycrack about Johnny O' Valdez and the Blarney Stone.

I don't share the story with Texas though, because her dunderhead fuse is a short one, and I've noticed her tolerance for our fellow country-men waning. I, too, inexplicably limit my harshest critiquing to my homeland comrades, deciding to forgive one cataclysmically overbearing and ethnocentric customer after discovering that he's actually Canadian, but happily, I find that the high expectations I have of my fellow citizens are not often misplaced. While serving the bus crowds, I notice that we can be a wonderfully bizarre people, and while those from other countries do enjoy our enthusiasm, frankly, they think we are too loud. Unfortunately, this means our worst moments are as highly visible as our best.

"Well, son of a bitch! How do you like that?" This man will clearly resent my accent to the grave.

"How about a Guinness? Myself, I prefer Beamish. Or, if you like cider, we have Bulmer's and a mess of others too."

"Where the hell are you from?"

"Calm down, Honey," the voice of the turquoise-bedecked woman seated at his side soothes while her eyes insist that he hush-it or else.

"Canada," I fib, hoping this might make it better for him. "I really fancy your hat," I don't fib, wondering how in the world this man ended up with my outlaw dream-hat of all time, and then wondering if they say *fancy* in Canada.

"My wife got this for me," he replies, and my smile to the turquoise woman next to him is met with the awkward realization that she is not his wife. We move on quickly to the order, whereupon a group of eight backpackers struggling toward bohemianism nearly lose their lives when

I explain to him that they have ordered all of the potato and leek soup. "They ordered *all* of the damn soup?" he roars.

"Yes. It's the only menu item that's vegetarian, and they were really hungry."

He rolls his eyes. "What about the French fries?"

The mystery woman interrupts, stroking his arm and seemingly trying to calm him, though her word choice doesn't quite match the undertaking, "Honey, remember they're called *chips* here." He glares through her toward the backpackers.

I answer quickly, "Plenty of potatoes left. But it'll probably be a spell before another batch of soup is ready. Sorry. The stew is delicious, though."

"No. I mean can't you just give *them* some extra French fries and I'll have a bowl of that soup?"

"Well you see . . ." I start, both amused and frightened by what I imagine will be his overreaction to my explanation regarding the chip dilemma. "I'm not certain if the potatoes are fried in a hundred percent vegetable lard, or if there might be some animal by-product involved, so they opted to play it safe with the soup."

"Oh, for the love of God!" He throws off the woman's hand. "Where the hell do they think they are?" Though the man's choice of words seems a bit excessive, I could somewhat understand his frustration on this point. While as an animal lover and part-time vegetarian (admittedly, for the part of the time when it's convenient), I could respect the backpackers' motivation, a part of me wanted to remind them of their surroundings and then ask them to more properly weigh their expectations when they asked me what kind of vegan dishes the pub served. Instead, I had gone into the kitchen and asked Swish, whose few rules for life include seasoning it with only the freshest spices and newly-picked herbs.

I found his thin frame hovering over an enormous tub of stew, the confines of his white chef's hat barely able to contain his flaming orange hair. He glanced up and waved me over, then turned back to the simmering pot, stirring it gently and closing his eyes, whispering, "Christ, that's beautiful." I paused to give him his moment with the stew before asking about vegan possibilities. He answered that there were fresh carrot tops and potato peels in the bottom of the garbage bin. "And of course back at the old caravan there's loads of mushrooms," he added with a wink, referring to the mildly intoxicating sort that grew wild there. "They're not English, are they?" he asked, referring to the bohemians.

"No. There are eight of them, though. And the one I spoke to said he was really hungry."

"*Blokes*? Ordering veggie?" He shook his head then glanced into a smaller pot, telling me there seemed to be enough potato and leek left and that he'd put up some extra wheaten bread with the order.

I nodded toward the rich, creamy mixture. "I think vegan means no dairy, Swish."

"Right. I think I saw some nice weeds near the river."

The backpackers eventually agreed to the dairy-friendly, if not dairy-free soup—a compromise I dare not share with the man now in front of me.

He continues his inquisition until his non-wife becomes exasperated and tells most of the pub and him in no uncertain terms what she will do with a leek and a potato if he persists in having to have them. At this, he announces to us all that he is soon leaving for home and he can't believe he came all the way over here and still can't get away from the "California hippie-commune meat-nazis" that are denying him soup.

"I believe they're Australian," I offer. His look tells me I've just joined their ranks.

Polishing off several pints, a bowl of stew, and one of Swish's baked apple concoctions swimming in cream, the angry man eventually leaves to return home, yammering through a succession of four-letter-word combinations that he will never return. I quietly thank him. The French twosome who sat nearest them thanks him also, but not at all quietly.

"Probably headed back to his cowboy ranch in Texas," surmises Swish.

"Watch it," I caution—in defense of my sister's name used vainly, not the vain man, who I reckon probably raises veal there. Relieved by his departure, the pub is granted respite for a brief interval before being visited upon by a weary young couple with outright weariless small children who scream through their entire meal while squishing the bits of food they don't throw across the pub deep into the table's wood grain.

At first, I mistake these parents as the type whose children can do no wrong—children whose waste is even made precious and perfect by brainsick parents who hollyloller to a thirty-foot range the nature of their prodigy's bodily functions, oftentimes broadcasting the chronicles while committing the Cardinal Sin of diaperdom: very public changing. This slays me, despite Mama's reminders that one day, I too will generate tiny replicas and become unsound. But until then, I am content in my misunderstanding of these After Delivery duos who were otherwise normal individuals Before Children.

But this particular couple takes no notice of their children's behavior, scarcely acknowledging the explosion about them, an impossible feat that is clearly envied by the rest of the crowded dining area. Yet no one seems angry or irritated, recognizing the pair's desensitization as a manner of coping, not disregard. Even Texas, who is a harder nut to crack, realizes that this kind of unconsciousness comes at a price. They haven't ordered it, but she brings them two whiskeys, double jiggers. They nod in gratitude and nourish their numbness, he with several small swallows, she with a single swift swill.

Startled by a hollered announcement indicating the direct departure of their bus, they scramble to put to use a neglected pile of napkins—the single item on the table that has remained undisturbed by their offspring. But there is no time, and we wave them away. Their group's abrupt departure ushers an instant change in the atmosphere and signals the start of the off-peak hours between lunch and supper, a significant portion of which Texas and I will spend clearing the heap of mess on, under, and surrounding their table—including a large puddle of vinegar, a broken plate, several anthills of salt, a used diaper, and numerous plastic packets of Heinz 57 the oldest child had apparently smuggled into the pub for the sole purpose of burnishing into the floor.

But we mind little, since during the lulls between meals and before the nightly sessions, when pub life slows to a crawl, the place seems overstocked with employees. Some are multinational momentaries like Texas and me, hired solely to help handle the crowds of tourists like ourselves. My own tranquility seems unmerited at these times, and I constantly look for ways to earn the money I'm being paid to relish this job.

When I have polished the last of Quinn's ashtrays to a shine and wiped the tables down to their original coats of varnish, I try to glean from my boss, Seamus Quinn, what more I can or should be doing. But he is preoccupied at all times with nothing in particular. An aura of frenzy surrounds Seamus, manifesting itself even in the wild curls atop his head. He moves quickly but without direction or purpose; and while the souls around him move at much slower paces, they seem to get far more accomplished. In fact, for one who is supposed to be in charge of everything at Quinn's, Seamus appears to have mastered the art of taking charge of nothing.

He hasn't volunteered a single word to Texas or me since handing each of us a bar rag and assuming we knew exactly where to start, taking for granted that the ability to pour the perfect Guinness is innate to the Irish only. He shrugs me off with the same words each time, spoken in rapid succession: "Two minutes two minutes." He utters these words in reply each time I approach him, sometimes before I even get my own words out:

"Seamus, what do I do with the tips from shared tables?"

He mutters hastily, "Two minutes two minutes." Then he frenzies off.

"Seamus, we're out of Fanta."

"Two minutes two minutes." Then away. Gone.

"Seamus, the person in the far corner just slumped over face-first into his roasted chicken and I can't lift him."

"Two minutes two minutes." Gone.

One particular time I have nothing to ask. I simply approach him as a test. "Seamus," I say.

"Two minutes two minutes."

Since Seamus continues to put me off indefinitely for two minutes, for most of my answers I turn to cheerful Eamon, chatty Bridget, and the lovely MaryO, three veterans of the permanent Quinn's staff—i.e. the ones not paid in cash. MaryO takes my questions seriously and answers them thoroughly. Full of smiles and encouragement, MaryO takes command of all within her vicinity, so I pretend that she is my boss and start to view Seamus as an outsider.

By our second week we have observed that Seamus is one who will live a short life. He will either suffer some kind of early failure due to the frenetic pressure of the blood that pulses through him, or he will meet his end in a love triangle. In one of my difficult conversations with Nigerian Richard, a fellow illegal coworker with whom I share universal gestures as neither of us speaks a mutual language, Richard alludes to the flirtatious relationship between Seamus and Careena—Careena being our prima-donna coworker with more issues than *Time* magazine.

Just as I'm about to gesture incredulously, Seamus frenzies by to indicate to Richard that he needs him in the back at the sink in two minutes two minutes. I assume that means Richard can stay up at the bar with me indefinitely, but he takes his cue from Seamus's gesture toward the dishwashing area and leaves to go suds up. Shortly after this, Careena saunters by, flashing Seamus a winning smile. At this, I consider that I've never seen Careena smile at anyone else like that. In fact, I don't think I've ever seen Careena smile at anyone else.

One evening about a day after our hire, while washing out my bar rag in the sink behind the counter, Careena flounced into work to introduce herself to me as spelled with a *C*, originating from the East Coast (of the New World), and having worked at Quinn's since the beginning of time. With the words of my red-haired brother itching to shuck off my tongue,

I tried to conjure Granny for a response, but all that came through was Mama, so I crossed my fingers and pretended out loud that it was dandy to meet her. Taking possession of my clean rag, she replaced it with her dirty one, and then pranced over to where Texas and Richard were busy bussing tables to make the announcement that *she* had no intentions of doing anything with *that*, pointing to the trash bin. Texas just kept clearing silverware, but I suspect Richard called her something foul in Fulani.

At this, I stopped washing out my latest rag to watch. Careena angrily stomped a single foot and furiously swished myriad blond hairs as she spoke to the tops of heads while they wiped tables. "You'd better do something about it right now," she demanded.

Texas stopped her work and looked up, genuinely baffled. "Who *are* you?"

Careena looked as though she'd been slapped, and I reckoned I should hurry over to save her from the next smack, which probably wouldn't be unintended.

"Texas, Careena. Careena, Texas. We are all coworkers." I could tell by his smile that Richard appreciated the way I gesticulatively emphasized the *co* in *coworkers*.

"*That*," pointing again, "is not my job."

While Texas was rolling the introduction, "Careena, trash. Trash, Careena," around on her tongue, Richard shrugged and Careena fumed away.

The scenario silently accelerated from there, Richard and Texas leaving the bin's overflow to grow taller and taller while Careena noiselessly rampaged here and there, trading rags with me each time I washed one out. I allowed this predilection of hers to irritate me more than it should, and I actually contemplated turning the water to scald moments before she swooped by the sink to pick up the clean rag lying within.

Careena finally reached her breaking point when the trash spilled over onto her, and she screamed at Richard and Texas, lashing out at them with my clean rag. Texas calmly and sympathetically informed her that all she had to do was ask nicely and they would have gladly taught her how to take out the trash.

It is after the garbage standoff that I start noticing cracks in our nonrelationship with Seamus, furthering the potency of Richard's allegations about Careena's role in Seamus's life and bed. However, Richard's implied innuendo would still remain unremarkable were it not for the fact that Seamus shares a bed and a long-standing relationship with another of the bartenders at Quinn's.

Curious, I put the Careena/Seamus question to Swish, who seems to know all of Life's Great Truths. Of course, whenever he speaks, one never knows whether it's really Swish or the mushrooms behind the words. I find him engrossed in the assemblage of a platter of seafood. He is carefully arranging the shrimp when he replies to my inquiry, "Absotively, mate! Christ that's a brilliant piece of salmon. I'd be quite surprised to learn which of our coworkers Seamus *isn't* sleeping with." He scrutinizes the platter from different angles and then concentrates his focus on creating a floret design with a few stray chips.

It is definitely the mushrooms with whom I am conversing. I answer them, "Well, it's highly unlikely our boss will be bedding me, as he won't even give me two minutes two minutes of his time. And MaryO doesn't strike me as the swingin' kind, which I'm glad of because she sort of reminds me of a fairy godmother and Mother Cosma—two figures I'd rather remain pure and virginal in my mind."

Virginal is all it takes to shift Swish's salacious and psychedelic thoughts into high gear, and for the rest of the evening, I notice subtle and not-so-subtle phallic symbols arranged into all the seafood platters that I deliver, put to the blush each time.

Later, back at the hostel, the wind does its best to push the farmhouse into the river. The gales have been going for about an hour now, erasing electricity and closing the pubs early. Texas throws on another brick of turf and checks for batteries on a small peat-dusted tape-player nearby, pressing play and letting loose a fiddle, a guitar, and the voice of Andy Irvine. I melt half a chocolate bar and add milk, handing my sister a mugful. Swish tumbles through the door with Lark, each completely soaked on half their bodies.

"It's a killing wind out there, mates."

I melt the remainder of my candy bar and hand them two cups of steaming chocolate. We listen to the wind scream and the old farmhouse howl back, and my heart yearns to stay right in this very moment, floating in a realm where hours are slowed and days stretched to their fullest. But the fluid time I feel here is an illusion. Like the beat of my heart, the rhythm of seconds will continue to measure minutes and then hours and then ultimately, change.

Texas is laughing at something Swish has said, but I've missed it, my thoughts now swarming around Granny's lap, where I often sat laughing with my family on Uncle Hap's porch for Sunday gatherings. Sometimes, when the laughter had shifted to the backyard with the afternoon sunshine and potato salad, I'd slip away to the wide and shadowy front hall where an old grandfather clock marked time. Especially loud in the late afternoon solitude, its cadenced tock filtered through the downstairs, ordering the rhythm of life.

Sharing a wall with the grandfather clock was the adjacent library, where on rainy Sundays I'd curl up and get lost in the pages of the books that lined its walls and littered its furniture, including the Latin book that my red-haired brother and I kept stashed in a secret place behind the couch, pretending it was a secret code left expressly to us by beings from another world who we communicated with by leaving coded messages folded and stuffed into the slots of the heavy oak doors. Even on these fantastic days, the clock's frequent chimes would interrupt our escape to remind us that the regular measure continued.

And so, in the quiet Sunday shadows, I'd carefully open the glass door on the lower portion of the tall old timepiece, reaching through the winding chains to seize hold of the pendulum, wondering if by the actions of my eight-year-old fingers I had put the world on pause. I'd stand there motionless, daring my ears to prove to me that time was still advancing. Eventually, the shrill merriment of my aunts or the boisterous antics of my uncles would shatter the silence and the possibility that maybe I had indeed stopped time. One day, I released the pendulum before my ears were able to testify to fact. I did it on purpose, because I wanted to believe it was possible.

Swish's voice calls me back to the present, and it's then that I notice Lark is gone. I ask about his exit, but neither my sister nor Swish can recall it. "I'm telling you, Texas, he can vanish into nothing."

"I've seen it too. He's a bloody leprechaun." Texas laughs, but Swish fixes his dark eyes on her and asserts sincerely, "I'm not taking the piss, mate. Elf. Sprite. Fairy. Whatever you want to call him. He is not of this world in the way that we are." He turns to me, "Stick around. Your eyes are open. You'll see what I mean." Heat from the fire swirls up my face and laps at my lashes, but I don't blink away its dryness as I stare into Swish's eyes, looking for the mushrooms' playful dance. Instead I see two liquid pools, black and steady, reflecting only the flame's flicker.

The gales howl and thunder, and I imagine how the storm is smashing waves into the rocky coast, grinding to sand bluff and shore. An unwise idea works its way into my head; and while I know that we'll be able to see very little, the sound alone will be enough to stir the soul.

"Let's drive to the pier," I foolishly suggest.

"B-l-ood-y h-ell!" Swish shouts, emphasizing each syllable and every consonant. "Smashing idea. Texas, grab my keys."

We nearly change our minds while sprinting the short distance from the hostel's door to the car. We shout to one another, but can't hear what the other is saying over the gales. Unable to hear each other's affirmations that this is extremely unwise, our bodies continue to do what our minds warn against. Swish's car is being rocked violently, and when the weight of our bodies hits the seats, it does nothing to curtail the swaying.

The night is black, and the horizontal rain smacking the car appears first in the headlights and then rushes toward us like a space-bending time-warp. Astounded to silence, we all jump when an enormous white dollop of froth whacks the windshield. More follow in rapid succession. Approaching the pier, we find ourselves steering through a wind tunnel of sea foam lifted from the water and hurled inland.

When we reach the pier, we find it consumed in a fury. The car doors are nearly ripped from their hinges immediately upon opening. Anything inside the vehicle not bolted or welded turns instantly from harmless debris into lethal projectile. Texas refuses to get out of the car with Swish and me.

The waves hammer the wharf and pummel the shore. We can see nothing beyond where the pier should be, but I know the tumultuous sea has swallowed the small island that lies just offshore. I wonder what the next crashing waves will envelop. In the darkness I hear their deafening thunder and feel the lash of their turbulent spray.

Listening to the roar and wondering how the surrounding cliffs have not yet tumbled, we stand staring into a blackness that howls and screams back at us, raw, intense, magnificent. We are saturated—pelted with rain, foam, saltwater . . . and instead of frantically craving shelter, we stand in awe of a force that could crush us in a single breath.

Host

Texas MacJerplin

"Are you telling me I have worms?"

The response from the doctor is a smile and a slight nod as she pens something in my chart with furrowed brows. "Little like that. Parasites go through stages. Your cyclical symptoms suggest . . ."

Dr. Maria T. Tsing's office is a minefield of erupting bodies at all times. I've never been to a medical facility's waiting area so peopled with intense ailers—hacking, spewing, and sweating as they shift uneasily in their seats. While sitting among the wasteland of victims waiting to hear themselves called each time I am here, I always wonder that I seem the only person who hasn't waited for the threat of the coffin to seek out medical intervention.

Today's flu season is in full swing. A child has vomited down the plastic slide in the play corner, which in turn has ignited an explosion of stomach spasms from the unfortunate bellies surrounding the area. The problem is made worse by the fact that the door from the waiting area to the patient rooms—also behind which is located the single restroom— can only be opened by either someone from within, or a button conveniently located near the floor behind the copy machine.

I'm not sure what it used to be, but the device used by the receptionist to reach the button now serves as a crowbar of sorts, cranking the door of the paper holder into a position that apparently guides the copier into the proper angle for it to be slammed against the wall, thus opening sesame.

A man swallowing bile clutches his gut with one hand and pounds pleadingly at the door with the other, while a child not belonging to him skips back and forth below, yelling that he has to be a big boy *right now*. The attention of the desensitized receptionist is finally garnered, and the boy elbows at the man's knees, preparing to sprint. She is reaching for the device at the same time an unsuspecting nurse steps through the door to rescue me with the words, "Next up, 523."

That's how they call patients back to the rooms, like a short-order cook might announce the advent of a hamburger platter. I suppose it's to be expected from a doctor's office with a neon *OPEN* sign hanging in one of its only and tiny windows. Except the *N* has long since lost its luster and the *E* has begun to flicker, so the sign now reads *OPE*, some- times *OP*. From the outside, the glow of the letters is the only evidence of life within the one-storey, sprawling, brick pancake that sits in blacktop syrup surrounded by stacks of other unremarkable concrete.

An urgent-care specialist in internal medicine, Dr. Tsing shares the building with two other practices—a urologist and a chiropractor. Separated by glass partitions, it is possible to peer into the waiting areas of the other two offices where demure and healthy-looking patrons sit quietly turning pages of magazines.

Mama had met Dr. Tsing several years ago in an aquatics class at the college-town Y. They got on straight away and spent the remainder of the class ignoring the instructor. Stepping out of the pool, Mama was less surprised to learn Maria was a doctor than to discover how diminutive the frame that was attached to the large, bobbing head she'd been chatting to.

It wasn't simply because Dr. Harbar had just been electrocuted by the sky that Mama chose Dr. Tsing as our new family physician. It was more because she'd immediately felt like a friend, and Mama liked having that kind of rapport with the person in charge when things went wrong within. Almighty Everything knows Mama'd never have chosen the place on appearance; the office had changed little over the years.

Dr. Tsing hands me a prescription for something that should kill the invading organism I've apparently been hosting since my return to the States. She seems confident that I picked up my worm overseas, and she urges me to make sure Sass gets treated. I'm about to spill down from the examining table when she stops me and shuffles close. "Heart. Heart. I must check the heart." She is standing in front of me with stethoscope suspended, giving me the go-ahead nod to shuck my sweater when she notices my eyes widen in fear. "You alright?"

"You mean I have *heart*worms?" I've seen the pictures of grotesque, enlarged, and strangled hearts at the vet's office, warning patients to have their pets wormed. I'm a goner for sure.

"No, no! I must check the heart because I always check the heart." She can't stifle her giggle. "Sorry. Sorry. Didn't mean to make you afraid. Must always check the heart and lungs. Now say *eee* for me." A hand extends from her short body and places the cold metal circle to my chest.

"Eee."

"Again." She pronounces both *a*'s longways as her short self stretches up to reach my chest.

"Eee."

"Again." She moves to another portion of my trunk.

"Eee."

"Again." She's on the other side of me now, on tiptoe.

"Eee."

"Again."

"Eee." The strangeness of this routine occurs to me, as it always does after the third or fourth time we exchange the same two-worded conversation. No other doctor has asked me to make noise while they listen to my insides. Wouldn't silence be preferred? Or would it work if I stopped saying *eee* and tried some of the other vowel sounds? What about *ooo?*

"Why do I have to say *eee* and not *ooo?*"

Dr. Tsing stops outright and gives me a quizzical look, "Because I check your heart and lungs that way." Of course. She resumes. "Again."

"Eee."

"Whoa! That's some powerful stuff!" the young hipster broadcasts to me and the rest of the pharmacy as he takes the scribbled prescription from my hand. The woman behind me carefully steps back and casts a concerned look in my direction. To my right, a man pities me. I suddenly feel like the acutely afflicted inhabitants of Dr. Tsing's waiting room. I want to say something to convince them I'm not a carrier of the next capital Death disease, but stop, considering that explaining my malady might only confirm their horrors.

"Thanks," I say to the hipster, but he is oblivious to the acid in my gratitude.

"Hey, no problem," he nods-winks-snaps-points at me all at the same time. I wonder at this choreographed gesture, speculating that its executor probably wouldn't aggravate me so much if I hadn't just been told I had a maggot hanging out in my gut. "We'll get this ready for you ASAP." He punctuates the *sap* with a single clap.

And then I see We—the same man who read Evie the entire contents of the information packet contained within her birth-control pills before he would let her have possession of them. By heart. She tried to tell him she'd taken them before and knew how they worked and how they might, just might, kill her.

The pills had kept Evie from partaking in the full Mass for several years. She'd gone to confession over it, but knew Reconciliation didn't work when treated as a debate. I'd spent the whole morning trying to talk Evie out of birth control and into something less damaging—like a bona fide love match, so I let We go.

And We did persist, adding that consultation was one of the most crucial aspects of his profession. It *saves lives*. She grabbed hold of his wrist then and told him his would end shortly if he kept going.

As Evie and I walked from the store that day, I mentioned how ironic it was that he was trying to save lives by consulting with her about a medicine that was designed to prevent them. She glared at me, called me a mini-Aquila, and then tossed her pharmacy package into the nearest dumpster. When I saw her in the line for Communion that Sunday and smiled, she covertly wedged a middle finger out from underneath her pray-folded hands.

I realize that today my pharmaceutical goal is to end life too—that of a modestly-celled organism that depends on me for its livelihood, one that has been with me for weeks, perhaps months. The thought starts to get me all fretful and low about loss until I recognize that this feeling has been around for a while, and the dog is going to hang for some time.

I'd felt it coming on soon after I turned and saw Sass with jubilation stretched all the way across her whole big smile. Vaden was his name. She'd run into him at the Louvre, literally, and then again at Quinn's, the day after the storm that demolished the pier and remodeled the boulders along the beach. We'd been watching with absorption two honeymooning newlyweds tucked into a snug, embracing one another with their eyes, so lost in each other they remained oblivious to all around them—save for the entire seafood platter Sass ended up dumping on top of them as her eyes lit on Vaden.

Later, after Swish and I had gotten the newly-married cleaned off and tidied up so they could resume their visceral lovemaking, I was marveling at how each spouse, without exchanging a single physical touch, managed to grope and fondle the other, when Swish noted that a narrator and bad music were the only things needed to turn the scene hard-core. "Who do you suppose is on top?" he'd asked.

"I can't tell. I think maybe she is. Wait a minute." The female half of the picture blinked slowly and breathed in, inducing from her counterpart a deep and euphoric sigh that raised by several degrees the temperature of the vicinity surrounding them. "Yes. She is. Definitely."

"Christ, mate, I think you're right. Does it feel a little scatty and all that . . . you know . . . watching your own sister have sex with another person's core?"

"What in the butternut are you talking abou . . . ?!" I started as I turned toward him, and then, "Shut. My. Mouth." There they were. The couple Swish had been referring to, Sass looking like pure bliss, rapture across her face and jubilation on her lips.

It wasn't simply the look of a crush kindled, infatuation sparked. It was riddles illuminated, mysteries answered. Love limitless. The kind that saves lives.

I should have warned Sass, should have told her I knew that soulfire, like the swelling sun inside, bursting against the sky's welkin bounty and into the stars a jillion strong. I knew its touch, reaching from the starry arc in moonshine grace against my flesh. I knew its taste, lips pressed soft, unraveling me, arms solid and tender holding me aloft, hands strong and hungry and cradling, reaching inward, all over, solving me.

But I'd kept closed. I didn't tell Sass. And I didn't tell the one who had kissed my skies for a moment on fire. I'd kept quiet, returning my nighttide to the slow burn of its dark. Closing my eyes, I pitch my reckoning deep and wide. I leapfrog it across waters, foothills, bluffs, oceans, mountains, deserts, and land it square inside my sister's next suss, where I hope she will find it saddling cowboy crazy into her thoughts, pressing her to splinter the impractical heavens, littered with wishes and hope, spurring her to reach inside the mystery of its dark and blaze infinite the evanescent stretch of horizon's twilight flame. I opened my eyes, grateful that though Sass and I were on opposite sides of an ocean, we were at least on the same side of fire-forged wishes.

The customer in front of me has made the mistake of asking We for assistance in selecting an elastic bandage wrap. As he dutifully and far too eagerly demonstrates its proper use, I consider strangling him with it in a counterdemonstration on its contraindications. But I don't, and not because removal from one store is enough for one lifetime, but because I know my frustration has naught to do with the words coming from his mouth and everything to do with the ones I kept inside.

We is in his element, unstoppable, and I wonder words, about where they live when we don't say them, and if they leave that place, can they come back for visits or do they grow forgotten, and can we ever really bury them.

We calls me. I step to the counter. "Have *we* taken this before?" I shake my head and brace myself.

"Well then, *we* must be *very careful* in doing so." The litany of side effects pouring forth from his grave expression makes me immediately want to forgo treatment and learn to live with worms. The woman and man who fear and pity me are staring in terror as well, as they are now assured I am a scourge.

When We finishes, I feel compelled to ask him if anything at all advantageous will happen as a result of taking this medicine. "Well now, *we* just can't be too cautious. Treatments always have downsides. We *always* look for remedies without acknowledging the *price of our cure.*"

"*We* do? Both of us? Really?"

He sighs hard, looks me square, and won't hand over the bag until sounding out the last consonant in the statement that follows his huff, "Be sure to take it with *plenty* of food."

As I leave, the hipster is assisting at full volume a mortified woman with over-the-counter advice on curing her yeast infection.

At home, I eat a mammoth slice of date cake and swallow a pill, thinking very carefully about my worm, my mailman, my sister, and the price of a cure.

Hyperbolic Hair

Texas MacJerplin

" . . . thicker, healthier, stronger, shinier . . ." she continues to explain as her shears move rapidly above my scalp at odd angles. My attention drifts.

My well-groomed friend—the perfection goddess called *Alexi*, or *hot*, depending upon your sexual preference—decided my venture overseas with Sass had been hard on my hair and necessitated a complete "make-over spa treatment" at the beauty shop . . . excuse me . . . *salon*, where she chooses to wax, color, electrocute, pluck, perm, and otherwise abuse her body hair. The salon aspires to be Parisian, but for the most part simply comes across as pricey.

And thus it is that I find myself in the hands of the animated Kelly—spelled with one *l* and an *ae* in place of the *y*, she has informed me—a pair of phonetical misinterpretations with which it makes no sense to comply. Kelly terrifies me. Aside from her predilection to derive joy from hour-long one-way conversations surrounding the merits of keratin, cuticles, and protein-cell follicles, she also takes great pleasure in the habit of extracting from its root my every facial hair.

I haven't experienced this kind of pain since Montana slipped on the bathroom floor while squeezing to my eyelashes a rubber and metal curling mechanism she'd insisted Sass and I experiment with just as our prom dates showed up at the door. My entire left set of upper eyelashes ended up on the floor with Montana, held fast between the jaws of the curler. Gaping up at me with an expression of horror that closely mirrored mine of pain, she moved to hug me and then thought the better of it. Perhaps to keep my body from entering shock, Sass took over from there, gamely declaring that I could not attend the prom with only one set of eyelashes unless she could too. Taking the pincers from Montana, Sass held them in front of my mouth and told me to make wishes, lots of them. Wishing the eyelashes back where they belonged, I blew hard and then watched my eyelashes trail to the floor with my hopes.

Sass brought the pincers to her left eye, ready to rip in solidarity. I commanded her to stop. With our dates in the living room and a spare set of eyelashes not likely to materialize, I reached for the lash tool. Inspired by Sass's bravery, I told her I would remedy the situation on my own.

And I did. Neither of our dates seemed to notice a thing as I emerged from the nether regions of a primping world so unfamiliar to me. And thus it was that I attended my senior prom with two matching, nearly bald upper eyelids.

Kelly jolts me back to the present realm of hairspray and nail-polish essence when her hair-care product dissertation reaches new, superlative measures, " . . . giving you the thickest, healthiest, strongest, shiniest hair you could possibly imagine." Enthusiasm oozes from her every hairless facial pore, weaving its way into teeny crevices that will soon be slathered with "the best, most effective age-defying cream you could possibly imagine."

"Your hair's terribly dry Ever had a highlight Are you healthy How's your diet Do you take vitamins?" Kelly assaults me. I continue my halfhearted appeasement smiles at her banter when it dawns on me: I have been called upon to speak—a most uncharacteristic consequence of a Kelaeconversation. I tell her that since my RDA of Foods-That-Eventually-Kill was sky high when I lived up north, I have been taking supplements to offset my time in the city. She looks at me shaken and wide-eyed before sprinting for cover behind a series of enormous shelves fortified with viscous hair-care products of various volatilities.

I must not have made it clear that people were not among the list of iniquitous things that I ate. Happily abandoned, I pick from my lap the parts of me that used to be attached and stare into the mirror at the bizarre makings of a new 'do that instantly causes me to wonder what goes on in Kelly's world.

She soon emerges from the coiffure-apparatus armory, eyeing me suspiciously. I'm about to reassure her that my dietary vices have improved significantly when she leans forward, looks me square in the eyes, tries her best to furrow well-manicured brows, and with grave deliberateness asks, "Have you ever taken these before?" In her hand she bears a stylish glass vase filled with neon-purple spheres and labeled *multivitamines pour des cheveux*.

I consider that here our encounter could go in many directions. I'm no stranger to multivitamins, but I've never actually taken a brand whose container I might use in home decor. Personally, I prefer the plastic-vesseled, chewable, animal-shaped tablets as a throwback to happy and healthy childhood memories, but for some reason I just don't feel like sharing in that level of detail with Kelly.

I end up answering her with a *yes* and a *no*, instantly regretting it as she braces herself and proceeds to recite from memory the entire contents of the promotional pamphlet that accompanies the ornamental urn.

Kelly is either truly concerned for the well-being of my hair or she has the work ethic of a hot-wired droid. Regardless, it is apparent that she takes hair, her job, and—right now—me, very seriously. And so I afford her the same.

After spouting a litany of affirmatives and negatives in response to her list of interrogatives, I suppose I pass the test because she recommences the physical assailment of my tresses—in silence, which seems awkward after the hearty marathon chat we've just exchanged.

She stops just short of a total scalp massacre and proceeds to inform me about what to do if I miss a dose of the chic vitamins that, apparently, I will be purchasing today. I laugh. Do bad things actually happen to people who forget a dose of their daily supplement? She is not amused, evidently having missed a dose of humor at birth. "*Don't* double up your dose," she says with such ominous alarm that she has my complete attention. "Simply resume the recommended dosage on the following day."

It strikes me square then: Kelly has simply got to get together with We. Together, their personal and emphatic mission statement in life will ensure that from medical necessity to material imbibement, we the world over will have read and understood completely the indications of each pill-shaped chemical ingested.

I look from Kelly to the mirror and start. Much of my hair is missing. And the rest of it is odd. I point to the supplements. "So those will make my hair healthier?" Kelly gives me a duh look.

I glance down toward the hair-animal lying dead on the floor beneath my chair. "Just to clarify, that means grow in thicker, shinier, *and faster?*" At this her eyes bulge, positively radiating duh.

I consider that the vase would make a splendid gift for Alexi.

Kelly is thrilled to squeals when I end up buying a vase of pills. As I leave, I begin to entertain the possibilities of what might occur if I were to double up on fluorescent supplements. I dismiss the thought and am walking to the car when the voice of Maggie's dad repeats itself to my memory—across a table full of veterans and a hand that guaranteed everything but the jack—spoken loud and clear right after I should never have refused his dare to bid four: *You don't have a hair on your ass.* . . .

Kelly eyes me suspiciously as I return for another vase.

Mystagogy

Arkansas MacTerptin

"By-god, Sass, you're headed for the goddam drop edge of yonder," Grandpa Jelly's reassuring words echoed through my head as I recalled our telephone conversation. Texas had made it back just fine, laughing as she told me how Mama'd shown up at the airport with blackberry pie in hand and Toddy'd gone down on one knee all over again just as soon as he saw Texas walk through the broken door at Tump's with Dad, Dog, and Grandpa Jelly.

Toddy had been proposing to my sister on and off since the sixth grade, but this time I'd wondered at the old joke as she related its latest punch line. "What was Toddy doing at Tump's?"

"Heard I was coming home is all."

"So he came all the way from Massachusetts for a 'welcome back'?"

"Well, he thought I might be headed back out to Arizona directly to try and catch the beginning of the semester, and he didn't want to go 'til Christmas without catching up."

"Catching up."

"What, Sass?"

"What about Chicago?"

"It's still there."

"And the frogs?"

"Arizona first."

"So you decided you're going back?"

"Yeah. Well, no. Grandpa decided for me. *Finish what you goddam start, by-god.* Don't laugh, Sis. You're in for the same when you get back."

"Yeah, I'm sure."

"I'm not." Then silence.

"When're you going?"

"Monday. I'm sure there'll still be some sublets off-campus. Did you hear what I said, Sass?"

"Of course I did. I've heard it for weeks. You're even less subtle when you're quiet, you know. You know I love the tar out of him, but are you sure Toddy is your Joseph?"

"I'm not sure of anything except I'm more worried about you than me. Don't you go thinking Vaden's the Answer, Sass. Don't lose your marvel to him. You'll just end up confusing wonder with wander.

Move your ass, Keegan. Just go away. I know, Mama. Sorry. Y'all, just let me talk to Sass, okay?"

"Holy Sebastian, Texas. You just said his name. And you cursed."

"You better be glad the Protector of Piety's not on this phone. I just got blessed out for my coal miner's cuss, but your sacred swear is bordering on blasphemy there, Sister."

"Seriously. How did you just get to say his name and live?"

"He's over it. I guess teeny-weeny Kathleeny finally uncovered his real name and adores it."

"Bless all! He didn't say a word about it to me."

"Me either. Delaware spilled it over gumbo last night. I'll bet he didn't tell you he calls Vaden *Darth*, either."

"Darth?"

"Vader."

"Nice. Listen, about the Prince of Darkness—"

"That's the Devil, Sass. You mean Dark Side."

"Whatever. It's just that—"

"Hush-it, Sass. Enjoy it. Just come back, okay?"

With the beat of drums still ricocheting from canyon walls, I'd thought of this conversation last night as I sat with Swish, Meg, Vaden, and the Berber tribe whose field of alfalfa might have been the final resting grounds of the mighty little Cromwell had it not been for a mystery named Ahmed. I'd run into Ahmed a week before in Marrakesh and then again yesterday afternoon, almost literally, when our brakes failed and his square of alfalfa slowed our freefall to an eventual stop somewhere deep in the Atlas Mountains.

Ahmed thinks in mysteries, like me. Much to the bumfuzzle of my three travelmates who had not eaten sheep's head a week ago, Ahmed and I embraced at once, recognizing in our second meeting surefire confirmation that chance is bunk.

It was because of the sheep's head I'd first met him, wandering a marketplace inside the walls of a city with one foot in the twentieth century and the other located somewhere around the turn of the fifteenth. I'd left Swish, Meg, and Vaden in the nineteenth century, the latter two fussing over figs at a marketer's stand, in a blusterstew of bother over the fruit's history given that not a stitch of either's rather astonishing measure of fig data was akin to the other's.

I looked to the seller and then to Swish, but neither seemed the least bit boy-howdied to discover themselves in the paired presence of the world's most accomplished fig experts, making me wonder briefly if Grandpa Jelly and I were the only blunderbusses on earth under the impression that, though tasty, the fruit's chief function was for letting people know you didn't give a turkey scratch—or a good goddam by-god in Grandpa's case.

I was about to put the matter to Swish, but he was absorbed in towering piles of mushrooms the likes of which his slobberjaws had never witnessed, which meant he surefire didn't care a fig to discuss the expression. Seeing as all were happy with their momentary whiskey diggings, I decided to skidoo in search of my own.

Moving off to a large square in the center of the time warp, I watched its heave as a lively collage of artisans, storytellers, musicians, charmers, drummers, magicians, and acrobats gathered to fever into a snaprattle the senses of all who hovered near. Crowds of locals soon joined the villagers and tribesmen in their ritual carnival of culture, and dozens of food stalls sprung to life, adding sizzle to the vibrant mix. Merging with the hungry crowd amid a buzz of energy, I realized just how far I was from a world of buttermilk, cowpeas, and red-eye gravy, walking among rows of cous cous, tagine, snails, brochettes, sheep's head.

"*Pardonnez-moi, Madame. Je recommande ceci.*" It took everything inside me to suppress a wiggle-dance upon hearing the sacred language accidentally spoken to me, house-proud to be mistaken for the French of my granny. I let the stranger land a few more mystery words into my heart, breathing them in like the purest tongue this side of the Holy Ghost hand-in-hand with my rump-shaking Mahalia Jackson, before admitting to English.

"Pardon. You may wish to try with this," he rephrased, and the stranger called Ahmed handed me a pinch of bright red spices before demonstrating with his own plate how to garnish and slice each cheek of a disembodied sheep.

"It'd win whole-hog at the Smokers Wild, duck soup," I told Grandpa Jelly about the strange crimson rub that very night in our phone conversation. I didn't mention the animal or cut that accompanied it, because he'd already worked himself into a swivet looking up Morocco in my *Funk and Wagnalls* and seeing it right next to Algeria. Countries that ended in *ia* affrighted him fierce, and he'd spent the next five minutes explaining in bizarre detail how to exact a blow and execute a deadly maneuver to another person's nose using my thumb.

Ahmed explained to me, as we chewed on cheek, the time-warped city, alive and pulsing inside a decaying body, with neighboring mountain villagers and tribesmen like himself continually making the journey to sell and trade their goods and celebrate their way of life. He described how the religion and origins of his people remained distinct from those of Arabic Morocco, with Berber traditions influenced by a cockamamie combination of Saharan nomads, ancient Maghrebis from the African plains, and descendants of Sudanese and Senegalese peoples brought to the region through the slave trade.

I started to tell him about my own cloud-cuckoo jumble of roots—trying my best to reckon what it meant to be catechized Catholic in the midst of Baptist brimstone, back-porch fiddle-fire, and backwoods corn-shine in a place blessed and cursed by the hybrid Appalachia and Ozark footprints surrounding it—and for the first time, I found myself on the separate side of my own familiarity. I couldn't suss it well enough to make a snaprattle of sense out of anything, much less my whole existence, so I just told Ahmed all about Slug instead, hoping to realize somewhere amid the native soil of crazy my tangled spirit for the first time all over again.

After mapping our way through the wrinkles of identity, Ahmed and I left each other deep in the folds of notion, understanding only and very little why—surrounded by wide paths paved with possibility—byways were our chosen routes. He would return to wander with his tribe deep in the yonder hills, leaving me to wonder if I would mine.

Filling up on figs, mushrooms, and muddle, we left Marrakesh a few days later for the Atlas Mountains beyond it, careening to a halt in the alfalfa field. Ahmed saw the divine in our second meeting, and we spent the night in festivity with him and his tribe between the walls of a gorge. A huge feast was prepared, and at first I'd wondered what was being celebrated. By the end of the night, sitting amid a circle of drums, I realized it was us, treated to our own soiree—rhythmic waves of warmth and generosity, resounding from walls of stone.

Leaving its echoes behind, we begin preparations to join Ahmed on a trek into the Sahara before sunsquint—a journey he was considering the exact moment our rattletrap came to land in his alfalfa field. Swish and Vaden request that we put off the journey long enough to work the alfalfa field in exchange for our damage to it. But Ahmed insists that we accompany him.

Awakening to a dramatic sweep of yellows and oranges against deep blue sky, I watch wisps of violet flare and fade with the peeking sun as we load up and cram into the car whose brakes have somehow been restored overnight by what means I'll never know. Ahmed's English doesn't cover the realm of car repairs and my Berber covers the realm of nothing. Still, I'm glad we'll be following behind Ahmed's car should our little Cromwell's brakes decide they don't operate in Berber, either.

Squat trees gradually lose their silhouettes as the east gives way to light and the west to rocky rises. I'm on the edge of a daydream where a group of old men in hooded robes sit weaving and twisting reeds on the crest of a rolling field flecked with patches of hazy gray purple; and amid the blushing rays of a newday sun, barefoot boys tend herds of sheep and chase one another among green hills. One of them laughs, waves, and dances for us as we weave by, reminding me that what I see is real, not a picture window out of another place, another time.

We pass women swathed in magnificent scarves washing colorful robes in a river, working fields, and carrying gigantic loads of firewood on their backs, heads. We steer through mud-brick villages that look as though they were hewn from the towering red rocks surrounding them. We see children trek—literally—to school through mountain passes that most people wouldn't traverse without gear. We watch men guiding pack mules over stones that spill into dried lakebeds stamped with animal tracks leftover from a time of plenty. Every bend draws us deeper into another time.

Stopping in a centuries-old, multi-storey, sprawling realm of mud and straw, we follow Ahmed through a maze of dirt-hard passages in search of the man who sells the typhoid pills we will apparently be needing. We wander past cattle, chickens, and goats amid the twisting array of mud-packed walls and inner courtyards that make up the kasbah commune. Begun in the eleventh century, it is occupied by nearly a thousand others who continue to repair and maintain the effects of weathering by using the same building methods and materials as their ancestors.

After an hour of searching, we find the man's wife, who welcomes us onto a balcony overlooking part of the village below and then serves us mint tea and cheese sandwiches. We start to refuse politely until Ahmed quietly instructs us not to. While Ahmed and the woman talk to one another, we sit barely in the fall-apart plastic chairs provided.

I peer over the wall and watch the goings-on in the dusty scatters of the courtyard below. A little boy taps a goat with a stick. When the goat ignores him, he moves in front of it and turns upside-down to gape into its face as it stares toward the ground. The goat continues to ignore him, so he starts singing to the animal, then just sings. He turns in circles and finally spies me. Beaming, he speaks in Ahmed's native tongue. I have no idea what to say back, but I discover that peek-a-boo is universal. A few minutes later, Ahmed translates his conversation with the woman and apologizes that we will have to wait several more hours for the man to return.

I would have waited years in that taped-together chair eating nothing but warm cheese sandwiches for the opportunity to experience each of this day's senses, impressions, notions—transporting us into a world so foreign, so old, so otherworldly, and so affecting we are moved to a hush. Even Swish. I nearly cry when the sun finally sets and draws a curtain of darkness over the beauty that has been playing before my eyes.

When the typhoid man returns, he insists that we stay through the dark hours and rest. This time Ahmed lets us refuse when we are offered to take the place of the family in their beds, and we sleep on mats out on the balcony, dreaming in the star space surrounding us. In the morning, goats hail the arrival of dawn, and we are loaded down with tea and extra bread before being allowed to stock up on pills that look as frightening as their size.

Although they are supposed to prevent against the fever, these tablets look and smell like they could cause a worse malady. Against what would surely be the better judgment of my mama, I follow instructions and swallow several of them, overcome by a moment of invincibility. After all, I know how to kill a man with my thumb.

Descending into the Saharan world of sand-baked huts the same color as the paths running to them, the landscape becomes rugged and dry, the country rural and isolated, oases infrequent. We pass camels wandering freely and the occasional man on a donkey. The road narrows until there is no road at all. Ahmed navigates through sand-dusted fields while Swish and Meg light up and begin singing.

Ahmed continues to lead through the nothingness that surrounds us, and without a trace of any road or path, I have no idea how he will locate our ultimate desert destination. All I know is that we are dune-bound.

When the Cromwell refuses to trudge through the thickening sand any longer, we park both cars and walk. I wonder if we'll ever be able to find them again. Then I think of Granny and coincidence, the language of the mystics, the unconscious wisdom of life.

After an hour's walk, somewhere in the middle of sand and sky, we come across a nomadic family and trade a portion of Swish's kif for the use of three of their camels, which we will apparently be returning to their possession once our journey is finished. I wonder how we'll find them again.

Closer to Algeria than I'll ever reveal to Grandpa Jelly, we plod onward into a vast expanse, trekking hours into the endless and towering dunes, surrounded by nothing but mountains of sand in all directions. A sandstorm two sunsets ago has removed all traces of prints on the dunes, having blown them into an array of silky smooth valleys and knife-edge peaks set ablaze by the deep orange of the African sunset.

The sky directly overhead is perfect powder-blue, and opposite the setting sun low on the horizon is a bloated haloed moon that peeks from behind the highest dunes as we plod onward. The weight of my backpack shifts slightly with each camel-step, and I wobble gently back and forth in a dream-like stupor soaking in the most stunning scene my eyes have ever witnessed. Ever.

Swallowed by miles and piles of sand in every direction, we eventually arrive at what will become our camp. Located in a valley of soft, it soon consists solely of two low tents made from nothing but wooden sticks and thickly woven blankets. The tents now raised and bare, Ahmed instructs us to remove the blankets from our camels and spread them on their floors. Our saddle-blanket will also serve as a bedroll, separating our sleeping bodies from the sand.

The sun has long since vanished from the horizon, and the light of a full moon turns the dunes into pink puff pastries. We are eager to explore our novel surroundings on foot, and Ahmed can tell, so he encourages us to set off on our own while he feeds the camels, warning that the desert can be a disorienting place even in broad daylight and to stay in a group, keeping constantly alert as to our whereabouts.

In typical Aussie-fashion, Meg locates the largest dune and vows to climb it. She and Swish met when she ordered a seafood platter, I delivered it, and she recognized immediately the sexual overtones in its arrangement. "I've got to meet this chef," she'd said, in more demand than request as she rose from her chair and marched directly into the kitchen. Swish looked up from a similar creation, ready to order out the intruder. "It's brilliant," she smiled. And it has been ever since.

Vaden and Swish reach the top of the monster dune next while I trail behind, dumping buckets of sand from my shoes. The retreat of the sun has left a slight chill in the still night air, and as a result we have all added layers. Swish has donned his brand-new brown *djellaba* and, wandering atop the dune, looks just like Obi-Wan.

He continues his wanderings while the rest of us happily scramble up sand slopes and slide down them for nearly an hour when we notice that something is nibbling at the moon. We consult Obi-Wan about the phenomenon, who thinks the culprit is a low cloud, but Vaden suggests a partial eclipse. Meg is just relieved to discover that it's not the kif causing hallucinations.

We climb again the slope of the monster dune, transfixed at the moon as the chunk slowly gets larger, barely believing we are being treated to an eclipse on this of all nights, at this time and in this setting. When over half of the moon has disappeared into shadow, I realize that our immediate setting has changed dramatically. The pink puff pastries are gone and have been replaced by deceptive dark mounds.

Starting back to camp, we are soon hopelessly lost. Following our footprints seems only to take us in circles. Recognizing landmarks is impossible as there are none—only gigantic black waves as far as the eye can see. At the top of one dune we see a tiny flicker of light in the distance, which we reckon, simply must be our camp. Unfortunately, the pinprick of light will disappear below the peaks of other dunes as soon as we climb down from this one.

As I gaze toward the vanishing moon, I am struck with a bang-up plan: I suggest that we angle our beeline toward camp against a satellite that has been shimmering brightly in the night sky. For hours the satellite has appeared stationary, and if *Funk and Wagnalls* doesn't let me down, this means it is in harmony with our own orbit; and unlike the constellations, it won't shift across the sky and skew the direction of our path. Of course the North Star would work just as well, but the satellite premise is far more novel and exciting.

My recommendation is received with much celestial fascination, turning my supposed fit of genius into a tangential impediment to progress when talk inadvertently turns from our camp-hunting endeavor to the satellite, then spy planes, then missile defense systems. After an exposition on world war, we navigate our way across the sea of sand.

The flicker turns out to be the firelight from a nomadic family of Berbers living in tents just like the ones back at our camp, wherever that may be. They seem a bit unwilling to help a group of intrusive, dunderheaded, satellite-guided backpackers who have lost their way in the Sahara. Relieved by the presence of other humans we can turn to should things get truly ugly, we are satisfied to leave the Berber family in peace for the time being.

For lack of any better plan we go by feel in the continuation of our search. Intuition rewards. Twenty minutes later we are back at camp, sipping tea around a small fire with Ahmed who knew we would get lost and eventually find our way back. He did not know about the eclipse, and by now the moon is almost completely gone. The sky is as black as the dunes, and I take my leave from the fire to gaze peacefully into the pitch night. I find the heavens in a downright blaze.

The moon has disappeared in complete shadow, and the Milky Way fires an arc across a sky so filled with stars I hardly recognize it. Never have I seen a black sky more densely packed with perforations of light. I am gloriously dumbstruck, and though famished, in no hurry to return to the cooking that started in the absence when we misplaced ourselves.

I trudge through the soft dark powder that meets my feet, farther out into the vast Saharan blackness that surrounds me (all the while taking care to stay in alignment with the satellite). The moon a faint memory, everything around is perfectly still. No wind. No noise. Nothing stirs. Complete quiet. Unreal silence. Absolute stillness. Total serenity.

Immersed in a world so utterly devoid of background noise, I become aware of the piercing ringing in my ears, and in the absence of all other perceptible sound, it feels deafening. Were it not for the ringing in my head, there would be nothing to convince me that time had not been frozen in a snapshot of charcoal turbulence. I wonder the silence of the stars a jillion strong, and when we were with them before time, what we did back then, up there.

Pressing my ears to my head, I listen for the footsteps and wonder where they are. I hear them within, in every wish ever made, every sin committed, every question raised. They plod forward in reply, "Understood, forgiven, answered."

And then I feel it, riding cowboy-wild across my heart, "Loved perfectly."

I wonder those footsteps, about each one ever pressed aiming a direction divine and now that I know, how can I ever bless them enough. I wonder cowboys, and like that song I only hear in diners anymore, where they have gone. Maybe back up there, to a time before, and did they leave because they thought nothing else would ever be new again, and how wrong they were.

I wonder my sister, and if we footstepped together into the night and shouted up to the starry arc, up to a jillion cowboy fires reflected lonesome and in welkin bounty across dark sky waters, would they hear and come back, and the world be even better. Or perhaps they're sated in their silence, where they can sit whittling poesy from flame and convince us of heaven's own febrility, that her argentine harmony, her burning euphony, may be the reason we breathe.

I watch the light shape and grow the moonsplinter slowly back to its larger self, like a Eucharistic shard knowing forever its whole. I remember always wishing for a piece of Father Manzelough's host, his beaming smile at my first receiving it, and then his telling me I was a wretch when all I had wanted was to call my granny Sacred, to give her a capital name, like the Mother Blessed she adored. I remember the very moment it happened, the moment he gave eternity pause, when I thought I'd landed on precisely why the archangel of light had fallen from heaven. I believed grace shed tears that day, and saints, their trappings. But that day is eclipsed.

The sliver of light continues to expand, intensifying its radiance amid the celestial campfires, where it takes over poesy and flame, speaks the language of incandescence, and reveals to the perfectly imprudent sky—naked and freckled with flickers across an empyrean curve—that the jagged shards of a jumbo God are never the same as the jagged shards of a gumbo God, but both together course through the All and Mighty of what we're after. Beneath the silence I understand that if grace shed tears that day, they were separate from mine; and though I typically ascribe these revelations to a whisper from Granny, in the saints' pigeon tongue, I recognize this one as a gift from Mr. Frank Assisi, who never trucked with trappings anyhow.

The three-quarter disc is now pouring from the sky, and I wonder if underneath all of this, there is nothing so perfect as the celestial side of a see-through moon, eclipsing safe the hope stored in wishes. Perhaps beneath her open-mouth beam she wishes she'd never been born to hold such dreams and promise as must a moon obliged by legend and myth to screen marvel and magic. But wonder knows we need her Eucharistic reminder, moonshine grace, the Cheshire of her smile, to pretend the mother perfect above us, unknowable, random rock, far-flung earth-debris, mysterious, landed, brilliant, all of this at once.

Stretching into soft sand, I inhale this communion so blessedly bumfuzzling it renders even the heart's tongue speechless—a beauty of such intensity it notions itself directly in the soul.

With mine nourished, I return to the communal tagine that would never have come to fruition without the capable hands of Ahmed. We sit around an enormous rough ceramic pot filled with steaming vegetables and meat. Eating in the traditional way—sans silverware, scooping the guts from enormous loaves of crusty bread and then using those crusts to shovel heaps of tagine into our mouths—we banquet gluttonously. We haven't showered in days, our hands are filthy; no one has soap or handi-wipes and no one cares. We feast. Our spirits feast.

The muffled sound of drums can be heard from a nomadic camp in the distance. The moon is back full, casting deep shadows among everything within its beam. I walk from camp once more into an environment that is radically altered from the black world of so short a time ago. The dunes are light puff pastries once again, and the sky a shadow of blue from the luminous lunar lantern it suspends. Most of the stars have been extinguished by the competing moonlight, and even the satellite has been transformed to no more than a dim pinprick in the sky. Standing in liquid light, floating on a dumpling moon, I reach for Texas's hand before remembering she's not there.

I think of the Holy Triune, Granny and the Blessed Mother I mistook her for, and the Communion of Saints.

I think about my sister's words. About leaving her side.

I think about our last exchange in each other's company, as we parted from one another at the airport on this side of the ocean, replicating a conversation we'd pirooted long ago between Dog, Dad, and Stretch. That conversation took place on the day Stretch hauled the last of his mules away. He said he needed a change. We all knew what he meant.

Whenever Dog and Stretch found themselves in each other's company, Dad usually stood between them to replace the silence called *Maisala* that would otherwise have stood there. But on that day, Dad stood just off to the side.

"Have good roads," Dog had said.

"Will do," replied Stretch.

Silence followed, until Dad filled it in. "All roads are good."

"They are," agreed Dog. "And the best ones cross," he added as he clapped Stretch's shoulder through the open window of his truck.

Stretch looked long at Dog, nodding slightly, before pulling away. And when Dad and Dog walked back to latch the gate, Texas and I came out from behind the *SOLD* board and circled back behind the house to make it look like we'd come from the other direction. There was silence between them when we arrived. On the walk back to the truck, we continued to act as though we were completely ignorant to it all. The silence. The heavy air.

Dog stopped to look over the dip and swell of the fenced and vacant land. "So you think it's going to be alright the way we left it?"

"Don't think I've seen anything finer," Dad answered. Dog was quiet, his head nodding slightly. When he took his hat off and wiped across his brow, Dad took the cue. "Hell, no. It's all going to shit as soon as Squint gets his hands on this place."

"Have good roads," Texas had said to me as I wouldn't stop hugging her, even as the last boarding call was announced.

"All roads are good," I whispered back.

"Yeah," she said, separating from me, turning her teary gaze from mine to Vaden. "And don't you forget that the best ones cross." She picked up her sack.

"Hey, did you make that up?" I hollered and smiled as she walked backward, blowing a single kiss.

"Hell no. But I think it's going to be alright."

Suspended just above the dunes is a violet haze, and I blink several times, trying to determine if it's real or an optical illusion. The old dream comes back, alive and acute. Only this time, wide awake.

I marvel about the night's optical wonders and dream-come-true illusion of perfection. The sandstorm smoothness, the sunset, the full moon, the halo, the total eclipse, the fiery heavens, the liquid moonlight. And as if orchestrated, the meteor that blazes surefire right overhead.

It is as though someone created this, the most perfect and incorporeal of nights . . . for each of us.

And maybe He,
  or She,
  or They
    did.